KW-221-693

THE COUNTRY SISTERS

1922. After the horrors of the Great War, the close-knit Truscott family returns to everyday life on their busy Hampshire farm.

The two Truscott sisters are on very different paths. Kate is happily married to Albert, content to be a mother and farmer's wife. Her younger sister Dot sets her heart on becoming a teacher.

But an unforeseen tragedy means Dot must give up her place at college. Instead she resigns herself to becoming a lady's companion to wealthy Mrs Humboldt, who is a difficult woman to please.

Accompanying Mrs Humboldt to Eastbourne, Dot enters an intoxicating new world of cocktails, circuses and dance halls, a life far removed from her quiet Hampshire village. And she soon catches the eye of a sophisticated seducer. Dot must quickly learn the ways of the world if she is to forge her own path, on her own terms.

0 030 816 80X

SP**ECIAL** ADERS

THE ULVERSCROFT FOUNDATION
(Registered UK charity number 264873)

was established in 1972 to provide funds for research, diagnosis and treatment of eye diseases. Examples of major projects funded by the Ulverscroft Foundation are:

- The Children's Eye Unit at Moorfields Eye Hospital, London
- The Ulverscroft Children's Eye Unit at Great Ormond Street Hospital for Sick Children
- Funding research into eye diseases and treatment at the Department of Ophthalmology, University of Leicester
- The Ulverscroft Vision Research Group, Institute of Child Health
- Twin operating theatres at the Western Ophthalmic Hospital, London
- The Chair of Ophthalmology at the Royal Australian College of Ophthalmologists

You can help further the work of the Foundation by making a donation or leaving a legacy. Every contribution is gratefully received. If you would like to help support the Foundation or require further information, please contact:

THE ULVERSCROFT FOUNDATION
The Green, Bradgate Road, Anstey
Leicester LE7 7FU, England
Tel: (0116) 236 4325

website: www.ulverscroft-foundation.org.uk

SALLY TARPEY

◆

THE COUNTRY SISTERS

SEFTON LIBRARY SERVICES

003081680

F

MAGNA
Leicester

First published in Great Britain in 2023

First Ulverscroft Edition
published 2024
by arrangement with
Kate Nash Literary Agency

Copyright © 2023 by Sally Tarpey
All rights reserved

*A catalogue record for this book is available
from the British Library.*

ISBN 978–0–7505–5039–0

Published by
Ulverscroft Limited
Anstey, Leicestershire

Printed and bound in Great Britain by
TJ Books Ltd., Padstow, Cornwall

This book is printed on acid-free paper

For Andrew

1

Dot Truscott woke early. She lay still for a while, her eyes adjusting to the sliver of light escaping around the edges of the curtains. The window was open to let the heat of sleeping bodies out of the bedroom and the fresh air in. When she had first arrived back home for the summer from her college in Chichester, she had offered to sleep downstairs but her father would have nothing of it. He insisted that he and eleven-year-old Henry sleep in the sitting room. Dot was to share a bed with her mother, with Tilly and Ronnie topped and tailed on the truckle bed, leaving Kate and Albert the luxury of a room of their own.

Dot could hear the rhythmic breathing of her mother and the two children. The whole house was quiet and only the sound of birdsong accompanied her light step on the stair as she crept downstairs. She avoided the third step for it creaked and would arouse the lightest sleepers, alerting them to her presence. She wanted to be on her own, to enjoy this time without the clamour of voices heralding the start of another busy day. There were so few moments like these to savour.

She looked around the cottage where she was born. The clutter of the Truscott family's daily lives had been tidied away the night before and the breakfast tea tray made ready with a freshly laundered tray cloth.

The brown earthenware teapot snuggled next to the glass sugar basin that had been Dot's grandmother's and the knitted cosy lay to one side ready for the early morning brew. A few embers glowed through the grate of the newly blackened kitchen range and the cat curled up on the cushion in her father's wooden chair didn't stir. It was even too early for him. The clock on the mantle showed five o'clock.

Dot slipped on her shoes, threw a shawl around her shoulders and stepped out into the warm air. The sun was a promise, peeking through the veil of the trees and a light mist lay over the stream that trickled its way towards the river. She walked along the lane and through a field gate. Scabious and knapweed gave a purple haze to the meadow and the tall grasses rippled in the light wind. Dot's long, dark, almost black hair swung across her back to the rhythm of her stride as she delighted in the swoosh of her nightgown against the rough stalks of the rye grass and wall barley. A broad smile crept across her face and her slightly turned-up nose wrinkled with the pleasure of the early morning countryside smells.

The land sloped gently upwards and, when she reached the field edge, she turned and stood for a while, looking at the sprinkling of dwelling houses edging the Down. Micklewell was such a small part of England and she loved it. She loved it now, in the early morning, with no one in sight. She smiled to herself wondering what any wandering farm hand would make of her in her nightclothes, but she was completely alone. An unfamiliar feeling to her. City life was so different, so busy. She had enjoyed that busyness but for now she was happy to feel the expanse of the Hampshire countryside around her and take stock.

Chichester was an exciting city, a place steeped in history and she had met such interesting people since she had moved there to take up her place at teacher training college. People like Constance Bennett who had befriended her when she was a new face at the college and invited her to a concert in the cathedral. She would miss that side of life in the city, there was not much in the way of cultural pursuits in Micklewell. There was also an inkling of regret that she had been introduced to Constance's brother, Edward, just before she was leaving Chichester for the summer. He was so much more interesting to talk to than the young men she knew in Micklewell with their awkward conversations about the latest cattle auction, the different types of wheat seed and whether the harvest would be early or late this year. She couldn't imagine any of them enjoying listening to a recital or being able to discuss the style of architecture of the cathedral.

Being in Chichester had opened up a whole new world for her and she was enjoying the independence and the discovery of so many new and exciting things. Edward was so different to the young men of Micklewell with their rough ways. He spoke differently and he behaved differently. Perhaps they would meet again when she returned to continue her training, always supposing she passed her exams. She had no reason to think that she wouldn't. She felt reasonably confident that she had studied as hard as she could and felt hopeful of a positive outcome.

As the air warmed around her and she began to feel the rising heat upon her skin, she turned to retrace her steps across the fields. She walked along the village street, humming to herself. In the distance, she noticed a figure, struggling with some wooden struc-

3

ture. What was it? Who was he and what was he doing there at this early hour? She was both curious and a little concerned that the stranger might turn and see her, still dressed in her nightclothes. As she moved closer, she could see that the person was erecting a painting easel on the bank at the side of the road. She stood back behind a hawthorn bush and watched as he placed and replaced his easel and his stool until he was satisfied with the position. He then positioned a wooden-framed canvas on the easel, opened a wooden box and began sifting through its contents.

All Dot could see from a distance was the curve of his narrow back and his long legs, which seemed to get in his way and be forever at the wrong angle to his body. His movements were slow and fluid and, once he had selected his brushes, he sat for a long time surveying the scene he intended to paint. He raised one of the brushes from time to time, using it as a measuring guide. Dot watched him as long as she dared and then crept out of her hiding place, treading carefully in case he should hear her footsteps and she should be discovered. He must be a visitor at the Manor. She was sure that no one in the farm cottages would have the leisure time to paint or the spare money to buy an easel and painting materials.

Just as she turned into the pathway leading back to Mead Cottages, the artist stood, undid the buttons of his jacket and took off his wide-brimmed hat. The tumble of rich auburn curls that fell over the painter's shoulders shocked Dot. This was no man but a woman. Still not aware that she was being observed, the painter pulled her hair back from her face and adjusted a clip. She then wound the tresses around her hand and tucked them back under her hat. Dot

4

smiled to herself at the assumptions she had made. Was she so conditioned to assume that only a man could be out on his own engaged in this early morning creativity? Why should a woman not be as free to engage her talents as a man? But why the man's clothing? Dot was fascinated by what she had seen and wanted to know more about this mysterious creature, this stranger in their midst.

By the time she got back, the morning routines had begun. She peered round the door and took in the scene. Her older sister, Kate, was preparing the breakfasts for the children with their youngest sister, Tilly, trying to help. Dot still looked at Tilly sometimes and wondered how strange she would feel once she was old enough to understand that her playmate, Ronnie, was actually her nephew. Nature played strange tricks sometimes. Their mother, Ada, had given birth to Tilly within weeks of Kate having Ronnie. Ada was forty-six and Kate, twenty-four. A late pregnancy for Ada and an unexpected one for Kate.

Kate had found a good father for Ronnie in Albert. He was a gentle and patient man. He was at that moment attempting to teach young Ronnie how to tie his own shoe laces. Her father, Jim, was slicing the bread and her mother was pouring the tea. Her younger brother, Henry, was sitting in front of the range with a toasting fork, complaining that it was too hot and why did he always get that job? Dot entered the kitchen and tried to make it to the staircase before she was noticed.

'And where have you been in your nightclothes?' Ada said without lifting her eyes or spilling a drop from the brown earthenware teapot.

'Just taking the air. It's a beautiful morning and I

5

woke early,' Dot replied.

'Well, it's to be hoped Granny White didn't see you. It will be all around the village how she saw that hussy, Dorothy Truscott, parading in her underwear. Bringing her loose city ways to a respectable village,' Ada replied.

'I had a shawl round me,' Dot said.

'Now don't exaggerate, Ma,' Kate said in defence of her sister. 'Anyway, Granny White would do well to mind her own business and get her own house in order, her granddaughter's been seen with more than one ploughboy behind the Queen's Head.'

'I thought you didn't listen to gossip, Kate,' Dot said.

'I don't but I know what I saw,' Kate replied raising one eyebrow.

'And what did you see?' Dot grinned.

'That's enough of that,' Ada said. 'There's small ears listening.'

The two sisters smiled at each other and Dot went upstairs to dress. As Dot prepared herself for the day, she thought about how much their lives had changed since Kate returned home, how different their relationship was now to when she had first gone away to be in service. Compared to her sister, Dot felt she had experienced so little of life. It was true, she wouldn't have wanted to go through what Kate had to cope with, being left to fend for herself and her unborn child, but she had survived. She had come through it all, the birth of her son, the death of the man she loved, the loneliness and squalor of the workhouse.

Dot had led a cosseted life by comparison. Luck had fallen her way and she had been encouraged to make the best of herself by Miss Clarence, the headteacher of the local school and Dot's mentor and friend. She was grateful for the opportunity to become a pupil teacher and to study to become fully qualified. She loved what she was doing, but somehow there was one aspect of life that was passing her by. She was yet to experience any feelings of passion for a man and she wondered when something might happen to arouse such feelings in her. She had received plenty of attentions from young men, it was true, but somehow none of them seemed quite right. She didn't feel anything for them except annoyance sometimes that they kept pestering her. Not that there had been a huge number to choose from in Micklewell. Many had not returned from the war, like her brother Fred. The closest she had come to feeling any attraction to any of them was with Jack Williams, Fred's pal.

She recalled how Jack had come to see them when he arrived home at the end of the war. He hardly said a word but just sat there, screwing his cap up in his hands and looking down rather than into their eyes. He was devastated at the loss of his friend. Perhaps it was because of his closeness to her brother that they started seeing each other. At first it was just a friendship but Jack had become more serious and had started talking about how he wanted to learn all the skills of farm work and become a farm manager one day so that he could settle down and have a family. That was when Dot had realised that she didn't want to be a farmer's wife but a teacher and so she had stopped seeing Jack as often. She liked him but she didn't like him enough to give up her ambition to become a teacher. She didn't love him.

She knew that Kate had been deeply in love with Philip and had been overwhelmed by her emotions.

They had spoken of such things when Kate had come back home, once the raw pain of losing him had eased enough for such deep feelings to be revealed.

As Dot lifted the hairbrush to tidy her unruly hair, she recalled one night when she and Kate were lying together on the bed. It disturbed her to think of it now. How lacking in awareness she had been. Kate had just fed Ronnie. It was the early hours of the morning and Dot couldn't sleep. When Kate placed Ronnie back in the cradle and they crept back under the covers, Dot whispered, 'Do you miss him, Kate?'

As soon as she'd said it, she'd regretted it. What a ridiculous question to ask. How insensitive of her. Kate was lying with her back to her sister and didn't reply immediately. Dot moved her hand to touch her sister's shoulder but stopped when she sensed that Kate was silently weeping. At that moment Dot felt inept, unable to help her sister, unable to understand how deeply Kate felt that loss. She was only eleven years old when Kate had gone to work in Andover, still a child, but she was a woman now and she wanted to experience love too, even if that meant bearing the pain that might come with it.

Dot pulled her hair back and secured it with several pins. She could hear the morning bustle downstairs was in full swing. Albert asking for another quick cup of tea before he set off for the farm. How much life had changed for the better since Kate had met Albert. Calls for her to come down reached her ears. Tilly and Ronnie clamouring for her attention. She never had a moment to herself when she came home but she would not have it any other way. She smoothed down her rather rumpled dress and took a last look in the mirror. Now to face the day! The moment she came downstairs, the demands on her time started.

'Please can we go to the stream and hunt for stick-lebacks?' Ronnie asked.

'Yes, please can we?' Tilly joined in.

'Can we, can we, can we?' they both chorused.

'I need you to go to the mill,' Ada interrupted. 'I'm running out of flour. I promised to bake scones for the village fete and I've only got enough for one batch.'

'And when you come back, do you think you could help me cut up some more squares for the new quilt I'm making, Dot?' Kate asked. 'It's so much quicker when there's two of us. Then I could get on with the stitching.'

'Does anyone mind if I get some breakfast first?' Dot said, smiling. 'I'm sure we can do all those things but there's something I have to do for myself first. I promised I'd call by to see Miss Clarence. She's keen to hear all about how I'm getting on with my training and how the exams went.'

'Well, it's still early yet to pay house calls,' Ada commented. 'The mill will be open though.'

'I suppose that's your way of getting to the top of the list, Ma,' Dot said, throwing a knowing glance at her mother. 'All right, I'll go to the mill first, then I'll go to see Miss Clarence. I will help you with the quilt, Kate, later today. I promise.'

'What about us?' Tilly asked. 'What about the sticklebacks?'

'Best time for sticklebacks is in the late afternoon,' Dot replied. 'Too much bright sun on the water makes them difficult to spot.'

'Dot's right,' Albert said. 'The fish will see your shadow on the water and dart for cover. Best wait 'til tomorrow. I have a lot to do today.'

9

'Can you come with us, Dad?' Ronnie asked.

'Sorry, son,' Albert replied. 'It's a busy time at the farm. Coming up for the harvesting.'

'Will you be collecting the tractor engine for the threshing soon then?' Jim asked. 'There's usually call for my services at the forge, one way or another, when that arrives.'

'We're expecting to pick it up from Stoke any day now,' Albert replied.

'I'll be glad when that's all done for another year,' Kate said. 'I worry about you driving that thing, it's dangerous.'

'So's having babies,' Ada chimed in. 'But there's some things in life that just have to be endured to get the benefits.'

'I'll walk with you as far as the forge, Dot,' Jim said. 'Sounds like we're all in for a busy day. There's four horses to be shod this morning and a pair of new gate fixings to be made for Addison's Farm this afternoon.'

'Can I come?' asked Ronnie. 'I could help with the bellows.'

There was nothing Ronnie loved more than to be with his grandfather in the forge but it was a dangerous place and Dot knew that Kate didn't like him being there when their father was very busy. It would be too easy for him to get in the way or an accident to happen. Jim wasn't too old to work, he was still a fit man, but he did need all his concentration and couldn't manage a small boy at the same time.

Dot saw the excitement and anticipation in her nephew's eyes.

'I tell you what,' she said with a smile. 'Why don't you come with me to the mill and then we can call in at the forge on the way back. You'll be more needed

10

on the bellows once the fire is set, isn't that right, Pa?' Dot asked, winking at her father.

'That's right,' Jim agreed. 'I'll see you later then, shall I?'

Ronnie accepted Dot's suggestion and Tilly was persuaded to help Kate with feeding the chickens and rabbits so that she didn't feel left out.

'I'm going to hold the new baby rabbits,' Tilly said to Ronnie, not wishing to be outdone by Ronnie's invitation to the forge. 'I'm going to be the first to hold them since they were born. Isn't that right, Kate?'

Ronnie just nodded at her in reply. He clearly didn't mind missing holding the baby rabbits if it meant he could work the bellows. There were some things in life that were more exciting than others.

2

The walk to the mill was not especially long but Ronnie's legs were short and his patience even shorter. So, Dot kept him entertained with stories of the mill cats and what good mousers they were, particularly old Jezebel. She left out the part about how the cat got her name, though, and simply said that she often had a litter of kittens at this time of year.

'I'm sure Mrs Deary will let you hold them if their eyes are open,' Dot said, hoping that would encourage his legs to walk a little faster.

The noise of the rushing water met their ears before the mill came into view and Ronnie's pace picked up. As they made their way through the scented willow herb on the river bank, Ronnie almost disappeared from view, the tall plants towering over him. They emerged from the floral forest, right in front of the water wheel which churned and frothed the water. Ronnie stood mesmerised by the rhythmic rotation of the wooden paddles and questions gushed from him. He was on to the next before Dot could answer the first.

'Why is it so noisy?' he asked.

'Where does all that water come from?'

'Who makes that thing that goes around?'

'I don't know who built the mill, Ronnie. You'll have to ask the owners, Mr and Mrs Deary. It's been here as long as I can remember. The water comes from under the ground and then flows into the river. It's noisy because the water is held back in the mill pond and, when it's let go, it's very, very strong. We'll go inside and then you can see how the wheel turns the mill stones that grind the flour.'

Dot steered Ronnie away from the edge of the water and began walking towards the mill entrance. But Ronnie had other ideas and let go of her hand. He ran back to get another look at the water wheel. As soon as she felt him go, she turned and called to him.

'Ronnie, stop, don't . . .'

She ran towards him as fast as she could and grabbed him by the shoulders. She pulled him back towards her and wrapped her arms around his chest.

'Never do that again, Ronnie,' she said rather more roughly than she'd intended.

She turned him around and squatted down in front of him, holding on to both of his hands.

'It's dangerous near the wheel, Ronnie,' she explained. 'The river here is so fast, that no one could swim against it, especially not a boy like you. And the wheel is always turning. Make sure you never go close to it. Do you understand?'

Ronnie's face became serious and he nodded his agreement. She didn't want to frighten him but she didn't want him to place himself in danger either.

'All right,' Dot said. Now, let's go inside and see how everything works shall we?'

The clatter and clunk of the turning machinery greeted them as soon as they stepped through the door. Ronnie put his hands over his ears and looked up at Dot who laughed at him.

The world inside the mill was shrouded in a fine, white dust which floated in the air and tickled Ronnie's nostrils. He sneezed several times.

13

'It affects most people like that, the first time,' Mrs Deary said, as she looked up from her task of scooping the flour from the hopper into sacks. Her round face beamed at them and her eyelashes were heavy with the white powder.

'Welcome home, Dorothy,' Mrs Deary continued. 'I see your ma's got you running errands as soon as you've arrived. You're looking well, a life of study agrees with you then?' She didn't wait for an answer but carried on, her tongue blathering in rhythm with the turning of the millstones. 'Now, this must be young Ronnie,' she said. 'Most boys like to go upstairs and see the stones working. Would you like to?'

Ronnie looked up at Dot, as if asking permission. She nodded her agreement.

'Right ho, up we go then. Mr Deary's up there. He loves to explain the workings. Just you say when you've had enough, mind. He doesn't know when to stop.'

As they reached the top of the stairs, the noise got even louder. Ronnie stood hesitantly on the top step, until Dot pushed him forward.

'He's the spit of his mother,' Mrs Deary said. 'No doubt there's some of his father in there too, I'm guessing.'

Dot didn't reply but encouraged Ronnie to step forward. She could tell when she was being tapped for more information. There was still a certain amount of tittle-tattle surrounding Kate's reappearance with a child and no husband, even five years after the event. The Truscotts had agreed that it would never be spoken of outside the immediate family, except to say that Ronnie's father was killed in the war.

When Mr Deary's enthusiasm for explaining his

14

mill began to pale on Dot as well as Ronnie, Dot made her excuses that her mother wouldn't be able to start her baking until they arrived home with the flour.

'Well, now you know where we are, Ronnie,' Mrs Deary said, 'you can come visit us again.'

They hurried back to the village along the mill stream path, Ronnie's feet more eager now they were headed where he was keener to go.

The forge fire had been lit and was blasting out when they arrived. The glowing red of the coals and the searing heat was sucked in on each breath, a complete contrast to the cool, bleached, dusty atmosphere of the mill.

Ronnie went immediately to his grandfather's side. He knew not to stand too close. He'd been told many times before. He stood for a while watching, astounded by the power of his grandfather's arms, the muscles bulging and the tendons straining as he worked the stubborn metal to the shape he required, bending it to his will. Watching his grandfather at work was what pleased Ronnie most. The sharp sound of the hammer as he brought it down on the red-hot metal and the perfect timing of the clang and ring, clang and ring, as it reverberated around the space. Ronnie loved his grandfather, the smell of his sweat and the droplets on his forehead that trickled down over his cheeks until they were soaked up by his neckerchief. He loved the broad sweep of his back and the firm position of his splayed feet in black boots as he swung the hammer. All of these things spoke to Ronnie of his grandfather's strength and yet he was a gentle man. Ronnie had never seen his grandfather's face split in anger, or heard him raise his voice, but he had seen him cry. He didn't quite understand when his gran told him that they were tears of happiness because why could being happy make you cry? There was so much in the world of adults that he didn't understand but what he did know was that he wanted to become one and then he too could work the fire in the forge.

Ronnie waited until his grandfather's arm raised and fell with the final blow and watched as he grasped the tongs and placed the glowing horse shoe into the water bath. The hissing steam rose and engulfed his grandfather, making him invisible for a while. When the mist cleared, the old man turned and faced Ronnie and the two of them grinned at each other. They shared the joy of the moment passing between them and recognised a mutual pleasure in the perfect magic of molten metal, tamed by flowing water.

Dot handed her father a towel, to wipe his face and stop the sweat from running into his eyes. He paused for a bit to get his breath after such physical exertion and then turned to Ronnie.

'Get me some water, lad, would you?' he said. 'My mouth is as dry as dust. Then, why don't you and Dot fetch me a bucket of water from the pump? The bath needs topping up for the next round of cooling.'

Ronnie took the cup from a small wooden table and went out the back to the pump. He returned the cool water to his grandfather and then he and Dot brought in several buckets until the trough was full.

'We really should be going now, Ronnie, or Ma will be hopping mad waiting for her flour,' Dot said.

'But I haven't worked the bellows yet,' Ronnie protested. 'You said I could work the bellows, Grandad, didn't you?'

'And so you will, Ronnie but your nan needs her flour for baking and we don't want to put her in a

16

lather now, do we? I'll make sure you can work the bellows tomorrow.'

That was another thing Ronnie didn't understand about adults. It was always tomorrow and tomorrow. When he was older, he would never say 'tomorrow' but 'let's do it today'.

3

The following afternoon, Dot set out with Ronnie and Tilly in search of sticklebacks amongst the shallows of the river. They walked to join the many generations of Micklewell children before them, who had whiled away a summer's afternoon, lying flat on their bellies, trying to spot the elusive little fish in their favourite hiding place. The sun flickered and flamed between overhung trees and dazzled Dot's eyes as she tried to focus on the two children, winding their way in front of her along the riverside path. They were playing tag and their feet flew along the earth and stones, their bodies twisting and dodging this way and that, their laughter as light as the breeze in the trees.

Dot lost sight of them once or twice and called to them to slow down and stay where she could see them, but they were so engrossed in their game, that they couldn't or didn't want to hear her. At the second bend in the river, they disappeared again from view and a short while later the screams of joy and excitement turned to one penetrating scream of fear. Dot ran immediately towards the sound, her heart thumping in her chest and her open mouth struggling for breath. She kicked against her skirts which were threatening to wrap themselves around her legs and hastily raised them so that she could run faster. As she turned the bend, she could see Tilly standing on the riverbank calling Ronnie's name over and over.

Dot's eyes scanned up and down the fast-flowing

18

water trying to spot Ronnie but the sunlight through the overhanging trees blurred her vision. Tilly looked up at Dot, her eyes wide and stuttered some words that Dot couldn't make out.

'Ronnie!' Dot howled.

Dot searched for signs of her nephew, her heart hammering in her chest. She finally spotted the top of Ronnie's head as it emerged between the floating weed some distance downstream. She tried to control the sense of panic that threatened to overwhelm her and was about to jump into the river when she noticed someone ahead of her, already swimming towards the struggling boy.

In a moment the dark shape was upon him, lifting Ronnie's chin out of the water and kicking hard for the bank. Dot was rooted to the spot, barely breathing or taking her eyes off the two figures locked together in their battle against the current. The stranger managed to get Ronnie into the shallows and was struggling out of the water with him. He looked so limp and still. Dot grasped Tilly's hand and ran, dragging Tilly behind her.

By the time they reached the two figures, the stranger was wading out of the water, holding Ronnie, whose head and limbs dangled, lifeless. Dot rushed straight to them and placed a hand on Ronnie's head.

'Oh God, is he?' Dot sobbed, tears flowing down her cheeks. She looked at the stranger's face, her eyes full of fear and hope. It was her, it was the artist woman.

'I need to check if he is breathing,' the woman said. 'We have to get the water out of him.'

She lay Ronnie down, placed her ear next to his mouth, then tilted his head back and began pressing hard on his chest.

19

'Don't, you're hurting him,' Tilly shouted.

But the woman carried on. After a few minutes, a cough escaped from Ronnie's mouth, followed by spurts of water. His eyelids flickered and he coughed and spluttered more, his chest heaving as he struggled for breath. The stranger stopped pressing on Ronnie and sat back. She then turned Ronnie on his side and finally looked up at Dot and Tilly.

'He's breathing,' the woman said.

Dot had been holding her own breath for so long, while she watched this person fighting to save Ronnie's life, that she almost collapsed. Her body drew in oxygen with gulps of complete relief. She knelt beside Ronnie, stroking his damp hair and listening to the air flow in and out of his lungs, whilst whispering his name.

Tilly squatted on the grass in front of his still body and peered at him, her little face screwed up in lines of worry and fear, but as he opened his eyes and looked at her, her mouth drew upwards into a smile. She threw her arms around him and held him tight.

'I think he'll be all right now,' the woman said.

'Thank God!' Dot gasped. She moved closer to Ronnie and lifted him onto her lap, wrapping her arms around him to warm him. He was shivering and she rubbed his arms and legs, until he spoke to her.

'I'm all right,' he said weakly.

'Yes, you're all right, Ronnie, thanks to this brave lady,' she said.

The woman nodded. 'He'll live,' she replied. 'He's a lucky boy that I saw him fall in.'

'And that you're a strong swimmer,' Dot said, looking up at the stranger.

The woman's clothes hung off her, dripping into a

puddle of river water where she stood, her toes long and delicately formed. Dot's eyes scanned upwards over long legs draped in clinging, dark grey trousers. A loose, white shirt moulded itself to the shape of her breasts and her long hair stuck to the sides of her face and snaked down across her neck. Her eyes were wide and bright and her lips parted in the exertion of her brave efforts to save Ronnie.

'You saved his life,' Dot said, her voice wavering as she began to realise how close they'd come to losing Ronnie. 'How can we ever thank you enough? If you hadn't been there. If you hadn't acted so quickly . . .'

'And if I knew where I'd thrown my shoes,' the young woman interrupted, giving an embarrassed smile, 'I might be able to walk home and get some dry clothes.'

'We'll help you, it's the least we can do,' Dot offered.

'No, you won't,' the young woman replied. 'You'll get this young man home, before he catches a chill on top of everything else.'

The young woman's face held an expression that said: You don't argue with me, and Dot agreed that Ronnie looked strong enough to walk now. As they shook hands, Dot said, 'I don't even know your name. You're not local, are you?'

'Miriam de Clere,' the woman replied. 'And no, I'm not from this area. I'm staying with my aunt, Mrs Humboldt, at Frog Hall.'

'I'm sure Ronnie's parents will want to thank you,' Dot said. 'I'm Dorothy Truscott. My sister, Kate, is Ronnie's mother and Albert is his father. We live with Ronnie's grandparents at number two, Mead Cottages, just beside the watercress beds. Do call by, please, won't you, so we can thank you properly.

21

Tomorrow afternoon perhaps?'

'I will,' Miriam replied, fixing Dot with her dark eyes. 'I most certainly will.'

* * *

Ada Truscott almost dropped her rolling pin when she saw the state of Ronnie. His clothes were soaking wet and he had little bits of river weed stuck in his hair.

'Whatever's happened?' she cried.

'Ronnie fell in the river and he almost drownded,' Tilly announced.

'But he didn't, as we can all see, Tilly. So just let me do the explaining,' Dot said.

'A lady saved him,' Tilly went on, undeterred.

'What lady?' Ada said, raising her voice.

'I said that I would explain, Tilly,' Dot said in a firm tone. 'Now, make yourself useful and go fetch a towel from the outhouse.'

'Well, are you going to tell me then or what?' Ada complained, holding her chest, her breathing heavy and laboured.

Dot glanced at her mother, concerned that the scare might bring on one of her turns which often made her feel faint. Dot had noticed that Ada's usual pace of doing things had slowed since the last time she was home. Her mother sat for longer spells between jobs than she used to and she seemed to have a constant cough, even now in the height of the summer.

'Where's Kate?' Dot asked.

'Here,' Kate said, appearing at the bottom of the stairs. 'What's going on?'

As soon as Ronnie saw her, he rushed to her side.

'Whatever's happened?' asked Kate, casting a severe look at her sister.

'Weren't you looking after him, Dot? He's absolutely soaked. He must have fallen right in. Where were you?'

Kate knelt down beside Ronnie and took the towel from Tilly who had reappeared.

'Let's get these wet clothes off, shall we?' Kate said gently removing them and wrapping him up in the towel. She lifted him and sat with him on her knee.

'Now, let's hear what happened,' Kate said, once she felt her son was settled and comforted.

'They were running on ahead, the two of them,' Dot explained. 'I told them not to but they went out of sight round the bend. By the time I got to them, Ronnie was being swept downriver.'

'A lady jumped in and saved him,' Tilly interrupted but stopped when the sharp stab of Dot's gaze reached her.

'What lady?' Kate asked.

'Her name is Miriam de Clere, she's visiting Frog Hall. Old Mrs Humbolt is her aunt,' Dot replied. 'I've asked her to call by tomorrow. I thought you would like to thank her yourself.'

'Yes, of course. We owe her a great deal,' Kate replied hugging Ronnie close. Dot noticed that Kate withheld any reprimands for not doing as he was told. She was obviously too relieved that he had survived his ordeal. That talk could wait until later.

★ ★ ★

The tapping on the front door came just as the family had just cleared away the dinner things and were

23

settling down for the evening. The whole family stopped whatever it was they were doing and looked, as one, towards the sound.

'Who the devil can that be at this time of the day?' Jim Truscott said, holding his shaving cup ready for his evening ablutions.

'Well, we won't know if someone doesn't answer the door,' Ada said, hurriedly taking off her apron. 'You go, Dot. You look the most respectable.'

Dot moved into the tiny sitting room just as a second rapping began on the door. She gently lifted the edge of the net curtain and saw a dark figure standing there. The person's face was turned away but the hat was unmistakeable. It was the artist, Miriam de Clere. Dot glanced at herself in the over-mantle mirror and was relived that she didn't look too dishevelled. Her mother would be mortified that she would be expected to receive a guest in her working clothes. Dot had to answer, though. She couldn't leave Miriam standing on the front step. She opened the door.

'I'm so sorry to call so late,' Miriam said. 'But my aunt needs me to accompany her tomorrow to Stoke and, having said that I would come to meet your family as you requested, I really couldn't leave you wondering what had happened to me. It would have been too rude.'

'Please, come in,' Dot replied. 'Do sit down,' she continued, noticing Miriam's slightly uncomfortable stance. 'I'll go and tell my family that you're here.'

Dot pulled the door to behind her, as close as she dared without looking like she was shutting Miriam out. The churchlike silence and stillness in the kitchen made Dot whisper the announcement that it was the young woman who'd saved Ronnie.

'But you said she was coming tomorrow,' hissed Ada.

'Never mind, Ma, she's here now,' Kate said. 'Ronnie, Tilly, upstairs. Henry go with them and keep them quiet.'

'But we want to . . .' Tilly began.

'Want never gets,' snapped Ada. 'Now, do as you're told. Dot, Kate and Albert, you go through and meet the lady. Your father and I need to make ourselves a bit more presentable.'

'She'll take us as she finds us,' Jim said.

Ada threw a disapproving look at him and went upstairs to comb her hair and put on a clean blouse. By the time Ada made her entry into the sitting room, there was a ripple of laughter around the room as everyone relaxed in Miriam's company. Dot was full of admiration at the personal magnetism of Miriam de Clere. She'd managed in a few words to set the family at ease.

Miriam rose and greeted Ada. 'Ah, Mrs Truscott. Pleased to meet you,' she said, extending her hand.

'Pleased to meet you too, I'm sure,' Ada replied, sitting down in the only remaining chair.

Dot couldn't help but notice the expression of restrained shock on her mother's face. Miriam's masculine clothing was not the sort of dress generally seen about Micklewell.

'Miss de Clere was just telling us of the time she fell in the duck pond as a child,' Jim said. 'She was throwing the bread for the ducks a bit too enthusiastically, lost her balance and went head first in after it.'

'Not that what happened to Ronnie was like that at all,' Miriam said. 'The duck pond was shallow and the river is fast-flowing. It could have been much more serious.'

'It could indeed,' Ada said.

'And we can't thank you enough for saving his life,' Albert added, taking Kate's hand.

'No, most certainly,' Kate said. 'If you hadn't been there . . . well, it doesn't bear thinking about.'

'Oh, I'm sure Dorothy would have done as well as I . . .' Miriam began.

'I am nowhere near as strong a swimmer as you,' Dot said. 'You reached him very quickly.'

'I only did what anyone else would have done,' Miriam replied.' How is the young man anyway? Has he recovered?'

'Perhaps we should let Miss de Clere see for herself,' Albert said. 'He should realise what a lucky escape he had.'

'No, no, please. I would prefer that you didn't make him relive that moment. The best thanks I could have is that you teach him how to swim. Then, one day he will be able to save himself,' Miriam replied.

'Oh my, what am I thinking of,' Ada said. 'We haven't offered you any refreshment, Miss de Clere. Kate, put the kettle on, would you?'

'Thank you but I'm afraid I must decline,' Miriam replied. 'I promised my aunt I would not be too long, as she is used to me playing a hand or two of canasta with her before bedtime.'

They all said their goodbyes and thanked Miriam again. Once the front door was closed, Ada said,' Well, she's a queer fish. What was she wearing?'

'She's an artist, Ma,' Dot replied.

'And?' Ada said. 'Being an artist doesn't mean you have to dress like a man, does it?'

'Well, perhaps it's what artists wear,' Dot said. 'I don't see why she shouldn't wear what's comfortable

26

for her.'

'Well, I don't know. What is the world coming to! It's all topsy-turvy, if you ask me,' Ada grumbled.

Kate and Dot's eyes met and they both raised them skywards whilst exchanging discreet grins. Their mother was so predictable.

4

It was several days before Dot met Miriam again. She was walking along the path beside the river, when she noticed the black-suited figure of Miriam de Clere, seated on a stool, with her canvas laid out on her easel. She was completely engaged in her task of mixing and applying paint, her head moving up to the subject of the mill before her and then down to her box of paints, then up again to take in the scene once more and down to touch her brush to the canvas. Dot was fascinated and stood for a while at a distance. She wanted to go and look over the young woman's shoulder but felt that would be rude and an imposition.

She decided to walk quietly by, keeping her distance and trying not to disturb the artist at her work. As if by a sixth sense that she was being observed, however, the young woman turned her head and looked out from beneath the wide brim of her hat. Her eyes were almost as dark as her suit and she had a serious expression, her lips pursed. Dot was taken by surprise then, when the young woman's face broke out into a wide smile and she inclined her head and said, 'Good morning.'

'I'm sorry. I didn't mean to disturb you,' Dot said, blushing.

'I'm not disturbed, at all,' the young woman replied. 'In fact, do you mind just walking forwards a little, towards the mill? I'll tell you when I want you to stop.'

Dot was not sure what to make of this request but

she said, 'All right,' and began to walk along the bank.

'Stop,' Miriam called. 'Now, turn around.'

Dot turned and waited.

'Put your arm through your basket and hold it in front of you.'

Dot did as she was told, yet at the same time she wondered what this young woman was about. Should she feel affronted by being told where and how to stand or flattered? Was Miriam painting her? Was she to be in this work of art?

Just as Dot was about to ask if she could move, Miriam called, 'Right, that's enough, thank you. I've got the broad outline, I can fill in the details later.'

Dot wasn't sure if she was being dismissed. Surely, she wasn't going to just expect Dot not to be interested in what she was painting? Should she ask to see it?

At that moment, Miriam put down her brushes, wiped her hands on a cloth and marched towards Dot.

'How rude of me,' she said. 'I apologise for being so abrupt. I get carried away sometimes, lost in my work. I'm a bit pushed for time. I'm doing a series of paintings for Lord Berrington at the Manor and he wants them finished for his wife's birthday. You know the Berringtons?'

Dot tried to conceal a grin. 'I know of them,' she said. 'I don't exactly move in their circles. My parents live, as you know, in one of the cottages beside the watercress beds. We are not familiar with the lords and ladies hereabouts.'

Miriam laughed. 'Of course, how pompous of me.'

Dot's eyes flickered in the direction of the easel and canvas and Miriam said, 'Would you like to see the painting so far? It's got a long way to go as yet but I think the addition of you in the foreground will make it more alive, more real. Don't expect too much, though. It's a work in progress.'

The two women walked back to the easel and Miriam encouraged Dot to stand before the painting.

'Well, what do you think?' Miriam asked.

Dot had never been asked to pass comment on someone's art work before and tentatively said, 'I think it's very good. You have captured the mill very well.'

'That is the usual, standard, complimentary answer, Dorothy,' Miriam replied, looking straight into Dot's eyes. 'Now, I want you to be more truthful. Have I captured the essence of this river? Don't answer straight away. Take your time. Look and tell me what you feel.'

Dot didn't know what to say, no one had ever asked for her opinions in that way and no stranger had been quite as forthright. This young woman was quite unlike anyone she had met before.

'Well . . . if I am honest . . .' Dot began.

'Oh, yes. I want you to be honest,' Miriam interrupted.

'I think that it all looks a bit as if nothing is happening. The mill wheel doesn't look as if it's turning and the river is too still. Look at it now, it's always moving. See how the weed all streams along with the flow, like a woman's hair in the wind?'

'Yes, I see,' Miriam said, pausing and holding Dot's gaze. 'I do see. Thank you, Dorothy. Now, I must get back to painting, immediately, before your words dissolve and fly away on the breeze. Good day to you. I hope we shall meet again.'

'Good day, Miss de Clere,' Dot replied. 'I sincerely

hope we do.'

'Call me, Miriam, please.'

'Miriam then,' Dot replied, feeling quite elated that her words had been accepted and that her opinion was valued. The encounter with Miriam de Clere had left a lasting impression upon her but she didn't quite know what the depth of that impression was, as yet.

5

The village fete was always an event to look forward to and the Truscott family were all there to join in with the fun. Early that morning, Jim and Albert had helped put out the trestle tables stored in Addison's barn and Kate and Dot had assisted the other women of the village in washing down and covering the tables with brightly-coloured cloths.

The village green looked a picture with bunting and flags hung from the trees, balloon sellers and an array of stalls displaying flowers and vegetables that were to be judged by the vicar during the afternoon. Jim Truscott had won the best in class entry for his carrots last year and was hopeful that, this year, his onions would win a prize. Ada had made scones to be sold in the refreshments corner and had also entered a Victoria sponge for the cake-making competition. Tilly and Ronnie proudly held their painted flower pots for the best decorated pot in the under sixes category and deposited them on the table with broad grins.

'Do you think one of us might win?' Tilly asked.

'I think you stand a very good chance,' Dot said.

'Can we go to the hoopla stall?' Ronnie asked. 'I want to win a jar of sweets this year. I'm much better at throwing. I've been practising.'

'And then have a pony ride?' added Tilly.

'One thing at a time,' laughed Ada, 'you're making my head spin.'

'I'll take them around,' Dot offered. 'You three take Ma for a well-earned rest at the tea stall. She's had a busy time with all the preparations for today and a slice of someone else's cake wouldn't go amiss, I'm sure.'

'I wouldn't say no to that.' Ada smiled. 'But I thought you needed to do a stint at the skittles, Jim?'

Jim looked at his fob watch. 'No, not yet. We've got the tug of war first, haven't we, Albert? So, we need all the energy we can get.'

'Oh! Can we have some cake?' Tilly pleaded.

'You can't do everything all at once,' Kate said. 'Now, which is it to be, hoopla, pony rides or cake?'

'Hoopla,' said Ronnie.

'Pony ride,' said Tilly.

They all laughed.

Dot accompanied the children and they added 'guess the number of sweets in the jar' to the fun, Dot making the guess on their behalf.

After about an hour, a bell was rung to announce the start of the tug of war competition.

'Come on,' Dot said. 'We mustn't miss this. Let's go and find the others.'

The family stood around the central arena and cheered as Jim and Albert's team came in and took up the rope. They were the Queen's Head team and the opposition were the men from the King's Head at Hatch. The competition had become a local tradition and was known as the Battle of the Kings and Queens.

'Take the strain,' the referee announced. Sixteen pairs of legs dug into the hard ground. Sixteen pairs of muscular arms tensed, faces grimaced and necks and shoulders strained. The tug of war began.

Shouts of 'Pull, lads, pull' and 'Dig in' were called

from members of the crowd and the referee kept his eye firmly on the knotted handkerchief in the centre of the rope, watching every movement to the left and to the right.

First the Queens had the upper hand and then the Kings. They seemed to be equally matched for a while. The sounds of the crowd cheering for their own side started as a murmur but soon accelerated into a roar, as people lost their inhibitions and children jumped up and down with excitement.

When the Queen's team finally won, there was clapping for both sides and a huge cheer for the victors as they departed the arena.

'What's Jack Williams doing in the King's team?' Dot asked. 'He's one of ours.'

'They needed some more muscle at the Kings,' Ada explained. 'Their team was hit hard after the war. If you remember, the fete didn't happen at all for two years. No one had the heart for it. So, when it got started again, some of our men volunteered to pull for the other side and Jack was one of them.'

'He's a good man, is Jack,' Kate added. 'He was a trusted friend to our Fred. I remember Fred saying in his letters how they always looked out for each other. There was one time when Jack saved him from a bullet by shoving him into a shell hole.'

Dot knew that Kate and Ada had a soft spot for Jack and since she'd been back at home, they had both been asking if Dot had any plans to see him during this visit. They weren't exactly subtle in their hints that he would make a good husband.

'I'm surprised that he hasn't married,' Ada said. 'The war took so many of our fine young men. I'm sure any young woman hereabouts would jump at the chance if only he would ask them.'

'He's obviously waiting for the right woman to say yes,' Kate replied, looking at Dot.

'I thought you and Jack were sweethearts at one time,' Kate continued. 'You spent a lot of time together when you were a pupil teacher and he started as a farm hand at Addison's. He's very good-looking and such a hard worker. What happened between you two?'

Dot didn't reply. It was true, they'd been walking out together before she'd become interested in qualifying to become a teacher. He'd kissed her on many occasions and she did like it, although sometimes he demanded too much of her time. They were often seen together at village events like the May Queen celebrations and the Harvest Supper dance. He was a good dancer and she liked being whirled around the floor in his strong arms. He was five years older than her and she felt the envy of the other local girls that she had the attentions of the good-looking Jack Williams. When he came home after the war and her brother Fred sadly didn't, he often came to see her parents and they would drink tea. Her parents were pleased to see him and talked about old times Sometimes she wondered why he came because he wasn't the best conversationalist.

As time went on, Dot realised that he came to see her as much as anything. His eyes constantly flicked in her direction and he seemed disappointed if she found an excuse to leave the room. Finally, he asked her out. She agreed. She had to admit that she found him attractive but he was too intense. There was an urgency sometimes in the way he held her. She felt his experience in his hands when he touched her. He'd become quite passionate on one occasion and she

35

recalled telling him not to go any further than touching her breasts. Despite this, she removed his hand from her skirts on more than one occasion and he'd apologised but said he couldn't help it.

'Life is short, Dot,' he'd said, 'and even shorter for us soldiers at the front. We never know if the next bullet has got our name on it.'

A few times, she had almost succumbed to his charms but she realised she had to be sensible. She wanted to become a teacher and to be unmarried and pregnant would see an end to her career before it even began.

She snapped out of her thoughts when Kate prompted her. 'So, what if he still holds a candle for you, Dot, and asks you out, what are you going to say? You'd better decide quickly because he might come over and put you on the spot.'

Dot's head was spinning and she felt as if she was reddening from her hair roots to her chest.

'I like him well enough,' Dot replied, 'I just don't want to give him a reason to hope . . .'

Her voice trailed off.

'Hope what, Dot? You are a dark horse. Sometimes I think that you're keeping things back from me. You used to tell me everything. Do you still have some feelings for him?'

Dot kept her council and did not reveal anything more to her sister. She wasn't sure herself what she felt, anyway.

'Well, he still likes you a lot, that's obvious. Look, he's talking to Dad and Albert now, but his eyes keep sliding over here in this direction. Now, I wonder why that would be?' Kate teased.

The three men came to join them and Dot's breath quickened.

'Good to see you home again, Dot. I hope you are well,' Jack said with a smile.

Dot acknowledged his greeting. 'Thank you, yes,' she replied, not wanting to engage with him too much in case Kate was right and he asked her out in front of the entire family. That could be very embarrassing.

Dot had tried to avoid him on her last two visits home because she didn't want to become too distracted by him. She needed to concentrate on her studies and, she had to admit, he was a distraction. Now, with him standing in front of her, his tanned skin highlighting his tousled blond hair and startling blue eyes, she could feel herself weakening. His broad shoulders and confident smile held her gaze. There was something about him, this time, that attracted her more. When his lips closed and he slowly licked them, there was a sensuousness about that simple action that stirred something in her. Something that she had not felt in the past. What was it? Was there something different about him or had something changed in her? She wasn't sure, she just felt that those lips were drawing her in, asking to touch hers.

'Jack's asked if we're all going to the Barn Dance tonight,' Jim said. 'I don't know about you, Ada, but I think I'll be ready for my bed tonight, after today. Too much excitement is not good for the old ticker.'

'Oh, there's nothing wrong with your ticker, Pa,' Kate said. 'You've got years in you yet. I'd like to go. How about it, Albert, Dot?

'You go with Dot,' Albert said. 'I'll stay and see the children to bed. You know what they're like after an exciting day. It might take a while to settle them down.'

'I think that's code for trying to get out of dancing,'

37

Kate whispered to Dot.

'We'll go, won't we, Dot,' Kate announced, without consulting her sister. 'We love a good barn dance.'

Dot threw her a look. Kate was matchmaking and she wasn't sure that rekindling a past association was the right thing to do, but there was one thing that Kate and Ada were right about, he was good-looking and the look in his eyes at that moment said how much he wanted to resume their relationship.

6

The two country sisters strolled, arm in arm, down Frog Lane towards Addison's barn. They both wore cool, loose-fitting cotton dresses, for they knew that they would get hotter as the evening went on.

'I intend to accept every invitation to dance that I get,' Kate said. 'It's been so long since I last danced and if no one invites us, then we'll dance with each other, eh, Dot?'

They talked excitedly as they anticipated who might be there and which dance tunes the band might play.

'I hope we get to dance 'Strip the Willow',' Dot said. 'That's my favourite.'

'Do you remember your first dance, Dot?' Kate asked. 'It was just before I went into service. I was fifteen, Fred was thirteen. and you were only seven. Henry was just a year old and we left him with Mary Suss so we could all go as a family. Ma and Pa took it in turns to take us round the floor and teach us the dances. Fred tried to get out of it as much as possible and disappeared halfway through the evening with his friends. When we finally found him, he was outside behind the stables, drinking scrumpy. He was so drunk that he fell into the duck pond on the way home.'

They both laughed and agreed that Fred was the best brother to them and how much they missed him.

As they neared the gates of the farm, they could hear the strains of the music filtering out into the evening air. People were sitting around outside on hay bales, laughing and drinking and the thump and skitter of feet on the dance floor stirred up dust that floated in clouds out of the open doorway. The two sisters stepped inside and were immediately swept up in the circle of bodies swooping around the large open space.

'Come on, Dot. It's the 'Old Swan Gallop'. We can do this,' Kate shouted above the sound of the music and grabbed Dot's hand.

Soon they were galloping around the floor, competing for space with everyone else. Couples narrowly avoided hitting each other and some, who were a bit over enthusiastic, careered into the onlookers sitting around the edges. But all was taken in good humour and, when the music subsided, some raced for the door for fresh air, others had red faces and were mopping their brows. All looked as if they were enjoying themselves immensely and were clapping the band and chatting to each other, nodding and smiling. The whole atmosphere was one of joy and abandonment, the most proficient dancers happily tolerating the ones with two left feet.

Dot and Kate took a short breather and glanced around the room. The caller announced that the next dance was to be the 'Dashing White Sergeant' and they were asked by the Carter brothers to join their group to make up the numbers. The Carter brothers were thatchers and their hands were rough, besides the eldest brother was renowned amongst the local women for his tendency to place his hand more on a woman's buttocks than her waist. People were quickly teaming up and it was the brothers or miss out on a dance. Kate looked at Dot with questioning eyes and

Dot nodded. They were swept up once again into the melee.

When that dance ended, Dot felt a tap on her shoulder. She turned to see Jack Williams, looking straight at her.

'Can I have the next dance, Dot?' Jack asked.

Kate winked at Dot, backed away and said that she was going to get herself a drink.

'I'm really quite out of breath,' Dot replied.

'Oh, come on. It's a 'Military Two Step'. It's easy,' Jack replied, taking her hand and guiding her back onto the floor.

As the band struck up their tune, Jack placed his hand on her waist and drew her to his side. When he took her in a ballroom hold, he held her close and Dot could feel his warm breath on her neck. It made her shiver with pleasure.

When the dance was over, she pulled away from him but he held her tight and whispered in her ear, 'Let's go outside. It's very hot in here. I'll buy you a drink.'

Dot scanned the room to see if Kate was in sight but she couldn't see her. She went with him. She could feel her heart pounding against her ribs and wasn't sure if it was the effect of dancing one dance after the other in quick succession, or something else. She was tingling with so many mixed sensations that she couldn't define one from the other. When Jack handed her a cup of cider, she downed it in one.

'I didn't take you for a drinker, Dorothy Truscott.' Jack grinned. 'Would you like another?'

'Yes, please,' she said passing him the cup.

Dot felt the cider seeping through her body and into her veins. She had spent so much time closeted

41

away with her books that she'd forgotten what it was like to really let her hair down and just enjoy herself. What harm was there in having a good time?

They sat shoulder to shoulder on a hay bale and she felt the heat of his body next to hers.

'So how is life in the town, Dot, and how's the studying going? Is it all what you expected it to be or do you get homesick for our little village?' Jack asked.

'Chichester is a really interesting place to live, actually,' she replied. 'And I've always liked studying.'

'Yes, I know. It was hard enough to tear you away from your reading and come out with me before you decided to train as a teacher. You seem to be even more difficult to pin down now. I know you've been back several times. I hope you're not avoiding me?'

'Studying takes up most of my time. That and seeing my family,' Dot replied.

'You're still sure that's what you want to do then, become a teacher?' Jack asked.

'Yes, I'm sure. It's all I've ever wanted to do,' Dot said.

'Not much room in your life for other things then?' Jack continued.

'I guess not,' Dot replied.

'No time for this, for example?' he said, turning towards her and placing his arms around her shoulders.

He kissed her fully on the mouth and drew her closer to him. She felt no desire to resist and gave in to the sensation that surged through her. She'd never known such a feeling. Somehow it felt different to the times in the past. She just didn't want it to end. Jack leaned away from her, stood up and took her hand. He held her gaze for a moment or two and then pulled her up and led her away from the hubbub and the chatter. They walked, hand in hand, behind the barn and towards the apple orchard. The sun was setting behind the trees, creating a glow that made Dot feel completely relaxed and at ease.

They didn't say anything to each other but just walked until they had left the noise of the barn dance behind. Jack stopped when they reached the edge of the orchard and leaned towards her, caressing her hair. They stood with their bodies close together, looking into each other's eyes. He kissed her again and she felt the passion in his touch. He took her hand and sat down on the grass, pulling her down with him. She lay beside him for a moment, looking up at the darkening sky and then closed her eyes in a wave of intense pleasure. She hadn't expected to feel like this. She sensed him lean over her and he kissed her again. His breath was warm and sweet on her face. He kissed her forehead and her cheeks, he kissed her neck and her chest. His hands were gentle and he touched her breasts, slowly and tenderly. The feelings that were coursing through her body threatened to overwhelm her but she didn't want him to stop. His tongue searched her mouth and she arched her back in a spasm of sheer joy. She felt his hands move down her body and he was lifting her skirt and whispering to her.

'You're so lovely, Dot. I've been wanting to do this for so long. You're beautiful. I love you, Dot.'

Dot suddenly panicked. She realised that she had let things go too far. She sat upright and pulled her skirt down.

'Please, Jack. Let's go back. I can't do this,' she panted.

'But you must realise that I love you. I don't want anyone else. Dot, will you marry me? I'm prepared to wait. I don't expect you to give up your studies. I know how important it is to you. Just tell me you'll think about it, please.'

Dot stood up and with more vehemence than she'd intended, she said, 'I can't make any promises, Jack. I want to become a teacher. I can't allow anything to stand in my way.'

'But I'm not standing in your way. You can't deny that you enjoyed what we've just done. I felt it in you. You want me and I want you. You can't let ambition stand in the way of true feelings, Dot.'

'I'm not. I'm just being sensible, that's all,' Dot replied.

'You're being a child. A child in the body of a woman. You need to grow up, Dot, and face up to what happens between a man and woman when they have feelings for each other. Tell me that you weren't enjoying me making love to you. Tell me you didn't feel something.'

'That's not the point, Jack . . .'

'That's entirely the point. Such feelings will out, Dot, believe me.'

They stood looking at each other for a while until Dot could bear it no longer and looked away, trying to make sense of what had just happened. He was right, she had felt such a yearning to give herself to him but she couldn't. She'd made plans for her future and she couldn't let a moment's passion weaken her resolve.

'I can't marry you, Jack,' she whispered. 'I'm sorry but I can't.'

7

The bringing of the traction engine from Stoke was an annual event. The great, heaving, steaming beast would arrive in the village, accompanied by gaggles of excited children and anxious adults, warning their offspring of the dangers of falling under the powerful machine. The clanking and grinding of the huge metal wheels and the plume of smoke rising into the evening sky, heralding its approach meant the cry would go up, 'It's here, the engine's here.'

So, it was with excited expectation that the children waited on the roadside that day and amongst them Henry, Ronnie and Tilly. The older ones stood up on the bank, promoting themselves to the position of lookouts, while the younger ones squatted on the ditch edges throwing stones and drawing patterns in the dirt with sticks.

'Is it coming yet?' Daniel Kimber asked his big brother.

'Should be here any time now,' fifteen-year-old Reuben replied. 'Father said he thought they would arrive after supper time and that's an hour gone.'

Up and down the village street, people stood at their garden gates or hung out of their upstairs windows for a first glimpse of the engine, grinding and roaring its way into their evening calm.

Old Mother White had dragged her stool outside her picket gate and was occasionally waving her walking stick in the direction of the little gang, warning

45

them to stay off the road.

'You hear me?' she squeaked, her ageing vocal chords straining to make them pay attention. 'Listen to your elders. Them's dangerous machines.'

A rumble of comments surged amongst the impatient group.

'Silly old biddy.'

'Daft old thing.'

'Wants to mind her own business.'

'Happen it is her business,' Reuben said. 'Her son got killed in the war and she's just fearful for your safety is all. So, show a bit of respect.'

Duly reprimanded, the children all settled down and waited for this most momentous event in the whole year. Apart from the Harvest Supper when there was music and dancing and the wassailing with warmed cider and mince pies, there was very little excitement in the village of Micklewell.

'Will my dad be driving?' Ronnie asked.

'Could be him or could be the other driver, Ernie Kimber. They take it in turns,' Henry replied.

'I hope it's Dad,' Ronnie said, getting to his feet for the fifth time since they'd arrived.

'It might be a while yet, Ronnie. So, you might as well play with Tilly for a bit longer,' Henry said.

'Look what I brought,' Tilly announced with a grin and out of one pocket she took five smooth pebbles. 'I've been collecting them. We can play five stones.'

Ronnie and Tilly were absorbed in their game and had attracted a little group of onlookers, when Reuben Kimber shouted, 'Here comes someone.'

'Is it the engine?' Daniel asked. 'I can't hear anything.'

46

'No. I think it's Davy Knight. He's running like the wind.'

As Davy approached, they could see something was wrong. The boy was sweating and breathing heavily. Henry went to meet him. Davy was struggling to speak, he bent over and tried to slow his breathing enough to talk.

'What is it, Davy? What's happened? Where's the engine?' Henry asked.

'An accident,' Davy gasped. 'Out on the road from Hatch. Need help. Got to get help.'

Reuben placed his hands on Davy's shoulders and did his best to slow him down but the boy's eyes were wide and he was babbling, not making a great deal of sense.

'Tell me, Davy. Is anybody hurt?' Reuben said.

Davy nodded, his eyes beginning to water and his chin quivering. By now one or two other members of the village had begun walking up the street. Walter and Mary Suss were the first to reach them. Walter's calm presence helped get more information out of Davy who kept shouting, 'Got to help them. Got to get help.'

'Now Davy, take a deep breath and tell us precisely what's happened,' Walter said.

'Haaaa,' he sighed. 'We were rounding a bend in the road on Nunnery Hill and a carriage was coming in the opposite direction. The drivers tried to avoid each other and . . .'

Davy fought to try to get the words out but his voice and his nerve failed him and gave way to sobbing.

'Who was driving the engine?' Henry asked, fearful of the reply.

'Give him time, Henry,' Walter said. 'The boy's run

a long way.'

Davy looked across at Henry. 'It's your Albert,' he said.

'Albert was driving?' Henry asked.

'No. He was . . .'

'Was what?' Henry shouted..

'He was walking beside. He went under the wheels,' Davy said.

Walter, noticing the fear in Henry, did his best to reassure him that things might not be as bad as they seemed, but Henry was already gathering up Ronnie and Tilly. 'I have to tell Kate,' he said.

'Mary and I will come with you,' Walter replied.

'Someone should summon the doctor,' Mary said.

By now, several other villagers had gathered round, alerted by the shouts. Offers of assistance came from all directions.

'I'll go for Dr Morrison,' Eddie Burton shouted.

'And I'll fetch Mabel Taylor. She's a nurse. Saw plenty during the war. She'll cope until the doctor comes,' Susan Burton added.

The crowd dispersed and watched as Henry hurried down the road towards Mead Cottages with Walter. Mary followed along behind with Ronnie and Tilly who asked questions that Mary was unable to answer, for she didn't know how.

Kate didn't have to enquire what Henry was doing home without Albert and the children. She could see it in his face, the look of deep concern, the inability to speak, the furrow between his eyes and the slump of his shoulders.

'It's Albert,' Walter said for him. 'There's been an accident.'

The words fell as straight as a stone down a well

and, before it hit the bottom, Kate was heading for the door.

'Wait, Kate,' Walter called. 'You can't walk there. It happened on Nunnery Hill. They're sending a cart.'

'Walter's right,' Ada said.

'I must go to him. I have to go, even if I have to run all the way,' Kate cried. Then she turned to Walter. The colour in her face drained. 'How bad is he?' she asked.

'We don't know. Young Davy ran with the message but he wasn't able to tell us much. The doctor's been sent for.'

Mary entered the kitchen with the two children and Kate immediately held Ronnie in her arms and clung to him.

'Is Dad hurt?' Ronnie asked.

'He'll be all right, Ronnie,' she replied. 'Don't worry. I'm going to him now.'

'I want to come too,' Ronnie said.

'Best you stay here with me and Tilly,' Ada said, going to her grandson. 'Dot and Granddad will be back soon.'

Ronnie held on to Kate's skirts. She bent down to him and kissed him. 'Be a good boy for Mum now, Ronnie. I need to go but we'll bring Dad home . . . as soon as we can.'

Kate glanced up at her mother and the two women exchanged a look that revealed their doubts and their fears. A traction engine could crush a man and they both knew it.

8

Kate's eyes searched the scene. The life had gone out of the engine and the mournful silence of the men standing around made a cold greeting. Samuel pulled the horses up and Kate was helped down from the cart by Ernie Kimber, his face grey with strain of what the day had brought them. Those villagers who had a means of transport gathered around, asking in whispers if there was anything they could do, trying not to look in the direction of Albert's body lying broken in the dust. Kate looked at Ernie with the question unspoken on her lips. Ernie knew what she sought: hope.

'It's bad, Kate,' he said. 'But he's alive, thank the Lord.'

Kate could barely see through her tears. She wiped her face on her sleeve and moved towards Albert. She prepared herself for what she was about to witness. He mustn't see the depth of her concerns. She drew on all her strength. The strength that had brought her through the most testing times in her life. But as soon as she set eyes upon him, she knew that all that she had suffered in the past was as nothing compared to what was before her now. He lay on his back with one leg twisted and crushed beneath him. His right arm lay across his chest and each exhale of breath brought a low moan as if the very effort of breathing caused him pain. His eyes were closed and, as she knelt by his side, she wondered if he knew she was there. She bent close to his ear and whispered, 'It's your Kate. I'm here, Albert. You're going to be all right. The doctor is coming.'

Albert's eyelids flickered but he could not seem to open them. There was a gash on the side of his head and the blood had dried and matted his hair. Kate took hold of the hand on his chest but he gasped in such pain that she placed it gently back and smoothed her hand across his forehead, continuing to whisper words of encouragement to him. She was aware of someone standing behind her and looked up to see Mabel and Nora Taylor with water, bowls, cloths and bandages.

'If you can move just a little to one side,' Mabel said, 'I will see what I can do. Dr Morrison is attending a difficult birth and will be here as soon as he can.'

Kate stood up and allowed Mabel to get closer. She checked his leg and said, 'I fear it is broken in two places but I need to look at his chest. Can you lift his arm?'

'He cries out if I touch it,' Kate said.

'All right,' Mable replied. 'We'll leave it for the moment but from his laboured breathing, I can tell he has broken some ribs. Nora, can you pour some water into that bowl and we'll clean up the cut on his head? I'm afraid I can't administer morphine but hopefully the doctor will be here soon. Here, Kate, roll up these old sheets and we'll make a cushion to support his leg. Don't try to straighten it. Nora and I will gently lift it and you slip the cushion underneath.'

Albert let out a scream as they shifted his leg and Kate felt sick as she saw the bone protruding through the tear in his trousers. He passed out and while he was unconscious, Nora lifted his arm and placed it on

51

the ground while Mabel moved her fingers delicately across his chest.

'There's definitely a cracked rib or two but now we've moved his arm he should be able to breathe more easily.'

The next few hours were an agonising wait. Albert slipped in and out of consciousness and Kate was grateful when his brain shut out the pain for him. She prayed that he would come back to her. Mabel and Nora did their best to reassure Kate but her attention was constantly drawn to the road in the hope that she would hear the doctor's pony and trap soon.

Finally, Dr Morrison arrived. He apologised for the delay and got straight on with examining Albert.

'You did right not to move him,' he said. 'But we will have to get him to hospital, that leg will need a plaster cast. That's something I can't do.'

The doctor administered a dose of morphine to Albert and sent two of the men in search of the straightest branch they could find.

'About the thickness of a woman's wrist,' he said.

He then took Kate to one side. 'Now Kate, once the morphine has started to work, I'm going to have to straighten that leg, if it's to be saved. Albert is not going to be entirely pain free and it will be distressing for you. If you want to . . .'

'I served in a military hospital in London during the war,' Kate said.

'Very well,' the doctor replied. 'In that case, I want you to tear one of these sheets into strips to bind his leg once I've straightened it.'

He handed Kate a pair of scissors from his medical bag and went to speak to the Taylor sisters.

'When the men return with the wood for a splint,

I'm going to need you two to help me,' he said. 'Is that all right?'

Mabel said, 'I know what to do but I'm not sure if Nora . . .'

'I dealt with the gash on Samuel White's leg when he didn't move out of the way fast enough before the cart horse kicked him, didn't I?' Nora said.

'I'm just saying, this won't be easy,' Mabel replied.

'If Kate can stand to see her husband in pain, then I'm sure I'll manage,' Nora replied. 'Tell me what you want me to do, doctor.'

The morphine did its work and the doctor acted quickly, directing Ernie to hold Albert down firmly by his shoulders, avoiding any pressure on his chest. Mabel pressed down on Albert's thigh, while Dr Morrison gave several sharp tugs on Albert's leg. Kate watched, feeling every movement but stood firm in her determination not to look away, even when Albert's anguished cry struck her like a blow in the stomach. Albert lost consciousness and they strapped his leg firmly to the branch.

'Now, we must lift him carefully to the cart and get him to Stoke Cottage Hospital before the morphine wears off,' the doctor instructed. 'Ernie and Samuel, you support him either side of his upper body, Miss Mabel, support his broken leg and Miss Nora, you take the other. Kate, it's probably best if you walk beside ready to comfort him, should he come around. Now move slowly and for pity's sake, don't drop him. He's been through enough.'

On the way to the hospital, Kate began to worry. How would they pay for Albert's treatment? She knew Dr Morrison did his best to help patients pay over a period of time, but she wasn't working and,

53

now Albert was injured, her father was the only wage earner in the house. How could they possibly manage?

Mabel Taylor had elected to travel with Kate, while the doctor and Nora followed behind in the pony and trap. Kate didn't know Mabel as well as she knew Nora. The war years had taken Mabel to the Middle East. She had served in the Queen Alexandra's Nursing Service and, when she returned to Micklewell, she continued to nurse those in need in the village. There was something about Mabel's forthright, no-nonsense character and air of capability that made people go to her with all sorts of problems.

Kate decided to voice the question that was troubling her. 'Will this cost a lot?' she asked.

'I'm afraid it will,' Mabel replied. 'But if his leg is to be saved, it's the only option.'

'Then I will have to find work,' Kate said. 'It's either that or Henry will have to leave school.'

'I know the cook at Andwell Hall needs a new kitchen maid. The last one left in a hurry, if you get my meaning,' Mabel said.

Kate put her hand on her own belly. She held the secret inside her. She had missed three cycles of her monthly bleeds. She should have told Albert but she hadn't. They were just beginning to get back on their feet after the war and she'd hoped to be able to find work so that they could afford a place of their own. If this pregnancy went to full term, then the new life inside her would begin to sap all her energy and she'd become too heavy and slow to work. It wasn't even worth thinking about. Once any employer knew she was pregnant, they would sack her anyway for sure. She had already been down that route once and knew the rules. She was not a deceitful person and she couldn't lie about her condition. If she was to find a job, then she would have to leave it within a few months. But a few months' money would help a great deal towards paying for the hospital treatment.

'Thank you for the suggestion,' Kate said. 'I'll talk to the family. Perhaps there might be other ways. With two young children in the house, my mother has enough to do and she's not in the best of health at the moment. If she loses me then I would worry she might not be able to cope.'

As they neared Stoke hospital, the effects of the morphine began to wear off and Albert murmured and groaned. Kate turned to see how he was.

'We're nearly there,' Mabel said. 'We can't stop now. He'll be all right for a while yet but we need to get there as soon as possible.'

Once they reached the hospital, they let the medical staff do their work. Mabel gave a report of the accident and her assessment of the extent of his injuries and there was nothing more to do but leave Albert in their capable hands.

The journey back was a silent one, with Kate deep inside her own thoughts and Mabel concentrating on getting them home. It had been a long day. At Hatch they stopped to water the horse and drink some water themselves at the old coaching inn. By the time they drove into Micklewell, the evening sky had turned the colour of a bruised eye.

The family were all waiting for news of Albert but Kate could only tell them that they were working to repair his leg and that they should return in two or three days to see how he was doing. Ada offered Kate some supper but she couldn't stomach it and pushed the plate to one side. The children were already in bed and the adults sat around with little to say to each other.

'This is bad news for Albert and for us all,' Jim Truscott finally said.

'It is,' Kate replied, 'and I don't know how we're going to find the money to pay for his treatment. Perhaps the Taylor sisters could help me? They did once before when I needed help. '

'I could work on the farm,' Dot said.

'No, you couldn't,' Kate replied. 'You've not finished your training.'

'I could finish once Albert is better. I'm sure the college would understand,' Dot continued. 'I'll go to the schoolhouse and see Miss Clarence first thing tomorrow, she'll know what to do.'

'Ma, Pa, tell her she can't do it. She won't listen to me. You know how headstrong she is,' Kate said.

Ada and Jim Truscott looked at each other but before they could say anything, Dot got up and said firmly, 'There's nothing any of you can say that will make any difference. I want to help and I will. There's no other practical solution.'

9

The day was already beginning to get hot. Dot stopped to splash some cold water on her face as she passed the village pump. She could hear voices approaching and two figures came into view just as she was wiping her face on her sleeve. She smiled to herself as she overheard Rose Wright moaning at her mother.

'Why is it always me has to fetch the water?' Rose complained. 'Those boys are stronger than me.'

'Your brothers are needed in the fields,' her mother replied. 'Which would you rather do on a day like today? Be out there in the heat or standing in a shady wash house up to your elbows in nice cool water?'

'It won't be cool by the time we get it home.' Rose replied, her face wrinkled in a frown, 'and neither will I.'

Every family had their tiffs, Dot thought. She recalled how she and Kate had argued, when they were younger, about who had done more work than the other and whose turn it was next. What she would give now to have such small worries.

'Morning Mrs Wright, morning Rose,' Dot said.

'Good morning, Dot,' Mrs Wright replied. 'Sorry to hear about your Albert. We're all praying for him to pull through.'

'Thank you,' Dot replied.

Mrs Wright put down her water buckets and dug her daughter in the ribs.

'Where's your manners?' she said.

57

Rose mumbled a reluctant, 'Morning,' and started filling the first bucket.

'You'd just better get used to working hard, my girl. 'Cos you're going to be working your hands to the bone for the rest of your life. Now, if you'd paid a bit more attention at school,' Mrs Wright continued, 'you could be more like Dot here and study to be a teacher.'

Then, clearly thinking better of the implication in her words, Mrs Wright hastily added, 'Not that looking after a bunch of children isn't hard work too.'

'Yes, it can be,' Dot replied. 'But I enjoy it.'

As soon as she uttered the words, she realised the true implications of what she'd just volunteered to do. If the college wouldn't agree to her taking some time off to support her family, then this might be the end of her teaching career. She was putting all her trust in Miss Clarence being able to help her.

Miss Clarence was in her garden, a wide-brimmed straw hat shielding her head from the sun and a basket over her arm. She was cutting fresh flowers from the colourful display of lupins, delphiniums and cornflowers and, as she bent and stooped, her long skirts brushed the gravel path.

'Good morning, Miss Clarence,' Dot called, as she opened the gate.

The gate dropped on its hinges, making a scraping noise as she pushed it. Miss Clarence looked up.

'Good morning, Dorothy,' she replied. 'I really must get someone to repair that gate. Another job to do! This house is falling apart.' She sighed. 'But I'm being rude, complaining to you about my little problems. More importantly, how is Albert? I heard about the accident.'

'He was taken to Stoke hospital,' Dot said. 'Dr Morrison and Mabel Taylor did their best to save his leg. We're hoping that the doctors at the hospital will be able to mend it enough so that he can walk.'

'I'm sure that they will do their very best,' Miss Clarence replied. 'Would you like to come in for some tea?'

Dot was grateful for the suggestion. It would be far easier to discuss things over a cup of tea.

'Now, let's talk of brighter things. I can't wait to hear all about your studies,' Miss Clarence continued. 'Would you mind putting these in water, while I put the kettle on?' she said, passing the basket to Dot.

A vase was produced from a corner cupboard and Dot trimmed the stalks, whilst taking in the surroundings of a tidy and efficient looking kitchen. A place for everything and everything in its place. So different to 2 Mead Cottages where there was always something on the table waiting to be constructed into the next meal or things flung across chairs, half mended or patched.

The small pine dresser along one wall held a set of plates and bowls all of the same design, a pretty floral centre with an intertwined leaf pattern around the edge. The table in the centre of the room was scrubbed clean and, at either end, two stick-back chairs were tucked neatly to attention. The only other chair in the room was a captain's chair, next to the range, with a hand embroidered cushion. It looked very comfortable.

Dot filled the vase with water from the tap over the butler sink and placed it next to the basket of flowers on the table.

'Now, tell me the news of your training,' Miss Clarence said, pouring the tea and nodding her head towards a plate of biscuits. 'Help yourself.' She smiled.

'It's everything you said it would be,' Dot replied. 'There's so much to learn. Being a teacher is something I've always wanted to be but this past year has made me realise that there is a great deal that I still do not know.'

'You're not put off by the challenge, I hope?' Miss Clarence asked.

'No, not at all,' Dot replied. 'Quite the opposite, in fact. Actually, it's the teaching that I've come to see you about. I have a question to ask you.'

'Go ahead and ask then,' Miss Clarence said, lifting her cup to her lips.

'You might not know the answer,' Dot said.

'Well, I won't if you don't give me the question.' Miss Clarence smiled gently.

'If I want to stop studying for a while, will the college allow me to go back?' Dot asked.

'I thought you were enjoying it you said?' Miss Clarence replied.

'I am but . . .'

'But?'

'Albert's accident has changed things,' Dot continued. 'I need to find some work. Father's earnings from the forge won't be enough. Albert may take a long time to recover and there's no other money coming in.'

'I see,' Miss Clarence said. 'Well, I don't know the rules on such things, Dorothy, I'm afraid. But I will try to find out for you. I'll write to the dean and explain your circumstances. I can confirm your love of teaching and my confidence in you. I'm sure if they can, they will agree to your temporary absence.'

10

Dot felt disappointed that Miss Clarence could not be more positive about her request. She had hoped for some reassurance. She didn't feel ready to go home and face the family's questions. There would be more waiting, waiting for Albert to get better and waiting for a reply to Miss Clarence's letter to the dean. It was much better that the enquiry came from Miss Clarence, though. The dean of the college might be more prepared to listen to a well-respected teacher and member of the community and one that was happy to vouch for Dot's character and her determination to complete her training despite her current circumstances.

She was so lost in thought, that she didn't notice someone walking towards her and only looked up when a voice said, 'Hello again, Dorothy.' It was Miriam de Clere. This time she was without her easel and paint box but still wearing the same masculine attire.

'I was on my way to the forge on an errand for my aunt's cook,' Miriam said, holding a toasting fork up as evidence. 'One of the tines is broken and the bread keeps falling into the grate. Poor Gertie is tired of sifting the grit through her teeth. The few that she has left that is!' Miriam continued, drawing her lips back over her teeth to imitate the gummy servant.

Dot couldn't help but smile and her smile made Miriam's lips part in a grin.

'Ah, there is a little sun behind the clouds,' Miriam said.

Dot wasn't sure whether she should take this as a rude comment on her demeanour, which she felt entirely justified in having, or as a kindly attempt to cheer her up. She decided to give Miriam de Clere the benefit of the doubt. She had an engaging way with her that succeeded in lifting Dot's spirits.

'You looked preoccupied,' Miriam said. 'Were you on your way somewhere or on your way back?'

'I've been to visit a friend,' Dot said.

'And now you are?'

'Going home, I suppose,' Dot replied.

'There's something in that 'suppose' that makes me think you might appreciate a diversion. Would you care to accompany me to the forge?' Miriam asked.

'I would but my father might wonder what I was doing strolling about like a lady of leisure with so much to do at home,' Dot said.

'Your father is the blacksmith? I didn't realise,' Miriam said. 'Then you can say that you are showing me the way. A poor, ignorant visitor who can't find her way down the village street.'

'The visitor must also be short-sighted, if she can't see her destination just a few paces away,' Dot said, indicating with her arm that Miriam was almost there.

The gentle banter made Dot forget her worries for a moment but she declined Miriam's request to accompany her, saying that she had a lot to do at home and half the day was already gone.

'Your day must start very early then,' Miriam replied.

'Indeed, it does,' Dot said. 'When you have a large family, there is always plenty to do.'

'Point taken,' Miriam said. 'But you must have some time in the day when you can have a few moments to yourself?'

'Yes, once the children are in bed and the dishes washed.'

'Then, perhaps you would take an evening stroll with me and show me the delights of the countryside around? I'm always on the lookout for potential subject matter for my paintings and the evenings are a cooler time of day.'

Dot found herself agreeing to meet with Miriam the following evening.

'Now that you know where the forge is, shall we meet here at seven o'clock?' Dot suggested.

'Under the spreading chestnut tree?' Miriam asked.

'No, it's an oak actually.'

'I was just quoting . . .'

'Longfellow. I know. I may be a blacksmith's daughter but I do know poetry,' Dot said.

11

By the time Dot reached the oak tree, Miriam was already there, sitting beneath it, a small sketch book on her knee.

'Do you always carry some drawing or painting materials with you?' Dot asked. 'I think every time I've seen you, you've had a brush or a pencil in your hand.'

'Or a toasting fork,' Miriam joked.

'Yes, of course. Did my father manage to mend it?'

'Yes, he did. That made old Gertie happy and anything that makes Gertie happy, makes my aunt happy too.'

'Well, are we going to sit here all evening or are we going on this walk?' Dot asked.

Miriam stood up, pocketed her sketchbook and pencil and they set off towards Down Lane.

'I thought we'd go this way,' Dot said. 'If we climb up past the ford, we can visit the chalk pit where my brother Fred used to work before he joined up. From there we can go on to Five Lanes End where we can look back and see the view over the church green. It will be beautiful with the sun setting.'

'Your brother fought in the war? Did he . . . ?' Miriam began.

'No, he didn't come home. Fred died along with so many others,' Dot replied. The words still caught in her throat when she spoke of him. 'Such a waste of life but let us talk of something brighter. Tell me about

64

yourself. What made you want to become an artist? And, if you'd pardon my directness, why do you wear men's clothing? Doesn't it attract comments? I've never seen a woman dressed quite like you before. I assume it's something to do with practicalities.'

'That's a story for when we pause for a rest,' Miriam replied. 'Now, lead on, my guide.'

They walked in quiet harmony and turned into a narrow lane with high banks, covered in yellow toadflax and vetch which competed with purple knapweed. The whole scene formed a tapestry of colour, the vetch clinging on with its many tendrils and refusing to be left behind in the clamour for the light.

'A pity we weren't here earlier in the day,' Dot said, 'for we would've seen such a fluttering of butterflies as would take your breath away.'

'Then we must come again,' Miriam replied.

They rounded the side of the chalk pit and began the climb up.

'Stay well away from the edge,' Dot warned. 'The soil is crumbling there and unsafe.'

They both needed all their breath to make the last few feet, which was very steep and when they reached the top, both flopped down in the grass to regain their strength. Dot lay back into the long grass and looked up at the sky. Clouds danced above her in a gentle breeze and their hypnotic effect made her close her eyes. A tickling sensation on her nose made her raise her hand to rub it but the tickle just appeared on her forehead and then on her neck. She sat up, brushing away whatever it was that was settling on her and found Miriam holding a long, feathery grass and smiling to herself.

'It was you,' Dot laughed.

65

Miriam leaned forward again and stroked the grass across Dot's chest, just where her dress dipped down, exposing her collar bone and that delicious little indentation where they met.

They held one another's gaze until Dot began to feel uncomfortable and sat up. She felt as if an invisible band was pulling them together, like a drawstring around the waist of a skirt. The only other woman she had been so intimately close to was her sister but this felt different. It made a tingling sensation run through her similar to the feeling she had when Jack had kissed her. She was confused and the only thing she could think to do was to talk quickly, distractedly.

'This is a perfect spot to sit and draw, don't you think?'

Not waiting for an answer, she moved on. 'I know many such places around the village. I could show you more but I don't know how long you're staying. In fact, I don't know much about you at all. Why you wear such strange clothes, for example?'

'Are they strange?' Miriam replied. 'I only think of them as practical. If you're traipsing around the countryside with easels and paint boxes, it's far easier to do so dressed like this, than to be encumbered with lifting skirts. I am not the first woman to wear such clothing, anyway. George Sand predates me by many years. Almost a century in fact. She took to wearing trousers because they were more practical when travelling, which she loved to do and also as a means of having access to some more masculine establishments and events.'

'Such as what?' Dot said. 'Did she not like the company of her own sex?'

Miriam laughed.

66

'And what's so funny?' Dot asked.

'You really are quite a country girl, aren't you?' Miriam replied.

'I don't know what that's supposed to mean,' Dot said, getting up. 'But if you're suggesting that my life is simple, then you're wrong. Everything has just been turned upside down by my brother-in-law's accident. His leg was crushed in a steam engine accident, he's in hospital. I don't know how we'll pay the fees. Henry is too young to do anything more than work in the fields and he would have to leave school to bring in no more than a few pennies. My father provides the only source of income for the family. I don't know what tomorrow will bring and I don't know how I can possibly finish my teacher training. We need to find some more money from somewhere. I have to work.'

Dot's words came out in such a flurry of emotion that Miriam appeared stunned into silence.

'I'm sorry, I didn't mean to upset you,' Miriam finally said, getting to her feet. 'I didn't realise things were so difficult for you and your family.'

'No, you live in a different world, so you couldn't,' Dot said sharply. 'But now you do know.'

The two women stood beside each other, looking out over the valley, each occupied in their own thoughts. Once Dot had regained her composure, Miriam suggested that they walk back.

Before they parted, Miriam said that she wanted to help and that she was sure there would be a way around this problem.

'I wish I had your confidence,' Dot said. 'Perhaps that's the difference between us. You can afford time to think and I must act.'

'Nevertheless, will you let me try to help you?'

Miriam said.

'I don't know what you can do but thank you for the thought,' Dot replied.

Miriam said that she would do her very best and they parted ways at a path junction just above the church, Miriam heading back towards Frog Hall and Dot to Mead Cottages. Dot didn't know what Miriam thought she could do to help. She was not convinced that any solution Miriam proposed would be one that would enable her to continue on her desired path of becoming a teacher.

12

'Was that the artist woman, Miriam de Clere, I saw you walking with?' Kate said, when both she and Dot arrived at the corner of the churchyard at the same time.

'Kate,' Dot replied, 'what are you doing here?'

'It was Ma's turn to do the flowers in the church,' Kate replied. 'She's not feeling up to much this evening, so I said I'd do them.'

'I told Miriam about Albert,' Dot said. 'She says she might be able to help. I don't know how, though. Will you be going to see Albert tomorrow? Shall I come with you?'

'I'll be walking to Hatch early tomorrow to get the carter's wagon into Stoke,' Kate replied. 'It would be more help to me if you could look after the children. Have you noticed how slow Ma is becoming? I think she finds the children very tiring. I've been sitting thinking while I was in the church, Dot. Do you think the Taylor sisters might help us out? They were so good to me when I returned from London with Ronnie and no husband.'

'Lending us some money, you mean?'

'Well not exactly lending, more of an advance payment. Henry could go and work digging potatoes and later in August there'll be the wheat and barley harvest and plenty of hands needed to help,' Kate said, placing a hand on her belly. 'There must be something I could do. Except . . .'

'Except what?' Dot noticed the position of Kate's hand and the slight bulge of her waistline.

'Kate, are you?'

Kate's eyes began to fill with tears. She nodded.

'Why are you so upset?' Dot asked. 'Aren't you and Albert happy? You wanted more children, didn't you?'

'Yes, just not now,' Kate said, tears running down her cheeks.

Dot put an arm around her sister.

'Some things can't always be planned, Kate,' she said. 'We'll find a way to help you and Albert out. I'm doing my best to find a way, you know that.'

'It's all right for you to say,' Kate snapped. 'You're not the one who has to go through with this knowing that we can ill afford another child at the moment. And I don't want you to say a word about this to anyone. I haven't even told Albert yet.'

'Not told him!' Dot said, pulling back from her sister.

'No. It won't help his state of mind to feel yet another burden,' Kate said.

'Is that how you feel, that your unborn child is a burden?' Dot asked.

'I wish I had your naivety, Dot. You really have no idea,' Kate said.

'I'm trying to understand but you can't keep this a secret for much longer, Kate.'

'Then what do you suggest I do?' Kate asked.

The bitterness in her voice shocked Dot. Kate was right, she wasn't the one having to cope with the blows Kate had been dealt recently. The only thing she could do was try to support her sister and give some practical help.

Dot hesitated. 'What you were saying about the

Taylor sisters,' she said. 'I'm sure if they can help, they will. Mabel helped straighten his leg. She saw how bad it was and will know how long it might take before he can . . .' She stopped. That train of thought was not helpful.

'When you return from the hospital tomorrow, we will go to see them,' she continued instead, taking her sister's hand. She hoped that the Taylor sisters would have some work for them. Although that hope was on fragile ground. She knew that farm work was not easy to come by at the moment, too many workers chasing too few jobs. The impact of ex-servicemen seeking work was having an effect, particularly in the small villages and she was aware that concerns of an impending financial depression was on everybody's minds. Town life and her own narrow focus on her career had left her largely immune to the news that filled the papers of small holdings and even larger farms struggling to survive. Now she had returned home to Micklewell, however, she could see the impact the lack of government help was having. She was not knowledgeable about economics but she could see the evidence before her eyes.

★ ★ ★

When Dot opened the door to Miriam de Clere the following morning, her surprise showed clearly on her face.

'Miriam! What are you doing here so early?'

Miriam passed the niceties by and immediately launched into an explanation of what she was doing on the Truscott family's doorstep at nine o'clock in the morning.

'I've spoken to my aunt about your difficulties . . .' she began.

'What do you mean. It wasn't your place to —' Dot interrupted.

'Who is it?' Ada cried out from the kitchen.

'It's all right, Ma. It's for me,' Dot called back.

But Ada appeared behind Dot, wiping her hands in her apron.

'Miss de Clere. Well, ask your visitor in, Dot,' Ada said. 'Where are your manners?'

'I'm sorry to call so early,' Miriam said. 'It's just that I have some news that I hope will be of interest to Dorothy.'

Dot stood back and opened the door wider for Miriam to enter.

'How are you, Mrs Truscott, and the rest of the family? How is your son-in-law?' Miriam asked.

'We're all well as can be expected, thank you. Albert's recovering, slowly. His leg's in plaster,' Ada replied. 'He won't be able to come home until he can walk with crutches and, even then, it will take him a long while to walk again. At least, we pray he will walk again.'

'Best to stay optimistic, Ma,' Dot said.

'Talking of which, I have some good news,' Miriam said. 'At least, I hope you'll think it's good.'

'Then please sit down,' Ada replied, indicating an armchair. 'I'll make some tea.'

As soon as Ada left the room, Miriam explained her plan.

'My aunt wants me to be a travelling companion to her on her yearly excursion to Eastbourne. Her usual companion has been taken ill and cannot go with her but I've told my aunt that if I'm going to Eastbourne,

72

then I want to be painting, not dragging around the sights. It's not the best use of my time.'

'So how does this affect me?' Dot asked.

'My idea is that you could be her companion and I could get on with what I do best,' Miriam said, leaning back and looking pleased with herself.

'What if I don't want to be a travelling companion?' Dot said, an expression of annoyance on her face. 'And exactly how does that help our family situation? Anyway, I don't know your aunt and she doesn't know me, we might not get on.'

'Who might not get on?' asked Ada, returning with the tea.

Miriam repeated her suggestion and Ada's practical side showed itself, as soon as Miriam had finished speaking.

'And this would be paid work, to accompany your aunt?' Ada asked, passing Miriam one of the best china cups.

'Of course.' Miriam said. 'Paid handsomely, I should add. My aunt is very well off, her late husband left her well provided for. It would be helping me out, too.'

'Will it mean giving up your training though? You've worked so hard, Dot. I'm sure Kate wouldn't want you to do that on Albert's account,' Ada said.

'It's not up to Kate,' Dot replied. 'We need the money and, if I take the job —' Dot looked pointedly at Miriam — 'I will request that most of my earnings be paid directly to you and Pa. As for giving up, I'm not giving up, just delaying things for a while, until Albert recovers. He might be walking again by the end of the summer holidays and I won't have to give up anything. Anyway, Miss Clarence has offered to help. She's informing the college of my situation and believes they will support any application for leave of absence on compassionate grounds.' Dot was aware that she was exaggerating the truth.

'So, can I tell my aunt that you are interested?' Miriam asked.

'You can tell her that I'm happy to accompany her to Eastbourne. But if Albert has recovered by the start of the new term and can return to work, then I will begin my studies again. I can only commit to that much,' Dot insisted.

'Then I will discuss things with her and report back, directly,' Miriam replied.

'She'll want to meet me, though, won't she?' Dot asked.

'Oh yes. She's completely in control of everything. But it will just be a formality. You'll be the most perfect companion for her,' Miriam replied. 'You're a good listener, aren't you?'

'Yes, I believe so.'

'And, being a teacher, you're practised in reading aloud?'

'Yes.'

'And do you know when to hold your thoughts and opinions to yourself when you consider it necessary to keep the peace?'

'Oh, I'm not sure about that one,' Ada interrupted.

'Yes, I can, Ma, if I'm in company outside the family,' Dot insisted.

'Then all will be well. You will get the job of companion to the formidable Mrs Humboldt,' Miriam said, her smile lighting up her face. 'And I will be free to paint. It's all quite exciting.'

Dot agreed, there would be no need for her and

Kate to go to the Taylor sisters now. Kate would be so relieved. She would try to talk to her sister privately about the pregnancy and encourage her to tell Albert. Keeping it from him was not going to help matters. Eventually the physical evidence would mean she could not conceal the truth.

'Well, that's a turn up,' Ada said after Miriam had left. 'Our guardian angel must have been watching over us. That's kind of her to do that. After all we're nothing to her or to Mrs Humboldt come to that. But what a strange young woman, she is. Whatever does she look like in those . . .'

'Trousers are more appropriate attire for an artist,' Dot said. 'Long skirts would be an encumbrance.'

She smiled at herself as she heard Miriam's words escaping her own lips.

13

A few days later, Albert was discharged from hospital. The Taylor sisters provided a cart to bring him home. Kate climbed down from the cart and took the crutches from her husband. The journey back from the hospital had been a quiet one, with Kate and Ernie trying to make conversation but Albert would not or could not join in. Kate kept her thoughts to herself and tried to encourage Albert with kind words about how well he was doing, when her eyes told her otherwise. Albert's face was pallid and grey. The strong man who had set out for work the morning of his accident had withered and shrunk away and what was left was not the same as the old Albert she knew and loved. There were dark circles under his eyes and his hair hung lank over his ears. A thick stubble covered his chin and his mouth was downturned, his lips dry and cracked. He sat immobile, his head hanging down until Kate spoke to him.

'We're home, my love,' she said. 'Ernie will help you down and I'll help you with your crutches. Now be careful, put your good leg down first and hold onto the side of the cart.'

'I know what to do,' Albert snapped. 'Just get those contraptions off me. I can walk to the door by myself.'

Kate wasn't fooled by his bravado. She knew that the bad-tempered complaining was to disguise the pain he felt when he put pressure on his leg. She placed his arms through the metal bands on the crutches and watched as he hobbled towards the gate. He stopped, his awkward stance showing that he couldn't open the gate for it would mean letting go of one of the crutches. Kate moved to help him but Ernie held her shoulder. Watching him struggle was agony for Kate but she understood why Ernie had stopped her. She mustn't treat him like a complete invalid, for his pride and independence needed repairing as much as his body did.

Albert took his weight on his good side and swung the other crutch over the gate. He wobbled for a while and by the tension in his back and shoulders, Kate could tell that the extra pressure caused him pain. He managed to get himself through the gate without falling over and Kate was relieved. She turned and thanked Ernie for fetching Albert from the hospital.

'You're most welcome,' Ernie said. 'You just call on me if you need anything.' Then he shouted goodbye to Albert and told him to rest up. 'We need you back at the farm as soon as ever that leg is better. There's no one builds a haystack as good as you, Albert,' he said.

The door opened and the whole family were there to greet Albert. Jim welcomed him home, while Ada fussed around, giving orders.

'Dot, put the kettle on. Henry, fetch the footstool so that Albert can rest his leg and Tilly, you get two cushions off the sofa.'

Ronnie hung back until Kate pulled him forward and lifted him to give Albert a hug.

'Now, let's get you settled in the kitchen,' Ada said. 'You take Jim's chair, it will be better for your leg and your back.' She took the cushions off Tilly and placed one at the back of the chair and the other on the footstool.

'It's good to have you home, Albert,' Dot said, handing him a cup of tea.

As soon as the tea was drunk and the children judged that the time was right, they asked if they could have a go with Albert's crutches.

'How do you work them?' Tilly asked, taking one from the side of Albert's chair.

'You can't work them, silly,' Henry said. 'They're the right size for a man, not for a girl.'

'They're not playthings, anyway,' Ada said. 'Albert needs them to help him get about.'

'Not for long,' Albert grumbled. 'I'll be putting them on the bonfire as soon as I'm able.'

'I'm not sure that would be a good idea,' Kate said. 'I think the hospital needs them back for the next patient. Now, we'd best get on and prepare some food or we'll all be very late to bed.'

'How will you get upstairs, though?' Henry asked Albert. 'Won't it be a bit difficult with the crutches?'

Everyone looked at Albert.

'I've been thinking that we'll need to make some rearrangements,' Ada said, breaking the awkward silence. 'It'll be best if Albert and Kate slept down-stairs. The children can all sleep in the same room.'

'And what about Dot?' Albert asked.

'Ah well, I'm probably not going to be here much longer, so don't worry about me,' Dot said.

'And where are you going?' Kate asked. 'You're here until the start of the new term, aren't you?'

'I'm taking that job I told you about. To help out,' Dot replied.

'What job?' Albert asked.

'She's going travelling with the owner of Frog Hall,

78

as a companion,' Ada said. 'It could be a longer position depending on —'

'Sshh Ma! Let me do the telling,' Dot interrupted, scowling at her mother.

'We need the money,' Ada continued, ignoring her daughter. 'If Albert's leg gets better soon, then she won't need to —'

'Won't need to what?' Albert asked.

'Won't need to give up her place at the college.'

Ada had blurted out the words before Dot could stop her.

'You're not giving up your place for me,' Albert said. 'I won't allow it.'

'And I won't allow it,' Kate added. 'I've already told you, Dot, I'd sooner go out scrubbing floors or picking potatoes than let you give up on what you've worked so hard to achieve.'

'Now look what you've done,' Jim Truscott said. 'Why don't you do like Dot said and let her explain the whole story, instead of you telling half a tale.'

'What would help now,' Dot said, 'is if you'd do what you're best at, Ma, and get the dinner started and I'll set the record straight with Kate and Albert, so they know exactly what I plan to do. You children go out and play. Take them to the ford, Henry, would you? But make sure they don't paddle downstream and fall in. We've enough trouble without that.'

That evening, after dinner, there was a manoeuvring of furniture and a sorting of personal belongings. Kate helped Albert get undressed and settled him into their makeshift bed and then arranged her own nightclothes. She turned away from him and as she took off her clothes, she decided that Dot had been right. Her belly was holding all the indications of what lay inside and her breasts were becoming fuller and heavier. She had to tell him. She slipped the nightgown over her head and climbed in beside him. Albert lay stiffly on his back, his eyes staring up at the ceiling.

'Are you comfortable enough?' Kate asked.

'It'll do,' Albert replied.

Kate took his hand and held it between them for a while.

'Albert, I have something to tell you,' she said. 'I know it's probably not the best time for this to be happening but some things have a way of planning themselves.'

She placed his hand on her belly and waited for his response.

His hand explored her abdomen and then reached up to her swollen breasts.

For a moment an image flashed through her mind of when she had lain beside Philip when he first returned home after sustaining dreadful injuries during the war. Would Albert react in the same way? Would he push her away?

She worried about his silence and reached across to touch his face, find his lips and kiss him. Her fingers stroked his cheek and the wetness of his tears both pleased and concerned her. Were these tears of joy or frustration?

'Albert, please say something,' she said.

'It's wonderful news,' Albert finally said. 'I only wish that I wasn't so useless. God knows how long it will take me to walk again. A husband should be able to provide for his family, Kate.'

'We have to be patient,' Kate replied. 'You have to be patient. The body takes a time to heal itself. What you have been through has been a shock to your body and your mind but you will recover, Albert. You survived a war and although you lost an eye, you learned to cope with that loss. Your leg will get better as long as you do like the doctors say and don't try to do too much, too soon. You are pleased about the baby, aren't you?'

Albert tried to shift his weight to turn towards her but winced at the pain.

'Of course, I'm pleased,' he said, reaching for her hand and bringing it to his lips.

'Now you'll have to kiss me goodnight. I can't turn on my side. And I apologise in advance for my snoring. You know that sleeping on my back causes it.'

Kate smiled inside. She was so relieved.

'And I can't dig you in the ribs or kick you,' she replied.

'Goodnight, my lovely wife,' Albert said. 'And goodnight, Baby.'

'Good night, Albert,' Kate replied, kissing him gently on the mouth. 'Now I can sleep soundly and tomorrow we will tell the family that a new addition will be arriving at the end of the year.'

14

After a few preliminary visits to Frog Hall when Dot had the opportunity to meet Mrs Humboldt and Mrs Humboldt had assessed Dot's suitability as a companion, it was decided that they would depart for Eastbourne as soon as possible. The anxiously awaited confirmation of Dot's leave of absence had arrived and financial arrangements had been agreed. They would be away for the entire month of August. A hotel had been booked and the journey would be made by carriage and train.

The morning they set out, the clouds were threatening rain. There was a cool breeze for the month of August and Dot had decided to pack clothes for both seasons, in case autumn should decide to descend upon them early. The carriage pulled up outside 2 Mead Cottages and Miriam got out to knock on the door.

'Let Barnaby do that,' her aunt said but Miriam was already opening the gate.

She'd hardly raised her fist, when the door opened and Dot was there in her travelling clothes, her bag at her feet. She wore a full skirt with a green velvet jacket which Miss Clarence had insisted she borrow, as the weather had taken a turn. Dot's protests were ignored and Miss Clarence declared that if she wouldn't borrow it, then she was giving it to Dot as a gift and that it would be rude to refuse. Not wishing to upset Miss Clarence, Dot accepted. She was setting off on an adventure, safe in the knowledge that her place would be kept open for her at the training college until she could resume her studies. Miss Clarence's influence had prevailed.

Henry carried her bag out to the carriage for her and Dot turned and waved at her family, all gathered to wish her a safe journey. Ronnie and Tilly were so excited that they began shouting their goodbyes and jumping around their grandparents, who were trying to calm them down.

'Hush now, you'll frighten the horses,' Ada said.

Kate was giving advice about being aware that the streets would be much busier than she was used to given all the holidaymakers and to watch out for buses and automobiles. As if Chichester wasn't busy too, Dot thought.

'And remember to write,' Kate called above the whooping of the children.

When her bag was loaded, she stepped up into the carriage. She was both excited and nervous. Old Mrs Humbolt sat on one side of the carriage with her maid and Miriam and Dot on the other.

'I do hope you'll be all right with your back to the driver,' Mrs Humboldt said. 'I couldn't possibly sit there, I need to face the way I'm going.'

'My aunt has a great many preferences in life,' Miriam whispered to Dot. 'No doubt you will find out more of them as the journey progresses.'

'And you will find out that my niece,' Mrs Humboldt replied, 'is very slow to recognise that, although my body is not quite as sprightly as it was, there is nothing wrong with my hearing.'

Miriam jabbed Dot in the ribs and looked heaven-ward.

'Or my eyesight,' Mrs Humboldt said. 'Now, Miss Truscott, I think we agreed that I will call you Dorothy and you can call me Mrs H, it's not such a mouthful. Except when we are in company, of course, then the full form of address will be required.'

Once these formalities had been agreed, Mrs Humboldt announced she would close her eyes for a while as she'd had a disturbed night.

'I never sleep well before taking a journey,' Mrs Humboldt said. 'So, I'd be grateful if you didn't converse loudly. I want to arrive at the station rested. This journey is going to take us all day and goodness only knows what state I'll be in when we get there if I don't rest. Dab some lavender oil on my temples, Elsie, would you? The fragrance helps me relax.'

The downtrodden looking Elsie lifted a small wooden box onto her lap and unfolded an Aladdin's cave of bottles, jars and powders. She cast an anxious eye over the contents, lifting and checking labels. Her hand shook a little, as she took out a clean handker-chief and tipped one of the bottles. The motion of the carriage did not make it easy.

'Not too much,' Mrs H barked. 'That has to last the whole trip.'

Elsie whispered, 'Please, could you turn your head, ma'am?'

'What, girl? Speak up,' Mrs H said.

'Your head, ma'am. I need to reach the other side,' Elsie said.

Dot was grateful that she wasn't in Elsie's shoes and hoped that Mrs H would prove to be a more ami-able companion than she was a mistress. In an effort

84

to put that concern out of her head, Dot amused herself trying to remember the names of the places they would be travelling through on their way to Eastbourne. They would be passing through Alton, close to Chawton, the home of Jane Austen. Dot so enjoyed her books that she'd asked Miriam if time could be spared to make a detour but Miriam had said that her aunt would not hear of it.

'She dislikes long journeys enough, without making them even longer,' Miriam said.

Dot had travelled to and from Chichester to study but she had little knowledge of the rest of her home county and she devoted every moment of their journey to observing the countryside around her. The country lanes, lined with trees that arched above them, soon gave way to the open fields. The rising and dipping land, criss-crossed with hedges of hawthorn, hazel and dog rose, swept away from them in curves and undulations. At one field opening, she was lucky enough to see a hare poised with its nose in the air, sniffing for danger. She leaned out of the carriage window, to see more and glimpsed a small group of deer, running across the fields in the distance. The spotted fawns trying to keep up with the adults as they leapt a ditch and disappeared into a clump of trees.

Time passed enjoyably in this quiet way and the carriage made steady progress, the driver taking care to avoid any pot holes that might lurch the passengers out of their seats and cause Mrs H to vent her annoyance. They were making good time, heading towards Midhurst where they would stay overnight before boarding the train for Brighton and then change for Eastbourne. It was going to be a long journey and

Mrs Humboldt had made it clear that she was not looking forward to it.

'But such trials must be borne if one is to experience life outside our little backwater, Miss Truscott,' the old lady had instructed.

As they approached Alton, Miriam leaned into Dot and whispered in her ear that they should wake her aunt, as they would be stopping soon to water the horses and to take some refreshment at the coaching inn.

Almost as if she had a sixth sense, Mrs H woke and enquired their whereabouts. She declared herself rested and even managed to twitch a slight smile in the corner of her mouth, when Miriam said they would be stopping shortly for some luncheon.

Dot climbed down from the carriage, taking in her surroundings. They were on the edge of the town and down the busy street she could see the many activities of the day unfolding in front of her. Groups of well-dressed people, parading up and down, looking in shop windows. Cars competing with some horse-drawn vehicles for space and store delivery boys weaving in and out on their cycles. One butcher's boy, dressed in his striped apron and flat cap, struggled to keep his bicycle upright with its heavy basket. He was trying to avoid two pedestrians crossing the road and almost wobbled off.

Dot wondered what her sister had felt, the first time she'd stepped onto the streets of Andover to become a nursemaid. She was so much younger than Dot when she left home, only fifteen and Dot was now twenty-two. Kate had so little experience of the wider world outside Micklewell. She must have been overawed with the busyness of it all. Dot's circumstances were quite different, she was a companion not a servant, but nevertheless she felt the uncertainty of exactly what her role would entail and how she should conduct herself. At least she had Miriam there to guide her.

Once they had finished their lunch, Mrs H was in a more amenable mood and they continued their journey. Dot was pleased when, after three more hours of travelling, they arrived in Midhurst. Mrs Humboldt's recovery had been short-lived and she had started to complain about the discomfort of it all and how she wasn't as young as she was and might soon have to give up travelling all together. As soon as they arrived at their overnight hotel, the Spread Eagle, she started barking instructions to the staff and to Elsie about her luggage and the need for tea in her room right away. She had had enough of jiggling about in the carriage and she had a splitting headache.

'If I don't appear for dinner then please dine without me,' she announced as she disappeared into the inn, Elsie scuttling after her.

Dot was relieved when Miriam suggested that the two of them might take a walk around the town. She quite understood how Mrs H, an elderly lady, must feel as she too was grateful that the world had stopped bouncing and lurching. She needed to stretch her legs and breathe the air.

Dot found Midhurst to be a delightful place. The beautiful wooden-framed buildings were attractive to look at and when they turned towards the church, they were greeted by a peal of bells.

'Must be bell ringing practice,' Dot said.

'Either that or they knew my aunt was coming and they're ringing out a warning.' Miriam grinned.

They both laughed. Dot felt comfortable in Miriam's presence. She might come from quite a different background to her own but she had no airs and graces about her and she had a real sense of fun. Dot had a feeling that Miriam was going to introduce her to a whole new way of experiencing life.

Mrs H did join them for dinner after all. She had made a remarkable recovery and talked excitedly about the plans she had for their stay in Eastbourne.

'If the weather is kind to us, Dorothy, I shall take my walks along the promenade after breakfast. The doctor says that the sea air is good for me and unless it is pouring with rain, that is what we shall do, walk. Then after morning coffee, I will have a lie down in my room until luncheon. The afternoons I always spend visiting one of the many interesting sights around the area or strolling around the shops to see if there is anything takes my fancy. There is a particularly good milliners who will copy any of the hats in two days if the design is to my liking but the fit is not good.'

'Will you be taking in the Italian Gardens, Aunt?' Miriam asked. 'I'm sure Dorothy would love to see them.'

'The Italian Gardens are on my list,' Mrs H replied.

'Then I shall accompany you with my drawing materials,' Miriam said. 'I wish to find a suitable viewpoint as I have an idea for a painting. I must also find the time to visit the School of Art where I met my good friend, Rav. You remember him, Aunt?'

'Are you referring to that young man who came to stay with us last summer and divided his time between flirting with young Elsie and philandering with all the daughters of Sir Henry and Lady Baldwin at their Summer Ball? What was his proper name? The one he was christened with? Eric something.'

'Eric Ravilious, Aunt,' Miriam replied. 'A name that will become very well known, in the future, believe me, for he has a remarkable talent.'

'Yes, as I said, for philandering. I felt I had to apologise profusely for his forwardness. You, of course, did not find it the least bit embarrassing. You've come to expect such behaviour from your bohemian friends, I suppose. At least you've introduced me to a more sedate and composed friend of yours this year. I'm sure Dorothy could never be accused of fraternizing in an inappropriate way with members of the opposite sex.'

Dot could have wished for a bowl of cherries to bury her face in at that point, for she would have matched their colour exactly.

15

The following morning, they all woke refreshed and ready to embark on the final leg of the journey. The brief carriage ride from Midhurst to Barnham where they were to join the train to Eastbourne passed without incident and even the connection at Brighton arrived on time and Mrs Humboldt could not find any cause for complaint. This meant that the rest of the group could relax and Dot felt a surge of excitement rise in her chest as the carriage pulled up outside the Queen's Hotel. The arrival of the party of four was met with a flurry of activity from the staff members on hand to assist guests. The doorman helped the ladies alight from their carriage and bell boys hurried to carry their baggage. Dot had to be encouraged to move from her stationary position at the bottom of the flight of steps where she was taking in the grand façade and the parade of curtained windows reflecting the early evening sun. The vast building soared up in white-washed layers towards a deep blue sky. Dot couldn't contemplate how many rooms there might be and found herself hoping that she might be in one with a sea view. The second- and third-floor rooms had decorative balconies and she let her imagination run with the idea of standing on the central one, watching the sun go down with a warm summer breeze on her face.

Mrs H's sharp tones interrupted her daydream bringing her swiftly back to reality.

'Come along, Dorothy. Your arm, if you please. Too many steps,' she complained.

Once she had deposited Mrs H in the nearest chair in the palatial entrance hall and Miriam had approached the reception desk to establish their room numbers, Dot stepped across the black-and-white tiled floor and took in more of her surroundings. She couldn't believe she was going to be staying in such a luxurious place. Goodness knows how much this was all going to cost. Try as she might her brain could not calculate the figure for this was a world of values beyond her experience. It made her head spin to think of it.

If Dot had not been craning her neck to look at the spiral staircase winding above her, it might never have happened. She was following the ornate, wrought-iron balustrades in their climb towards the glass dome far above, when she felt something brush against her and suddenly lost her balance. A pair of hands caught her by the shoulders.

'I'm so sorry,' a voice said. 'I should have watched where I was going.'

She pulled back from the person who was holding her and felt her blushes rising through her cheeks.

The young man had neatly trimmed hair and was wearing a trilby hat. He was clean-shaven and smelled of cologne. Her eyes fixed on the slight indent in his chin and the feminine curve of his lips. She glanced at his white shirt cuff on her left shoulder, the jet cufflink edged with gold. He was looking down at her with an expression of concern, his grey eyes searching her face.

'Are you all right?' he asked.

'I'm perfectly all right,' Dot replied. 'My fault entirely.'

He removed his hands from her shoulders. 'Are you quite sure?' he said and before she could reply, he called a bell boy over and asked him to bring some water.

Miriam, who had been watching all this unfold, whilst waiting at the reception desk, came over to join them.

'Are you unwell, Dot?' she said.

'No, I just lost my balance, that's all,' Dot replied.

'Due to my carelessness, I'm ashamed to say. I wasn't looking where I was going. Allow me to introduce myself . . . Ralph Bletchford,' the young man said, removing his hat and inclining his head.

'Well, if you're sure you're all right,' Miriam said. 'Then perhaps we should help my aunt up to her room, Dot. She's looking rather tired.'

'Of course,' Ralph Bletchford said. 'Would you do me the honour of taking a glass of sherry with me before dinner by way of an apology for my clumsiness?'

'That's very k . . .' Dot began.

'Thank you, Mr Bletchford, but I'm not sure my aunt would think it proper to take sherry with a stranger on our first night here,' Miriam replied.

Not to be dissuaded, Mr Bletchford walked beside them and said, 'I quite understand. Another evening perhaps? I am always in the Circle Bar before dinner. We're sure to meet again and I could introduce myself to your aunt and make recompense to this young lady for my carelessness.'

Before Dot could reply, Miriam took her arm and guided her away from Mr Bletchford in the direction of her dozing aunt.

'Really, Dot,' Miriam chided. 'You can't go accepting invitations from every man who pays you attention.

92

Do you know nothing of the wiles of the opposite sex? I can see you have a great deal to learn.'

Dot blushed. She didn't leap to defend herself, for it was true. She had little experience of such social interactions but she did find Ralph Bletchford very attractive.

Mrs H had opened her eyes and regained her position of authority pertaining to matters of her own comfort. She had chosen the Queen's Hotel because it had a lift and it was towards this marvel of engineering that Dot and Miriam steered Mrs H. Mrs H had asked for a bedroom with a view and an adjoining maid's room for Elsie. The box room was little more than a cupboard but Elsie knew better than complain. Miriam and Dot had rooms across the corridor (no sea view). After Mrs H's rest, Dot and Miriam accompanied her downstairs to the dining room. As they passed through the Circle Bar, Dot looked around expecting to see Mr Bletchford but the room was full of chattering groups of people and she felt conscious of staring too long at people's faces.

Once in the dining room, they were shown to a table in the centre of the room. Every table was draped in crisp, white linen and the upholstered chairs were covered in a yellow gold fabric that matched the colour of the walls. When seated, Dot looked up at the ceiling which had an embossed design picked out in white. Several leaf-patterned ceiling roses supported ornate, metal and glass pendulous light fittings, bathing the whole room in a warm light.

Mrs H's stomach was upset by the journey so she ordered the soup and some steamed fish. Miriam and Dot were more adventurous and decided upon the chicken fricassee. It wasn't until the dessert course that Dot noticed a gentleman sitting alone at the far end of the dining room. She felt sure that it was Mr Bletchford. Had he noticed her? There was something about him that made her hope that he had. Whatever was she thinking?

'I was thinking that we should go to the Italian Gardens tomorrow,' Mrs H said. 'The weather is good at the moment and there is no sense in waiting. The English weather will do as it pleases and we must fit in with whatever it has in store for us.'

'I'm all for that,' Miriam agreed. 'Last year I started some sketches of the stone pergola and would like to continue. If I'm lucky the wisteria should be in its second flush.'

Miriam and her aunt then embarked upon the fine details of the day and Dot's eye kept roaming in the direction of the young man on his own. She found herself hoping that he would finish his meal before them and pass by their table on his way out. Her mother always said to be careful what you wish for and, when he rose to his feet, she was filled with mixed emotions. Should she smile at him? Perhaps he wouldn't even notice her. Would Miriam rebuff him as before and cause embarrassment? Miriam and her aunt had their backs to him and couldn't see his approach. So, when he drew near, he was looking directly at her.

He paused and nodded his acknowledgement.

'Good evening, ladies,' he said. Then he addressed Dot personally. 'May I ask if you have recovered from our little accident earlier, miss?'

'Accident?' Mrs H exclaimed. 'What's this about an accident? Why wasn't I told? And who are you, young man?'

'Ralph Bletchford, pleased to meet you,' he replied. 'It was entirely my fault. I bumped into Miss . . . I'm sorry I don't even know your name,' he continued, smiling at Dot.

'My name is Mrs Humbolt,' came the reply. 'And I think you'd better explain yourself, young man.'

'Happy to,' Ralph replied. 'If you ladies have finished your meal, perhaps we could take coffee together in the lounge and I will order some after dinner mints.'

Much to Dot's surprise, Mrs Humboldt's expression softened as she succumbed to the charm of Ralph Bletchford. She agreed to the suggestion and also to the offer of his arm to help her through to the lounge. Miriam's face told a different story.

16

'So, is someone going to explain what's happened here?' Mrs H said, raising an eyebrow and looking first at Miriam and then Dot.

'I wasn't really hurt,' Dot explained. 'I just lost my balance.'

'I'm afraid I'm responsible for that. I bumped into her,' Ralph said. 'I should have been looking where I was going, instead of looking at my watch.'

'And why were you looking at your watch instead of paying attention to what lies in front of you, may I ask?' Mrs H said.

'A meeting. I was due to meet a business colleague and I was late. I was on my way to the door, when I brushed shoulders with this young lady, for which I sincerely apologise,' Ralph replied.

The waitress set down the tray of coffee and there was a convenient pause. Dot's face flushed. She wasn't sure how to respond. She needn't have worried, however, for Mrs Humboldt took control of the situation.

'I see. Now, let us do the introductions properly, Mr Bletchford. The age of propriety is not yet dead, despite the march of so-called progress. This is my niece, Miss de Clere and this is Miss Truscott. We are taking a few days' holiday; the sea air is good for my health. And you, I take it, are travelling for business rather than pleasure. Although not too successfully, if your absent colleague is anything to go by.'

'On this particular occasion, I am engaged in business but I too enjoy Eastbourne for its clean air and relaxed atmosphere. I did manage to meet with my colleague, by the way, and I would gauge the meeting a success,' Ralph replied.

'I'm pleased for you, Mr Bletchford. And what is your business?'

'I am in the automobile industry. The motor car is the transport of the future, Mrs Humboldt, believe me.'

'For the likes of my aunt, perhaps,' Miriam interrupted, 'for she could employ a driver. But surely, Mr Bletchford, this is a luxury most families could not afford.'

'You would think so, Miss de Clere, but our company is constantly mastering new feats of engineering and developing new models. We are working on one at the moment, which we intend to market at a price that many more people could afford.'

At this point Mr Bletchford looked around in a rather theatrical fashion and lowered his voice. 'But I should be careful of divulging company secrets. One never knows who is listening.'

'And what is your company, Mr Bletchford?' Mrs H asked.

'The Morris Motor Company, based in Oxford. You must have heard of us?'

'A motor car is a motor car to me, Mr Bletchford,' Mrs H replied. 'Noisy, smelly things. Give me a horse and carriage any day.'

Ralph took up the challenge and clearly saw this as his opportunity to persuade her of the benefits of owning a car.

'There's nothing so convincing as positive proof,'

he said. 'Please allow me to demonstrate the advantages of motor travel. If you have no firm plans for tomorrow, I could take you all for a spin in my Morris Oxford. It's a four-seater, so I could take all three of you. What do you say?'

'We had planned the Italian Gardens,' Miriam said. 'And I've driven in motor cars before. One is much like another, I would guess. My aunt has problems with her back and legs and her body will not stand being shaken up on a bumpy ride.'

'Then you would guess wrongly, pardon me for saying so. The Morris Oxford has incomparable road handling and far superior suspension to any other automobile. I'm sure your aunt will find it a very comfortable ride.'

Dot hoped Mrs H would say yes. A ride in a motor car would be so exciting.

Mrs H paused, glanced at Miriam and then at Dot, whose expression gave away her feelings.

'All right, Mr Bletchford,' she agreed. 'We will give it a try. We'll go to the gardens in the morning and then I will take my usual rest. Let's say three o'clock tomorrow afternoon, shall we? Perhaps we could go to Michelham Priory?'

Dot glowed inside.

17

The morning began well, with a benign sun showing itself occasionally from behind clusters of ballooning clouds. The stroll along the promenade had brought a welcoming breeze, preventing the three women from getting too hot. Mrs H was in good spirits. Once in the gardens, Miriam went in one direction, to begin her sketches and Dot accompanied Mrs H on a leisurely tour of the gardens. They began with the deep flower borders, lining the main pathway through the centre of the gardens and Dot commented upon the beautiful array of colours.

'Mmm,' Mrs H grunted. 'Dahlias, too blowsy for me. Not to my taste. And there are far too many people on this path. We will turn here and seek a quieter area, away from the crowds. It's the price one pays for journeying at this time of the year, I suppose.'

The two women turned into a secluded area, where the sizzle of reds and oranges gave way to an area of muted greens. Tall trees fringed the edges of a grassy bank, backed by a pergola in the Greek style, its austere stone columns forming a perfectly symmetrical curve. The stone steps led up to a shaded seating area and Dot assisted Mrs H up to the raised platform, where she could rest and take in the lush vegetation.

'Ah, yes. This is much better.' Mrs H sighed. 'Now, tell me, Dorothy. What are your plans for the future? Miriam has told me a little of your determination to

99

become a teacher. You have just a short time left to qualify, as I understand it. Very commendable for one who comes from a country labouring background.'

Dot took the comment in the spirit she hoped it was intended, rather than take offence at the social prejudices that the statement implied. *We can all be victims of a narrow upbringing*, Dot thought, *whichever end of the social spectrum we are born into*. She let Mrs H ramble on.

'Now, my understanding is that your family are in financial straits at the moment as a result of your brother-in-law's unfortunate accident and the need to pay hospital fees. Miriam has told me that once the new term commences, you may be forced to seek permanent employment elsewhere in order that you can help with household costs. Is that correct?'

Dot was about to agree when Mrs H launched into a speech about the injustices of this world and how Miriam would do well to appreciate the privileges of the family she was born into and be more like Dot, prepared to sacrifice personal ambitions for the good of the family.

'I'm not talking out of the top of my hat, Dorothy, as you might think. I too have had to put personal desires aside . . . but that is another story and one that I don't often talk about. Suffice to say, I have decided that I want to help you continue your ambitions, my dear. You are a young woman who strikes me as having the right sort of influence upon my niece and I am sure that there must be a way that I can assist you in completing your training. As you are such a good friend of Miriam's, I am prepared to organise some financial support.'

Dot opened her mouth to comment but she was

met with a firm hand on her own and Mrs Humboldt's fixed expression.

'No protestations, Dorothy, please. Do not insult me by turning my offer down. We will talk of this again but for now, let us get to the rose garden before my legs give up on me.'

It was in the rose garden that the sky began to darken. Mrs H looked up at the approaching purple clouds and said, 'We must seek some shelter, Dorothy, or we'll soon take on the appearance of drowned rats. My new bonnet will be entirely ruined.'

Dot scanned the immediate area and, although there was a small gazebo within a few yards, several people had already noticed the impending change in the weather and there was not enough room for two more bodies inside its cramped space.

'Is there somewhere we could get out of the rain?' Dot asked. 'A glass house or cafeteria perhaps?'

'Ah, yes, very sensible of you, my dear,' Mrs H replied. 'Of course, the Garden Tea Rooms. As I remember it, we go through that archway there and walk to the right. Let's see if we can outrun Mother Nature. Take my arm, Dorothy, and the extra support will enable speedier progress.'

Dot didn't think that the words 'run' and 'speedy' could possibly apply to Mrs H, but it became apparent that she could put on a spurt if her good appearance was being threatened.

The two women made it to the doors of the tea rooms just as the heavens opened. Dot gave a thought to Miriam and hoped she had managed to shelter and save her precious drawings from a soaking.

'That was a lucky escape,' Mrs Humboldt said, smiling. Dot looked at her employer. The little

101

excitement had brought a high colour to her cheeks and she detected an expression of light-hearted pleasure in her eyes.

Dot guided Mrs H towards a vacant table in the corner of the room and helped her sit down, placing her stick against the low window ledge. A prim waitress arrived with her pad and pen to take their order and announced that there were no more teacakes but that the scones were very nice or there was boiled fruit cake or Victoria sponge.

'I will have the fruit cake, thank you,' Mrs H replied. 'And do you have Earl Grey tea? It's far superior to other teas. It's all I drink at home these days.'

'We do, madam,' the waitress replied, thinly disguising her indignation. 'We only serve the finest teas here.'

'Is that acceptable to you, Dorothy?' Mrs H asked.

'Yes, Earl Grey would be lovely,' Dot said.

'And some cake?' the waitress asked.

'Yes, the Victoria sponge, thank you,' Dot replied.

'Well done for not ordering the scones,' Mrs H said, once the waitress had left them. 'In my opinion, whenever a waitress pushes a particular item on the menu, it's because they need to get rid of it. They were probably baked yesterday and more like rock buns than scones.' Mrs H winked.

Dot was beginning to think that she had formed an image of Mrs H that was not her true character. After their earlier conversation, she was beginning to see another side of Mrs Humboldt, one who had possibly done a fair amount of pushing the social boundaries herself in her younger days.

When the rain began to ease off, Mrs H suggested that they should finish their tea and begin the walk back. 'Let's walk along the promenade rather than through the gardens,' she said. 'That way we may meet up with Miriam and if the rain comes on again, we could always hail a cab. There are plenty along the sea front.'

As they reached the main gates at the top end of the gardens, Dot noticed Miriam scanning the area, looking out for them. She waved as they approached and, when they got closer, greeted them enthusiastically. She then stood to one side and, with a flourish of her arm, revealed a poster advertising the travelling circus.

'Look!' she said with a grin. 'We must go. You'd like to go, wouldn't you, Dot?'

Dot detected that Miriam was enlisting her support in case of any objections on her aunt's part. Miriam had a way of getting what she wanted. If there were thrills out there to be had, she would find them and Dot could feel the pull of the tide that was swiftly dragging her in a direction not entirely in her control.

18

Stepping into Ralph Bletchford's car that afternoon was thrilling for Dot. She felt as if all eyes were on her as Ralph closed the door and walked around to take up the driving seat. Miriam insisted that Dot should sit up front, as this was her first experience of car travel.

'Such a pity your aunt was not up to coming. Perhaps she will feel better after a rest,' Ralph said. 'She had expressed an interest in seeing Michelham Priory. Would you ladies care to see it today or do you have other suggestions?'

'Aunt Phoebe does not always recognise her own limitations,' Miriam said. 'The long walk this morning exhausted her. Still, I'm sure we can find plenty to entertain us. The Priory sounds rather dull, though. All those monks with their drab habits. How about the Long Man of Wilmington or Beachy Head? I've been dying to see these sights since I've been visiting Eastbourne but my aunt has always had other ideas.'

'The dramatic views from Beachy Head on a clear day can be invigorating,' Ralph agreed. 'On a windy day it can be too much fresh air but today should be perfect. Let us drive to the cliffs,' he announced with the flourish of a showman. 'Hold onto your hats, ladies, the charabanc tour will depart forthwith.'

As the car topped each rise, Dot held her breath in expectation but the road seemed to dip and curve continuously, until she felt they would never reach their destination. It was difficult to conduct a conversation with the wind rushing past her ears, so she settled into just enjoying the ride. After about thirty minutes, Ralph announced that they would be able to see the cliffs very soon. When the anticipated sight came into view, Dot gasped at the dramatic beauty of the greensward and the contrasting vast expanse of white cliffs before her.

'The best views are to be had if we walk a short distance,' Ralph said as he parked the car. 'A pity you didn't bring your sketch pad, Miss de Clere,' he added.

'Ah, but I did,' Miriam replied tapping a shoulder bag. 'Never go anywhere without it.'

The three set out along the cliff top path. The afternoon was warm with a gentle breeze and they chatted about the delights and powers of the sea as they walked. The land dipped a little and then rose to high point. As they reached the top, a sudden gust of wind lifted the front of Dot's hat and she placed a hand on it to prevent it from sailing over the edge and into the sea surging below.

'I suggest you tie the bow with a stronger knot, Miss Truscott,' Ralph said and took a step towards her.

'I'll do it,' Miriam said forcing herself between them.

The hat secured, Dot stood and took in the views.

'I had no idea it would be so breathtaking.' She sighed. 'The white cliffs just go on and on. Oh look, a lighthouse!' she said pointing to the foot of the cliffs in the distance.

'This is a scene that has been the subject of many works of art,' Ralph said. 'Will you make a study of it today, Miss de Clere?'

'As you say, many have drawn and painted the lighthouse, Mr Bletchford. I am not one to follow the crowd,' Miriam said. 'I shall choose a different viewpoint. I may not even sketch at all. I have to want to capture it on paper. Creativity is a force that comes from within. It cannot be commanded or summoned by outside influences.'

'I stand corrected, Miss de Clere,' Ralph replied, a tight smile sliding across his lips.

'Is there any way we can get down to the beach from here?' Dot asked. 'I should love to walk along the sand.'

'I'm afraid not,' Ralph said. 'The only way down is straight down and I wouldn't recommend that.'

They walked on. Ralph Bletchford began talking of all the other interesting places they should see in and around Eastbourne. Miriam declined to join in the conversation. Dot felt awkward at this and compensated with over-enthusiastic nods and smiles at Ralph's continuous commentary.

'You go on,' Miriam announced suddenly, putting down her bag. 'The light is changing and I want to capture the pinkish glow on the cliffs. It contrasts so beautifully with the darkening blue of the sea, it's almost indigo. Luckily, I have brought my pastels with me.'

'If we go just a little further it's possible to see the curve of the bay back towards Eastbourne,' Ralph said.

Dot didn't reply immediately and Ralph, clearly noticing the anxious look on her face, added, 'We will not go out of sight and we'll meet up together in a short while for the walk back to the car. Will fifteen or twenty minutes be long enough, Miss de Clere, for you to capture the moment?'

'Indeed,' Miriam replied.

As they climbed above the place where Miriam was sitting, Dot could feel the air cooling and gave a little shiver. She wished she'd brought her shawl but the climb soon made her body temperature rise and she was so mesmerised by the views that she wasn't paying as much attention as she should to keeping on the path.

'Take care,' Ralph warned. 'The edge of the cliff is not safe, the soil crumbles easily.'

His words sailed over her head. She was so exhilarated by the climb that she didn't hear Ralph's advice. In her excitement, she'd moved quickly on and was now ahead of him. When she reached the viewpoint, another gust of wind hit her in the face and took her breath away. She was startled. The violent blast affected her balance. She lost her footing. The clouds raced across the sun and released its beams in a rush of white light, blinding her. The sky became the sea and the sea collided with the sky. Her eyes were not telling her which way was up. She was trying to regain her balance and her sense of direction when a hand grabbed her by the arm and pulled her to safety.

Her face was buried in Ralph's silk waistcoat, his open jacket flapping in the wind. She took a deep breath and a tinge of sweat, mixed with the sweet smell of his cologne made her pull back. Too close, she was too close. She lifted her chin and looked up into his grey eyes, a worried frown making his dark eyebrows meet, his full lips turned down at the edges. He leaned down towards her and tilted his fingers under her chin. There was a moment when she thought he was going to kiss her and what shocked her most was that she wanted it to happen. Her eyes started to water. Whether it was the wind that had slapped her in the face, the narrow escape from falling or the tumble of emotions she felt surging within her, she couldn't say but the tears began to flow freely.

Ralph put his arm around her and walked her gently away from the edge of the cliff. Once a safe distance away, he stopped and held her steady by both arms, looking at her.

'I thought I'd lost you there for a moment,' he said. 'You seem to be making a habit of falling into my arms. Are you all right now?'

'No, she is not all right,' a breathless voice said. 'What do you think you are doing, Mr Bletchford, letting my friend get so close to the edge? She could have died. I saw everything and ran as fast as I could.'

Dot could just make out Miriam's face through her tears. Miriam exploded at Ralph, calling him irresponsible and accused him of taking advantage of Dot.

'It wasn't his fault. He saved me, Miriam.' Dot tried to explain but her words were useless against the power of Miriam's tirade.

'As soon as Miss Truscott feels up to walking, I insist we go straight back to the car and you take us to the hotel,' she snapped. 'Goodness only knows what my aunt is going to say when I return her in this state.'

'Of course, I will drive you back immediately,' Ralph replied.

Not a word was said all the way back and when the doorman held the car door open for them, Dot looked back at Ralph. She wanted to say thank you and goodbye but Miriam grabbed her by the hand

and ushered her up the steps before anything could escape her lips.

19

Dot was not so shaken by the experiences of the afternoon that her awareness of what was going on around her was blunted. As she ascended the steps, Miriam's tight grip on her arm only heightened her senses. Why was Miriam so angry? Dot twisted her neck to glance behind her and saw Ralph handing the car keys to a valet. His words were just audible. 'Park this, would you? Return the keys to me in room fifteen.' He was on the same floor.

Miriam insisted that Dot rested. She poured her a glass of water from the carafe beside the bed and pulled the curtains.

'I think we have both learned lessons from this afternoon's misadventure,' Miriam said. 'However, I do not think that we should mention this to my aunt. Her health is already fragile. We don't want to add to her worries. I will go to the lounge and order some tea and let you sleep. Dinner is not for another hour. Now do as I say, Dorothy, or you may find the repercussions of this afternoon will catch up with you.'

Dot lay for a while going over events in her mind but the more she thought, the less her mind was receptive to sleep. Miriam was behaving like a bossy sister, telling her what to do. She swung her legs over the edge of the bed and pulled on her shoes. There was still a little soil and grass attached to the heels.

Dot closed the door quietly behind her and walked along the corridor counting off the numbers: eleven, thirteen . . . fifteen. This was Ralph's room. She stood for a moment, gazing at the dark panelled door, listening. She looked up and down the deeply carpeted space and seeing no one, tapped gently. No answer came from within. She tapped again.

The door opened and he was standing there before her, his shirt open at the neck and his braces dangling from the waist of his trousers.

'I didn't order . . .' he began.

There was a moment when both mouths opened and no sound came out. Two sets of eyes stared and two backs straightened.

'Oh, it's you,' Ralph finally said. 'I thought it was room service, hence the attire or rather lack of it.'

Dot's mouth dried. Now she was here, at his door. She hadn't planned what to say. She only knew she couldn't leave things the way they were when they parted.

'I just came to say I'm sorry,' she blurted.

'Sorry for what?' he asked. 'You were the injured party as I recall. Have you recovered?'

'I have but I fear Miriam is in such a lather about the incident that she may never recover.'

'Forgive me for saying so but I think Miss de Clere has too much of the artistic disposition and is prone to hysterics.'

Ralph pulled a face whilst saying this and Dot giggled.

They stood looking at one another for a while and Dot felt a tingling feeling move from her chest, down through her body and settle in her groin.

'I would invite you in but it would not be appropriate, I feel,' Ralph said. 'Times are changing but not fast enough for a man to entertain a young woman in

111

his room unaccompanied.'

Dot heard voices at the far end of the corridor and hoped it wasn't Miriam and Mrs H coming to find her. Her attention was drawn to the voices.

'Could you meet me later this evening after dinner, perhaps?' he added, hurriedly. 'Do Miriam and her aunt retire early?'

'About nine usually,' Dot replied.

'There is an orangery at the rear of the building, through the lounge and along a corridor. It's busy during the day but after dinner we would probably have it to ourselves. What do you say?'

Dot nodded. 'Nine o'clock, then,' she replied.

★ ★ ★

Nine o'clock couldn't come soon enough. Dot managed to excuse herself early, feigning a headache but instead of returning to her room, she went to find the orangery. The lighting along the corridor was dimmed and when she reached the orangery doors, she hesitated. It seemed very dark inside. She turned and looked behind her. No one was about. The heavy glass and metal doors gave way and the scent of jasmine enveloped her. The moon was beginning to show through the glass roof, giving an eerie backlight to the tall plants. The air felt damp to her bare arms. Fronds brushed her face as she moved amongst the dense planting and a tall tree fern loomed above her, casting a shadow over her. She didn't know whether to call out Ralph's name or remain silent.

She turned a corner and there, standing beneath a tree in the centre of the pathway, was Ralph. He held out his hand and presented her with the perfectly formed fruit. It settled in her palm, the weight of it promising all its fragrant juiciness. She lifted it to her nose and inhaled the sharp, bitter sweetness of the deep, orange skin.

'The only ripe one on the tree,' Ralph said. 'For you.'

Dot smiled.

'There's a bench just over there. Shall we sit?'

They sat and talked in whispers. After more apologies and a slightly awkward silence, he began to talk about himself. He told her of his aim to become the general manager of the Morris Oxford car factory, where he worked and then to eventually set up other factories throughout the south of England.

'There's so much potential for a man of ambition, Dorothy. I may call you Dorothy, may I?'

'Of course,' she replied.

'And do you have any ambitions, Dorothy?'

'Well, I'm training to become a teacher in Chichester College but I would like to be married some day and have a family of my own. I love children.'

'So would I,' Ralph said, taking her hand. 'It seems we have a lot in common.'

He leaned into her and kissed her gently on the cheek. 'You are very beautiful, Dorothy Truscott. You must have been told that many times before.'

Ralph's hands slipped around her waist and he drew her closer. His lips were on her lips, their breath mingled and Dot's heart thumped in her chest. She had never been kissed like this before. Drunken farm boys trying to grope her while they were dancing at Harvest Festival, their sloppy, beer-soaked mouths flapping about her face, only served to make her run for the door. Even Jack's kiss had felt less exciting than this. This was tender and sweet-tasting. She wanted more. Then Ralph pulled away from her and sighed.

'Oh Dorothy,' he said. 'If only . . .'

'If only what?' she prompted.

'Nothing. There is no point in wishing. We might have become firm friends. More than that perhaps, but I must return to Oxford and you to the Hampshire Downs. You must think of it as just a kiss, a token of affection, that's all.'

Dot couldn't believe he was dismissing it in that way. It was more than just a kiss to her. She had never felt this way before. Jack's kisses had not been as tender as Ralph Bletchford's. He was clearly more practised in the art of seduction and that both excited and troubled her. He was so much more mature and refined than anyone she had ever met. He was both attractive and charming. She was captivated.

Ralph took Dot's hand and pressed it to his lips. He stood up and looked at her for a long time, then said, 'Goodnight, my dear, Dorothy. If only we had met at another time, in another life,' and left her sitting there alone.

Dot remained perfectly still for a long time. She was stunned by what had just happened. How could he kiss her like that and then just walk away? The taste of him still lingered on her lips, the press of his body against hers. He was denying his own passion, while she could not escape from hers. He had awakened something within her, feelings so strong they could not be denied. There was so much she still had to learn about men, about life and about love. Miriam had been right, she was just a simple country girl, but not anymore. Something was beginning and she wasn't sure that she wanted to control it.

20

'What is it?' Miriam asked. 'What's happened? Tell me. Something has upset you, I know it. I can tell. You've lost your smile and you're not looking at me when I speak to you.'

'Nothing, it's nothing,' Dot replied, looking away.

'It most definitely is something and I'm going to get to the bottom of it. You might as well tell me now.'

'Good morning. What can I get you this morning? Tea, coffee?' the waitress asked, hovering at Miriam's shoulder.

'Tea, we always both have tea,' Miriam snapped. 'Thank you,' she added as an afterthought.

'Well, if you won't tell me, then I will just have to devise a Dorothy recovery plan, regardless of the cause of the ailment. My diagnosis is a decline in spirits due to a dearth of excitement. We have nothing planned, except strolls along the promenade with Aunty and interminable amounts of tea, cake and maudlin conversation. Plus, you had quite a shock on the cliff tops with that Ralph Bletchford. I don't know what he was thinking about letting you get ahead of him like that.'

At the mention of his name, Dot fought to hold back the tears and her throat dried so that, when she tried to reply, no words would come, only a low moan.

'That's it, isn't it?' Miriam said. 'What's he done now? He hasn't touched you, has he? If he has, then by God, I'll . . .'

'What if he has?' Dot whispered, her voice wavering. 'What if I wanted him to?'

The waitress arrived with the tea and Miriam ordered them scrambled eggs and toast.

'What if I didn't want scrambled eggs?' Dot complained.

'Don't you want them? I'll call her back. I just wanted to get rid of her so that we can talk about this, Dot.'

'I don't want to talk about it,' Dot said, the tears escaping now, despite her best efforts to contain them.

Miriam handed her a handkerchief.

'All right. We won't,' she agreed. 'But it is better to share these things. I'm listening whenever you want to talk.'

The two of them ate their breakfast in virtual silence, Dot constantly scanning the room in case Ralph appeared whilst at the same time conscious of being under Miriam's over protective gaze.

When they returned to their rooms, Miriam said that she was going to work on her painting of the Italian Gardens and Dot went to prepare for her stroll with Mrs Humboldt.

The day passed without event. Dot did a good job of covering up her feelings and Mrs H did enough talking for both of them, punctuating a stream of comments about passers-by with the occasional complaint about her legs and the need to sit down.

At the evening meal, Miriam sat down at the table with a broad grin on her face and presented her aunt and Dot with tickets for the circus.

'Whatever did you get those for?' Mrs H sighed. 'All those smelly animals and loud music. Not to mention sitting amongst all those people harbouring all sorts

116

of germs.'

Used to her aunt's mood swings, Miriam simply said, 'Of course, Aunt, if you'd prefer not to come, I'm sure Elsie would love to take your ticket.'

'And who would look after me for the evening, pray?' Mrs H blustered. 'On the other hand, I don't like to think of my money being wasted and it is my money, Dorothy, whatever Miriam tells you. She doesn't exactly earn a living from her paintings. We should give the ticket to someone else. Mr Bletchford, for example. It was kind of him to take you out in his car.'

Miriam glanced at Dot whose face had turned pale.

'I don't think that would be a good idea,' Miriam said. 'Anyway, he's probably left by now. He had business to attend to, I think.'

'Oh no, he hasn't. I saw him this afternoon when I took tea in the lounge. He was with a very attractive young woman. His sister, he said. They helped me to the lift and then went along to his room together.'

Mrs H paused, pursed her lips and placed her hands on the table. She retrieved her napkin and placed it on her lap, smoothing it methodically.

'They didn't look at all alike,' she said.

After dinner, Dot went to her room early saying that she felt unwell. The lift was full, so she took the stairs. Just as she reached the top step on the first landing, she met the gaze of Ralph Bletchford who was walking towards her with a young woman on his arm. She lowered her eyes, intending to walk straight past them without exchanging words, but he greeted her which forced her to look up at them.

'Good evening, Dorothy. I'm so glad that we've managed to meet again before I leave. Let me introduce you to my sister, Meredith. She's here in Eastbourne for a conference, the suffragette movement. Meredith, this is Miss Dorothy Truscott.'

The young woman smiled and said, 'Pleased to meet you, Miss Truscott. Ralph has mentioned your name. He took you and your travelling companion touring, I understand?'

'Yes,' Dot replied. Her skin was crawling. She desperately wanted to escape this encounter but didn't know how.

'I assume you've finished your dinner,' Meredith said. 'A pity. It would have been nice to make your acquaintance. Perhaps I could have enlisted you to our cause?'

'Miss Truscott is far too busy with her companions to come and listen to a room full of women bemoaning their lot,' Ralph said.

'He's on our side, really.' Meredith smiled. 'He's taken a vow of secrecy not to tell our parents. They would not approve.'

'They certainly wouldn't. So, you'd better not get yourself arrested or your name in the papers, Merry,' Ralph added.

'Don't worry, I shall keep a low profile. Wouldn't want to push Mother right over the edge. First her only son announces that he's going to America and then her daughter sullies the family name! We're not exactly model children, are we?'

The pressure in Dot's chest felt as if it would burst. She could feel little beads of sweat forming on her upper lip. America? What was all that talk of becoming a manager and wanting a family? Why he was nothing but a liar, a flirt and a liar. How could she have been so easily taken in by him?

'Please excuse me,' she said. 'I have a headache coming on and must retire. I wish you a pleasant evening.'

Her anger surged up from her stomach and made her spit out a few departing words to him. 'I wish you every success in America, Mr Bletchford. I hope you find what you're looking for. I'm not sure people speak the truth when they say the streets there are paved with gold. Truth is not always easy to come by, don't you agree?'

21

The morning of the bleed, Kate was standing at the wash house sink. The copper was boiling away with the week's white washing and she was scrubbing vigorously at the neck of some stranger's shirts. She'd managed to find extra employment by taking in laundry from some of the big houses around Micklewell. The Taylor sisters had put her in touch with the housekeepers and when word got around, she found she was agreeing to take on more and more.

The sharp, stabbing pain deep in her groin made her wince and she went suddenly light-headed. She held onto the side of the deep sink and waited until the wave of nausea passed over her. She lowered herself onto the stool that was holding the door open and felt between her legs. There was a wetness. She peered down to see a bloom of red, stark against her white undergarments. Fear gripped her. She was losing the baby.

She grabbed a towel and staggered into the kitchen. Thankfully no one was about. The children had gone with her mother to the market and Albert was taking his time trying to get to the forge on his crutches. He needed to do something useful, he said, and her father had suggested he could help with some of the finishing jobs that could be done whilst seated.

Kate made her way upstairs, found some monthly rags and fixed them in place. Then she lay down on the bed, the towel under her and her feet raised on two pillows. She remained still and prayed. She thought she had lost her faith when her brother and Philip were taken from her but she didn't know where else to turn. If there was a God, perhaps he would help her now?

She and Albert were so looking forward to the birth of their child. A brother or sister for Ronnie. Albert was such a good father. There were not many men who would take on another man's child but he had done so with a glad and open heart. He had become a respected and valued member of the community in Micklewell and she so wanted to bear him a healthy child. Now they might never meet their little one. She was miscarrying.

She lay still for a long time, hoping that the bleeding would stop and must have drifted into sleep. She was woken by the sound of calling below.

'Kate? Ada? Anyone about?'

Kate tried to sit up and swing her legs over the edge of the bed but the effort made her dizzy.

'Is there anyone at home?'

She recognised Mary Suss's voice. She trusted Mary. She had born four children of her own and been present at the births of many more in the village besides. Mary was the one to call.

'Up here, Mary,' Kate replied.

When Mary came into the room, she gasped at the sight of Kate who was pale and shaking.

'Oh, Kate, my dear. You poor darling,' she said. 'Here, let me help you sit up.'

'I'm going to lose the baby, aren't I?' Kate said, tears pouring down her face.

'I can't say that yet, my dear,' Mary replied. 'Let's have a look at you. Where's Ada and Albert?'

'Albert is at the forge with Pa. He's taken to going down there of a morning. He can't do much but he's so bored with being at home all day and he's beginning to get depressed. Ma's at the market, she's taken the children,' Kate said. 'They won't be back for a while yet. I can't lose this baby, Mary. It will be my fault. I shouldn't have taken on the extra work.'

'Now hush, Kate. Don't upset yourself. These things sometimes happen and it's no one's fault. Some babes just don't want to stay with us and we don't know yet that yours has gone. Sometimes the bleeding just stops and everything progresses as normal. Try not to worry, Kate. Easier said than done, I know, but worrying is not going to make things any better.'

Mary helped Kate change her undergarments and took a look at how much blood Kate had lost.

'I've seen worse and the mother gave birth to a healthy boy,' she said. 'Now let's get you downstairs and get a nice hot cup of tea in you. And I'll finish that washing and get it on the line. There's enough of a breeze. It should be dry before dinner time. But you must promise me that you'll slow down and stop taking on too much.'

Kate nodded. 'I'll do whatever's best for the babe,' she said. 'Mary, please don't mention this to Ma,' she added. 'I don't want to worry her.'

'She needs to know,' Mary replied.

'She can't,' Kate said.

'Why ever not?' Mary asked. 'If this should happen again . . .'

'Please don't say anything, Mary. I don't want to create more worry,' Kate insisted.

Mary grunted. 'Now, who's the midwife here?'

'You are,' Kate replied.

'And who knows best about pregnancies?'

'You do,' Kate said.

'So, let me know best and tell Ada.'

That was Mary's last word.

Mary told Kate to lie still with her legs raised while she bustled about, getting everything done before the family returned. She had just sat down and Kate had come downstairs when excited shouts alerted them both to the return of Ada and the children. Tilly and Ronnie burst through the chain curtain simultaneously, each carrying a bag which they proceeded to dump on the floor and began rooting through the contents.

'Look what Nan bought me,' Ronnie said, holding a brightly coloured spinning top aloft.

'And me,' Tilly said. 'I chose my colours. They're my favourites, red and yellow.'

'Now what's going on here?' Ada said as she joined them, looking tired and frazzled by the children's constant energy. 'I told you that bags must be unpacked first but not all over the floor.'

Then she noticed their visitor. 'Mary, what are you doing here?'

'Well, I came to ask if you had any bottle green wool. I'm knitting Walter a balaclava for the winter and I've run out. Thought I had enough but it turns out I haven't. Kate said you were out so I thought I'd keep her company for a bit,' Mary replied.

As she said this, she looked long and hard at Kate, her small mouth giving a little twitch and her eyes widening in expectation.

'Mary kindly helped me hang out the washing. There was rather a lot today and . . .'

'And I thought she was looking worn out, Ada,'

Mary continued.

'I told her she didn't need to do it. That she was taking too much on. Her father and I said we could manage. Dot's money should be coming through soon. She's done two weeks already,' Ada replied.

'Have you heard from her?' Mary asked.

'Not a peep. I suppose that Mrs Humboldt is keeping her busy. I've heard tell that she's a bit of a tartar. Works her staff hard. Will you stay for a glass of cider? Jim thinks the bottle's finished but I kept a bit back.' She grinned.

While Ada went to fetch the cider from the pantry, Mary gave Kate another meaningful look and whispered, 'You have to tell her. No time like the present. Tell her when I'm here, that might be best. Allowances must be made for you if you want to carry this babe to full term.'

'But things are hard enough for Ma without . . .'

Kate's comment was cut short by Ada's arrival. She brought down two glasses and struggled with arthritic fingers to remove the wired glass stopper.

'Here, give it to me, Ma,' Kate said.

The children let out several whoops of excitement as they challenged each other to see who could keep their top going the longest.

'Why don't you two take those outside?' Mary suggested. 'There's more room in the yard.'

The children departed and Mary continued as they shared the cider between them. 'I think Kate needs to rest more.' She gave Kate a long, hard look.

'I had a bleed, Ma' Kate said.

'A bleed?' Ada gasped, looking grey. 'How much?'

'It wasn't too much but from now on she mustn't do any heavy lifting and no standing for long hours at a sink,' Mary replied, looking from mother to daughter.

The three women sat absorbed in their own thoughts for a while until Kate broke the awkward silence.

'Please don't speak of this to Albert,' she said. 'He'll go out of his mind with worry and be watching me like a hawk every time I fetch and carry. He had to watch me pull back from the Spanish Flu when it was determined to take me. I can't bear to see him suffer such worries again.'

The two older women looked at each other and nodded their acknowledgement of Kate's wishes.

When Mary had left and everyone retired for the night, Kate slipped into bed beside Albert and asked if he was beginning to learn how things worked at the forge.

'If I'm honest, I feel a bit useless,' Albert replied. 'I made it home from the trenches with only a minor wound compared to some and now I know how the men who were really badly injured feel. There are so many of them, Kate. Good men who went to war with able bodies and strong minds. They came home broken and will never be the same again. Take Gordon Crowther, he's never been able to work again. His mind has gone, they say. He's not able to hold his tools steady anymore, his hands shake uncontrollably. He lost his job at the woodturners because he made such a mess of everything he tried to make. They said they had to let him go. As for me? I don't know what's to happen to me in the long term. This leg is taking such a time to heal.'

Kate turned towards him and placed her arm across his chest.

'It will be all right, Albert,' she said. 'You just have to give it time. We have each other, that's the main thing.'

'I don't know what I'd do without you, Kate,' he said. 'You and Ronnie mean the world to me. I just hope we can manage until I'm fit enough to go back to the farm. There's nothing that would make me happier than for us to be able to rent a place of our own. I want to provide for you and Ronnie and the new little one.'

He placed his hand tenderly on her swollen belly.

'I'm going to get stronger, Kate. My leg will get better and I'm going to make everything right for our family.'

Kate hoped that he was right.

22

Mrs H had declined to come to the circus so Miriam ordered a taxi cab to take just the two of them to the show. When the doorman announced that their transport had arrived, they made their way down the stone steps where several cars were waiting on the turning circle.

'Which one's ours?' Miriam asked.

The doorman pointed to a shiny black and grey vehicle with the passenger door held open by a woman wearing a neat blouse with a tie neck. A flurry of tight curls peeked from beneath her felt hat. She wore dark, leather gloves and threw a cigarette onto the ground, grinding it with her foot before straightening her trim jacket. She looked directly at them.

'But that one's taken,' Dot said. 'Look, that woman is about to get into it.'

'That's your driver, miss,' the doorman answered. 'Miss Scott. She's well known in Eastbourne. Good driver apparently too. Been driving since the war. Owns her own taxi company now.'

'Well,' Miriam exclaimed, 'who'd have thought sleepy old Eastbourne would have stepped into the twentieth century. Good for her, I say.'

Miss Scott greeted them with a smile.

'Where to, ladies? The Gaiety Club?' she asked.

'We've got tickets for the circus,' Miriam replied.

'Right ho. Devonshire Park it is then,' Miss Scott replied. She walked to the front of the car and proceeded to wind a crank. On the third swing, the engine sprang into action.

Miss Scott invited them to 'jump in' and they settled into the back seat, exchanging looks and nudging and smiling at each other.

'This is turning into quite an adventure.' Dot beamed.

Her mood had lightened after her upsetting experience with Ralph Bletchford. This excursion to something completely new and exciting was just what she needed. She took Miriam's hand and squeezed it.

'Thank you, Miriam,' she said. 'I'm so looking forward to this. Just wait until I tell my family. They'll never believe it!'

Miriam paid the fare and asked Miss Scott to return for them in two hours.

Dot stood and gazed up at the huge tent that rose up into a deep blue sky. The stark whiteness of the canvas soared like a billowing cloud and a flapping flag at its apex announced that the Barnum and Bailey Circus was in town.

Two young women wearing feathered headdresses and sparkling gowns handed them a flyer listing the circus acts, as they headed towards the gaping entrance.

'Watch out for the guy ropes,' they trilled. 'Candy floss and candy cones inside. Buy yourself a clown chocolate bar and find the lucky ticket.'

As they took their seats, the brass band struck up a tune and the parade around the ring began. Long-legged, sinuous young men and women stood on the backs of beautiful white, prancing horses with flowing manes and tails. A tumble of clowns spilling over each other and turning somersaults, grinned, white-faced and red-mouthed at the crowd. Jugglers threw blue and gold clubs into the air and caught them behind their backs.

The ringmaster mounted a podium and cracked his whip and the parade filed out of the ring. The music reached a crescendo and then silence hovered over the audience's heads, the sense of anticipation held on everyone's breath.

The ringmaster announced, 'Welcome to the wonderful world of Barnum and Bailey's Circus. An evening of delight and remarkable feats. Marvel at the contortions of the Zither Sisters, be astounded by the aerial acrobatics of the Flying Martellos and prepare to be introduced to the dark and dangerous animals of deepest Africa.'

At this, a roar was heard from outside the tent and the audience let out a collective gasp. 'Fear not, my friends,' the ringmaster announced with a sweeping gesture of his hand. 'For the mighty lion-tamer, Fearless Felix, will tame these beasts for your entertainment and no hair on any head shall be harmed.'

A muscular man dressed like a Roman centurion leaped into the ring accompanied by a glamorous young woman in flowing white robes, who handed him his whip and a chair. He held both items above his head to the rapturous applause of the audience.

'Let us hope that his performance lives up to his bravado,' Miriam whispered.

'I'm not sure I like the idea of wild animals in the ring at all,' Dot replied.

But she was soon distracted by the antics of the clowns who had appeared with their oversized shoes and trousers and riding the smallest bicycles Dot had ever seen. They laughed along with every mishap and misdemeanour until a bucket of water threatened to douse them. How they laughed even more when the bucket released nothing but tiny scraps of paper which fluttered about their heads and settled in their hair.

There was an interval when a huge iron cage was constructed around the ring to keep the audience safe from the lion and Miriam and Dot bought themselves ice cream cones and listened to the excited chatter of the children around them. How lucky these children were, thought Dot, to experience such sights. How she would love to be able to bring Ronnie and Tilly to see such a spectacle.

The afternoon was over all too quickly. On the way out of the big top Dot couldn't stop talking about the high wire act and the trapeze artists and how wonderful it must be to fly through the air like that.

'I'm not sure I could place that much trust in another human being,' Miriam replied.

'Better than trusting a lion,' Dot replied. 'Although I felt sorry for the creature. It can't be right to keep a wild animal caged up like that, no wonder it was angry at being poked and made to jump through hoops.'

There were so many people pressing through the narrow entrance trying to get out that Dot almost lost sight of Miriam in the crush. Excited children wheeled around their parents' legs. People pressed in on all sides and elbows dug into Dot's side. She got pushed to the edge of the tunnel and was finding it difficult to make her way to the exit. As she finally managed to emerge from the tent, she noticed Miriam talking to a group of strangers.

'There you are, Dorothy. Come and meet my old friends from art school. This is Bettine and Arthur, Florence and Clive,' Miriam said, grabbing Dot by the arm and presenting her to the group.

The strangers all shook her hand in turn. Dorothy hoped that her mouth was not gaping for she was astounded by their outlandish appearance. The women wore brightly coloured shawls, tasselled at the ends. Florence's abundant hair was free-flowing across her shoulders and Bettine's was cropped short, showing off her elegant neck. The men were equally colourful, brightly patterned waistcoats glinted beneath their dramatic black cloaks and they wore wide-brimmed hats. The four of them looked like they were gypsies or a music hall act, about to break into song.

'What a coincidence that we should bump into you,' Miriam said. 'Are you staying in Eastbourne for long?'

'We're here for a few more days,' Clive said. 'We simply must get together for an evening. What do you say?'

'Great idea,' Miriam replied. 'What do you suggest?'

'There's a wonderful assembly rooms where there's live music and dancing on Saturday nights, Caffyns, do you know it?'

'No, but I'm sure our taxi driver will. How about it, Dot?'

Miriam took a cursory glance in Dot's direction but didn't wait for a reply.

'It's a date then, Saturday, eight o'clock. See you there,' Miriam said.

They all kissed each other flamboyantly on cheeks and Miriam took Dot's arm, clearly excited at the prospect of dancing the night away and escaping her aunt's constant scrutiny. Dot wondered what she could wear to such an event. She didn't really have anything suitable. Dances in Micklewell weren't exactly high society affairs.

23

'What do you mean you can't go?' Miriam asked, when Dot said that she really didn't think that sort of thing was for her.

'What 'sort of thing'?' Miriam continued. 'It's only a dance. You've been to a dance before, haven't you?'

'Yes but . . .'

'No buts. It will be fun. Dancing is fun. She should come, shouldn't she, Aunt?' Miriam implored.

Mrs H looked over the top of her glasses and put down her morning paper.

'Well, if you call all that mad jigging about dancing. In my day we glided around the floor with elegance. As far as I can tell, today's dancing is just cavorting about,' she grumbled, wrinkling her nose. 'Perhaps Dorothy shares my opinion and does not wish to be seen flinging her limbs about with your outlandish friends. Now leave Dorothy alone to make up her own mind. I take it you have plenty to do, Miriam. Dorothy and I are heading off to the shops. I want to visit Dale and Kerley's Department Store. We will take lunch out.'

Miriam was summarily dismissed and Mrs H and Dot set out for the short walk to Dale and Kerley's. Elsie accompanied them to carry the parcels, for Mrs H was determined not to come home empty-handed. The elderly lady seemed to find herself a new set of legs as she hustled them around the various departments within the store and soon Elsie was weighed down with stoles, blouses, nightgowns, stockings and a warm pair of boots, ready for the winter.

'Now,' Mrs H said, turning to Dot, 'if you're to go to the ball, Cinderella, you will need a new gown to wear.'

Ignoring Dot's protests, Mrs H commandeered the lift and instructed the girl operating it. 'Kindly stop at the right floor for evening wear.'

Elsie stood amongst a mountain of parcels, while Mrs H directed operations from a comfortable chair.

'Such a joy to be able to shop for beautiful things,' Mrs H cooed. 'I'm past the time of life for such frippery and Miriam refuses to wear anything remotely feminine. I despair of her!'

Dot tried on dress after dress until Mrs H was satisfied that she looked the part.

'That pale blue is just your colour, my dear,' she said. 'Complements your eyes and shows off that lovely dark brown hair. It fits well, too, all in the right places.'

Dot blushed. She'd never had anyone point out her feminine curves before and it made her feel self-conscious. She wasn't sure that she could wear such a revealing dress in public.

Mrs H turned to the shop assistant and asked, 'Now, I'm not up to date with the latest fashion but would you say that this is what the young women are wearing in the dance halls at the moment?'

'Oh yes, madam,' the assistant gushed. 'This is our very latest design. The sequinned bodice and the fringed skirt are all the rage. The style suits you well, miss. You have a lovely figure.'

'It is beautiful,' Dot said, looking at herself in a mirror and not quite believing what she saw, 'but I really couldn't . . .'

'Oh yes you can and you will,' Mrs H insisted. 'Now, you get changed and we'll have it wrapped. Elsie can manage one more thing, I'm sure. Fabric like that must be as light as gossamer. Come on, Elsie, buck up. You look like you've lost a pound and found a penny. I'll get the doorman to find a boy to carry our purchases. Will that put a smile back on your face?'

24

As soon as Dot and Miriam walked into the assembly rooms, Dot felt as if all eyes were on her. They weren't of course. The whole room was a seething, writhing, living creature, expanding and contracting, winding and weaving. Bobbing feathers, pinned to headbands, collided with strings of pearls dangling from necks. White-shirted arms swung bare-shouldered women in circles and dapper black-and-white, laced shoes swivelled with dainty ankle-strapped sandals, stomping in rhythm to the music which reverberated around the hall. The whole scene made Dot dizzy.

'There they are,' Miriam shouted above the noise.

She guided Dot towards a table on the left-hand side of the room. Arthur and Ralph got up and Arthur offered to get them some drinks.

'You simply must try a cocktail,' Florence said.

'You look wonderful,' Bettine gushed, patting the chair next to her. 'I just love that dress!'

After two cocktails, Dot felt a little more relaxed and was even quite enjoying the whole experience. Her foot started tapping to the music and Clive caught her eye.

'How about a dance?' he asked Dot.

'I've never . . .'

'It's easy. There are only a few basic steps. It's the Charleston,' Clive replied.

'Look, step, tap, step, tap. What could be simpler?'

He took Dot's hand and led her onto the dance

136

floor. She soon found that the beat of the music carried her along. The dance was fast and furious and Dot was perspiring when she finally came back to her seat.

'What you need is a Tom Collins,' Bettine said.

'Who's he?' Dot asked.

Laughter rippled around the table and Miriam explained that it was a long drink, very refreshing, she said, and went to buy them two.

She came back with another man who was carrying the drinks for her. He was dressed in a cream suit with a matching waistcoat and wore a cream homburg hat edged with light brown. His shoes were tan and white brogues and he walked with a confident swagger towards their table, glancing first at Miriam and then, she thought, directly at her. Whatever he said to Miriam made her smile.

'Look who I found at the bar,' Miriam announced. 'He was drinking far too much and making a nuisance of himself, as usual. So, I thought I would drag him away and bring him to sit with us where I can keep an eye on him. You know everyone, I think, Douglas, except for Dorothy. Dorothy, this is Douglas Brooks-Grant, another penniless artist. Don't be fooled by the get up, he probably stole it from the valet service in some posh hotel. His father has disowned him and for all I know disinherited him, so he's not the catch he pretends to be. Apart from that he's perfectly harmless.'

'How do you do, Dorothy? Pleased to meet you. Don't believe a word that Miriam says about me. It's all slanderous nonsense. I'm told that this drink is for you,' Douglas said, handing one of the glasses to Dot. He dragged over a chair from another table and placed it next to her. She was slightly uncomfortable at his closeness but smiled at him.

'Now, tell me all about yourself. How do you know our dear Miriam and what you are doing in East-bourne?'

Dot didn't know quite what to say.

'Dorothy is my aunt's companion and my friend. So, be on your best behaviour, Douglas, or I will set the formidable Mrs H upon you.'

Douglas held up his hands in surrender.

'Anything but that,' he said.

She smiled at his repartee and agreed to dance with him. He impressed her with his footwork and how he seemed to just glide with her around the dance floor. He was an exceptional dancer and several times he made her laugh with his witty observations of the different dance styles around the room.

'He's the grab your girl and run type,' he joked, 'And his feet are so much like dinner plates that he keeps clumping all over his lady's delicate toes. She likes to think herself a real flapper but she's more like a woman drowning than dancing.'

Dot was having the best time.

As the evening progressed, Dot's confidence grew and she danced with anyone who asked her. Several of those who spun her round the floor held her waist tighter than she liked and one stroked her arm in a way that she found too familiar. It seemed as if certain social niceties were being ignored here but she didn't mention anything because she didn't want to appear prudish.

With all the drinking, Dot went to the ladies' room several times. The third time, she was aware of someone standing by an open window, smoking. It was

Douglas. He'd been drinking all evening and his former charms had started to pale on her when he became too familiar with her and was placing his hands inappropriately on her body. He tried to butt in when she was dancing with other men, becoming quite rude when the other men objected to the interruption. She noticed that he had lost his hat and his slick, black hair now flopped untidily over his face. His hypnotic eyes were fixed upon her and he pursed his lips and leered at her as she walked by. She was uncertain what to do, so she smiled at him out of embarrassment at his unwanted attentions. He seemed to have turned into a completely different man to the one she had been introduced to earlier.

When she came out of the ladies' room, he was still there. He offered her a cigarette and she said she didn't smoke. He really was becoming a nuisance and she wasn't sure how to get rid of him.

'Well, would you at least have one more dance with me?' he asked.

Maybe that would get rid of him, she thought, so she nodded. He walked towards her and pulled her immediately into a close hold. They were still in the corridor when he grabbed her. She was completely taken by surprise at his force and the strength of his grip. She pulled back and looked at him. He pressed his body against her and kissed her neck. She looked over her shoulder and noticed two women disappearing into the toilet area. She opened her lips to speak and he forced his mouth upon hers.

Two men entering the men's room wolf-whistled at them and Dot struggled to free herself from his arms. His grip tightened and he dragged her behind a screen, amongst piles of boxes and chairs. He pushed her up against the wall and she tried to shout but his hand was clamped over her mouth.

'I'm not going to hurt you,' he whispered. 'If I take my hand away will you promise me not to scream? I just want to kiss you, that's all. Don't pretend you don't want me to, you've been sending out the signals all night.' His breath was sour with beer and he had a bead of sweat on his upper lip. 'Just one little kiss. That's all,' he said.

Dot's eyes opened wide and she could see only his dark brows knitted together, his greased hair flopping across his forehead, his eyes narrowing until they almost disappeared beneath heavy eyelids. She nodded, frantically. Anything to make him stop, so she could breathe.

He took his hand away and she immediately tried to shout but no sound would come. His anger exploded in her face and he placed his lower arm across her neck. He was throttling her. He used his other arm to brutally massage her breasts, all the while whispering to her. She didn't hear what he was saying. She wanted to forget that this was happening. She tried to take her mind elsewhere. He lifted up her dress and began pulling at her underwear. He kicked her legs apart and she nearly lost her balance. The music pounding in her ears throbbed with her own blood surging through her veins. She needed to fight him. His nails scratched her stomach and his spittle ran down her neck. His breathing surged and subsided and the noise of the dancehall came back to her as if down a long and winding tunnel. She could hear voices. She had to find the strength to call out. She took a deep breath and let out a scream that came from deep inside her.

'Dot? Dorothy, is that you? Where are you?' someone called.

At the sound of another voice, he released her from his grip. She sank down to the floor and curled herself into a tight ball. She heard footsteps and shouts. She passed out. When she opened her eyes, she saw Miriam bending over her, calling orders to people to fetch a doctor, to bring her some water, to call the police. Miriam sat her up and held her closely in her arms, whispering to her, 'You're safe now. Everything will be all right. We'll see that whoever did this is punished for what he's done.'

25

Miriam lay next to Dot, one arm across her friend, holding her hand tightly. The doctor had given Dot a sedative and she was quieter now, although she was not asleep. She lay with her back to Miriam, unable to look at her, unable to move or speak. Her body was wounded and her peace of mind shattered into tiny shards of glass that pierced her heart and her brain. She ached all over. When she moved her eyelids, needles stung the backs of her eyes and when she opened them, even the dim light of the room was too bright for her. She squeezed them closed but that made her head spin. There was no comfortable position to be in, no escaping the dreadful truth of the present.

Dot struggled to get to sleep but eventually her body gave in. She murmured and sobbed and shouted her way through a disturbed night and when the morning came, she woke feeling hollow and empty. It was as if all that had filled her with joy had drained away during the night. The Dot who had danced and laughed so vigorously just a few hours ago had disappeared.

Miriam was standing by the window when she opened her eyes and Dot looked at the curve of her back and her loose, auburn hair over her shoulders. She both wished for and dreaded the moment when Miriam turned around. How could she face her friend, holding within her the deep shame of what had happened? She sat up and waited for her mind to clear.

Miriam must have sensed her movement and

turned. She came straight to Dot's side and held Dot in her arms, smoothing her forehead and talking to her in a soothing voice.

'My dear, dear, Dot. I'm here. I'm not going anywhere. I'm so sorry for what has happened to you. Did you get a good look at the man? It would help if you could give a description. You were in no fit state last night.'

What should she say? This man was a friend of Miriam's. Would Miriam believe her?

Dot was shaking and when she tried to speak all that came out were deep sobs that wracked her body and made her gasp for breath. The events of the evening surged through her mind. She'd been giving him signals, that's what he said. Had she? She was just enjoying herself.

Dot let her keep whispering words of support and when Miriam drew back and looked at her, she let the tears flow.

'We don't have to go anywhere today,' Miriam said. 'I will tell my aunt that you are unwell. We can take breakfast and lunch and dinner in your room if you wish. I'm going to order some tea and toast right away.'

'I don't want any breakfast,' Dot said.

'You must eat, my dear,' Miriam began and then stopped herself. 'Well, we can talk about that later. Let's just have some tea.'

Miriam moved towards the telephone. Dot got up and said, 'I'm going to run a bath. I feel dirty.'

'Of course,' Miriam replied. 'You go and do just that. I'll go back to my room for a short while and order tea for an hour's time. Does that sound all right?'

Dot nodded and took herself into the bathroom.

143

She undressed and lowered her bruised body into the warm, comforting water. She soaped herself and then lay there for a long time, until the water began to cool. She climbed out, dried herself and put on fresh clothes.

By the time Miriam came back, she was beginning to feel a little better, although her mind kept revisiting the worst moments of the previous evening. She kept questioning herself. Had she given him any reason to believe she wanted him to? No, she was sure she hadn't. Could she have fought him off more determinedly? No, he was too strong, too overpowering. What more could she have done?

She sipped her tea and nibbled at some toast but she really wasn't hungry.

'I've spoken to my aunt,' Miriam said. 'I didn't disclose the details. I just said you felt unwell today. So please don't worry. She's quite happy to have Elsie accompany her in a stroll along the promenade. She hopes you will feel better soon.'

The day passed in a blur for Dot. Miriam read to her, and they talked about Miriam's art projects but avoided discussing what had happened the previous night. Towards the late afternoon, Dot began to feel trapped between four walls and asked to walk outside. When they reached the foyer, she immediately regretted that request. She felt as if everyone was looking at her, their eyes piercing her clothing and seeing her bruises, their mouths open in shock at her sullied body. Somehow, she managed to quell the gorge of panic rising in her throat and get outside where she breathed the salty air deep into her lungs. Her head began to clear and she felt less dizzy. Miriam took her arm and they descended the steps.

144

As they strolled towards the Carpet Gardens on the waterfront, Miriam glanced from time to time in Dot's direction. When Dot's pallid complexion started to gain some colour, Miriam asked her how she was feeling.

'I'm feeling as well as a woman can feel after . . .' Dot said, her voice tightening.

Miriam reached for her hand. 'I'm so sorry, Dot. That was insensitive of me. Please forgive me. I would do anything to make the pain go away. Tell me what I can do to help you.'

'There's nothing you can do,' Dot said, wiping away her tears.

'I can,' Miriam said. 'I can go and report this to the police.'

'No, don't do that, Miriam. I don't want you to,' Dot snapped.

'Why ever not? Something as serious as this should not go unreported.'

'Because it was Douglas,' Dot said, unleashing all the anger she felt.

'What? Are you sure? You were a little squiffy, Dot. Douglas would never . . .'

'I knew you wouldn't believe me,' Dot replied.

'I just don't think he would do that,' Miriam reasoned. 'Is it possible you overreacted? You know sometimes men get a little amorous and find it difficult to hold back, do you know what I mean?'

'No, I don't know what you mean. Are you saying that it was my fault and I shouldn't have let it get that far? It was him who grabbed me, Miriam. I didn't encourage him. What was I supposed to do? Let him rape me?'

'Now you are overreacting, Dot. All I'm saying is

145

that you've got a lot to learn about the passions that drive people.'

'It appears that I have and you've got a lot to learn about what friendship really means,' Dot replied.

The two women stood looking at each other, neither able to speak.

'I don't want to talk about this anymore. I want to go back now,' Dot said, turning to walk away.

'Please don't be like that, Dot. I was just trying to help you understand that sometimes we just have to put things down to experience and learn from those experiences,' Miriam replied, trying to keep up with her.

'Well, there are some experiences I could do without,' Dot said.

★　★　★

The following day, relations between Dot and Miriam were strained. Dot did her best to cover up the atmosphere between them. She didn't want Mrs Humboldt to become aware of the rift. That would involve difficult explanations and complicate things even further. They would be going home soon and she could get back to what was important to her. She needed to put all this behind her and get back to living her own life.

★　★　★

Several days later, the group of women started out on the return journey home. Mrs Humboldt, oblivious of recent events, tried to engage her in conversation, enquiring about whether she had enjoyed her time in

Eastbourne. Dot managed to be enthusiastic about the Italian Gardens and Beachy Head, although all the time she was struggling to blot her most recent experience out of her mind.

'Well, I have so enjoyed your company,' Mrs Humboldt said. 'In fact, I would go so far as to say that you make by far the best companion I have ever had. Should you wish to accompany me on any sojourns in the future, I would be only too pleased to have you with me.'

Dot thanked Mrs Humboldt for her compliments but said that she really must resume her studies back in Chichester.

'I have a vocation to teach, Mrs Humboldt, and I intend to absorb myself in learning. I can think of nothing more I would rather do, than lose myself in my books. I must pass my final exams. This time next year, I hope to be teaching a class full of children.'

Miriam instructed the hansom cab driver to take them all to Frog Hall and when Dot tried to interrupt, Miriam said, 'We should settle my aunt in first and then I will arrange for you to be driven home.' She then whispered into Dot's ear, 'I want to say a proper goodbye to you . . . on your own. We can't part with bad feeling between us.'

Dot wasn't sure that what was broken could be mended but she was dependant upon Miriam and the carriage.

The two of them sat together on the stone bench beside the ornamental pond in the gardens of Frog Hall. Dot looked around her and wondered how she had ended up here. Just a few weeks ago, she'd been shelling peas in the kitchen of 2 Mead Cottages, laughing at the antics of Ronnie and Tilly. How things could change in such a short space of time.

'When do you go back to Chichester?' Miriam asked.

'Very soon,' Dot replied. 'Term starts a week from today.'

'Will you be all right?' Miriam asked. 'I can't bear the thought of you there on your own.'

'I won't be on my own,' Dot said. 'I've made friends down there and I have plenty to occupy me.'

'But I won't be there with you,' Miriam said. 'And that pains me, Dorothy. I've had time to think about my reaction to what happened with Douglas. I don't want you to think that I don't believe you. You were obviously very upset by his behaviour and I didn't do a very good job of supporting you. I wasn't very sympathetic. I can understand that you're cross with me but —'

'Yes, I'm angry with you and what makes me even angrier is that you think it's your job to educate me about the ways of men and of love. What do you know about either, Miriam?'

'I'm sorry. I know my friends are not the sort of people you would ordinarily spend time with and Douglas can be somewhat over the top sometimes when he drinks too much.'

'Over the top! I was frightened, Miriam. Can't you understand that? I was frightened and shocked by what he was trying to do and it's going to take me some time to get over it. It's probably a good thing that we aren't going to be seeing one another for a while. I need to get back to some normality. I need to get back to some real work.'

Miriam was silent for a while. When she finally spoke, she had tears in her eyes.

'But we will stay friends, won't we? Don't you see that I want to be with you? I've grown to love you and I hoped that you have some affection for me?'

Dot could see in Miriam's eyes that she was talking about a kind of love that she wasn't sure she could give. She was going to need time to get over what had happened in Eastbourne and she needed to put some distance between Miriam and herself. To regain her confidence in herself and immerse herself in her studies.

26

Kate's labour pains started in the early hours of a cold Friday morning. Outside she could hear the rain lashing against the window pane and the wind was whistling through the gap in the badly fitting frame. She lay awake counting the time lapse between the pains for a while, controlling a desire to get out of bed and walk around. She didn't want to disturb the household sooner than was necessary. *Fifty-eight, fifty-nine, sixty. That's six minutes. Time to wake Albert*, she thought. She prodded her husband on the shoulder.

'Albert, Albert wake up,' she whispered.

'What? What's the matter?' he groaned.

'The baby's coming,' she replied. 'You need to fetch the midwife. Fetch Mary Suss.'

'It can't be. It's too soon,' Albert said, his voice full of sleep.

'Babies arrive when they want to. We don't have any control over that,' Kate replied.

Kate swung her legs over the edge of the bed and struggled to get her heavy body upright. She bent over, clinging to the edge of the marble-topped washstand, while the pain washed over her. She tried to breathe deeply and stay calm. It was five years since she'd given birth to Ronnie. How was it possible to have forgotten exactly how excruciating labour pains were? At least this time she was in her home with her family around her, not in a godforsaken workhouse far from all those who loved her. When the pain subsided, she raised her head and could hear Albert struggling with his clothes. She shivered and groped for her shawl in the darkness of the bedroom. Albert lit the oil lamp and the pungent smell made Kate retch. She hoped this wasn't going to be a sick birth.

Albert's walking stick tapped on the wooden floor as they made their way downstairs. She followed him carrying the lamp, trying not to breathe in the fumes. When he'd poked the fire in the range into life and added some kindling, he took down his coat from the hook behind the door and dragged on his cap.

'Should we wake Ma?' Albert asked.

'No, not yet,' Kate replied. 'I'll wait until you get back with Mary.'

'Add some of the coal once you've got a blaze going,' Albert said. 'It's a bitterly cold night to be born into.'

He opened the kitchen door and a blast of freezing air came in, making Kate gasp.

'I'll be as quick as I can,' Albert said, going out into the black night. Kate knew that Albert would go as fast as his bad leg would allow him. She had purposely left more time than she thought she needed in order for him to get to Mary's and back before the babe was born. Although the doctors had done their best, Albert's leg would never be right and they just had to get used to the fact and make allowances.

Kate kept a close watch on the fire, feeding it carefully with the wood and then adding the smaller pieces of coal. She walked around the kitchen, still timing her contractions and when they lessened, she put the

151

kettle on the stove. After being dragged out of bed before dawn, Kate was sure that Mary would appreciate a hot cup of tea to get her through the next few hours.

Kate tried to keep as quiet as possible but she knew that her mother was a light sleeper.

'This is it, then?' Ada said, as she appeared at Kate's shoulder.

Kate nodded and grimaced as another wave of pain swept over her.

'She's early,' Ada said, rubbing her daughter's back. 'No sense of timing, just like her mother. You couldn't wait to get into this world either. Now let's get things ready for her, shall we?'

'Might be a boy,' Kate said.

'I have a feeling about this one. She's a girl all right,' Ada replied.

By the time Albert was back with Mary Suss, Ada had got everything ready, bowls and towels, soap and water. She'd checked that the children were still sleeping soundly and made sure that there were replacement sheets for Kate and Albert's bed. As Mary and Albert walked in the door, she poured hot water on the tea leaves and stoked up the fire.

'How far on are you?' Mary asked, as she took off her hat and coat. 'Have your waters . . .' She didn't finish the question for they burst there and then, taking Kate by surprise and leaving a puddle on the kitchen floor.

'Right, we need to get you upstairs and onto the bed,' Mary said.

A weak early morning sun was just beginning to filter through scattered clouds when Kate entered the final stage of labour. Ronnie and Tilly appeared at the bedroom door, woken by the unusual sounds, followed by Henry and Jim, who ushered them gently away.

'Is Mum all right?' asked Ronnie.

'Is the baby coming?' asked Tilly.

'Seems like it,' Jim replied. 'Your mum's fine, Ronnie. She's in good hands. Let's go and get some breakfast. I bet your dad's got the porridge pot going downstairs.'

The hours of the morning ticked by, tea was drunk, cooling flannels were placed on Kate's forehead and the baby made its slow progress into the world.

'Come on, Kate, one last push and your baby will be here,' Mary said.

Kate pulled together all the energy she could muster and finally her child was born.

'Is she all right?' Kate asked.

No reply came, as Ada was cutting the chord and Mary was hastily clearing the child's mouth of mucus. Kate tried desperately to see what was happening but she felt so weak she could hardly raise her head. She felt dizzy and nauseous. She was aware that there was frantic activity at the base of the bed. Why wasn't the baby crying?

'Tell me she's all right. Please tell me,' Kate cried.

After what seemed like an eternity, eventually Kate heard a whimper that turned into a full-blown yell as the baby filled its lungs with air and let the household know it had arrived.

Mary wrapped the babe in a torn-up sheet and Ada then folded her in the white crocheted shawl she'd made especially for this moment. Mary placed the little bundle into Kate's arms and said, 'You've a healthy baby girl. Congratulations, Kate.'

Kate wept tears of joy. She peeled back the covering to look upon her daughter's face. Her eyes were screwed up tight as if she wasn't quite ready to greet her family. Kate touched her skin, still covered in the white, creamy substance from the womb. She had wisps of dark hair on her head and her nose wrinkled up as if she wasn't sure what these new smells were around her. Kate felt a rush of love for this fragile being in her arms. She was so tiny and so vulnerable but she would keep her close and warm. She would protect and care for her.

'Shall I fetch Albert?' Ada asked, wiping Kate's face and arranging her pillows so she could sit up.

'Yes, please. Tell him to come and meet his daughter,' Kate replied, exhausted but happy.

Albert came rushing in. He moved straight to the bedside and kissed Kate on the forehead. His large fingers delicately pulled back the wrap to look at the child's face.

'She's beautiful, Kate,' he said.

'Would you like to hold her?' Kate asked and Albert took the baby in his arms, his face revealing all the love he felt for this tiny little thing.

'She's so small,' Albert said.

'That one was in so much of a hurry to get out that she came before she was cooked,' Mary Suss smiled. 'It'll take a while for her to grow into her skin but she'll soon catch up. She's a strong 'un.'

Kate then noticed that Ronnie was leaning against the door frame, waiting to be invited in. Kate beckoned to him.

'Come, Ronnie, come and see your new baby sister,' she said.

Albert bent down with the small bundle. There

were snuffling sounds and one arm poked out of the wrap.

'Look, she wants to say hello to her big brother,' Albert said.

Ronnie peeked into the bundle and said quietly, 'She's got hair already.'

Albert laughed. 'Yes, she's got hair and the tiniest fingernails. Everything is perfect.'

'Except she hasn't got a name yet,' Ada said.

'No name,' Mary gasped. 'Why ever not?'

'We didn't want to tempt fate by deciding, in case she was a boy,' Kate replied.

'Well, the poor child needs a name,' Mary replied.

Just at that moment, Tilly came running in, closely followed by Jim and Henry who looked thoroughly embarrassed about the whole thing.

'I told her to wait a bit,' Jim said, 'but you know what she's like.'

Tilly was so excited she started talking immediately about how they would play together and rushed off to bring the baby one of her favourite toys, a small doll that Dot had made for her.

'This is Rose and she can be yours when you're older,' she said, holding the doll up to the baby's face.

'Thank you, Tilly, that's very kind,' Kate said. 'Rose is such a pretty name. Would it be a good name for our little girl? What do you think, Albert, Ronnie?'

Albert and Ronnie agreed that Rose suited her. 'Rose Locock,' Albert said.

'R for Ronnie and R for Rose.' Ronnie smiled.

Once the family had been ushered out, Kate put Rose to the breast and she suckled happily. Mother and daughter lay together peacefully for a while until Mary said, 'I should check on you now, Kate. The afterbirth should be coming away soon.'

Mary examined Kate while Ada laid Rose in the wooden cradle that Albert and Jim had made for her.

'Good job that was finished a month ago, otherwise it would have been the chest of drawers for her.' Ada smiled. She gave the cradle a rock and gazed down lovingly at her beautiful granddaughter.

A shout of pain drew everyone's attention back to Kate who was drawing up her knees and breathing deeply.

'What is it?' Ada asked, her face pale. 'What's wrong?'

Mary placed a hand on Kate's belly.

'You've not finished yet, Kate,' she said. 'Those are more labour pains you're having. There's another baby.'

'Twins?' Ada gasped.

Mary nodded. 'We'd best get ready for another few hours' work. Though sometimes the second one can be quicker.'

Kate couldn't believe that she'd been carrying twins and no one had guessed, least of all her. Ada rushed downstairs to tell the family and Albert felt the need to step outside for a breath of air. Two babies? His excitement was tempered with concern. How were they going to cope? How would Kate feed two? She had looked exhausted after the birth of Rose. He hoped everything would be all right.

Thankfully, the second birth was much easier and it was only another hour before Kate had baby number two in her arms. Albert appeared without being summoned this time. He'd been pacing about, moving in and out of the kitchen, listening beneath the bedroom window and hovering close to the stairs.

When he heard the cries of the second child, he went straight to Kate's side.

Kate looked exhausted but happy as she lay back on the pillows. Albert kissed her and sat on the edge of the bed, holding her hand in his. Tears welled in the corner of his eyes and his voice was hoarse and broken as he whispered to her, 'My love.'

'You have another daughter,' Kate said.

He gently pulled back the cloth that his daughter was wrapped in and smiled at this second little bundle that had entered his life, her still wet wisps of hair clinging to her tiny forehead, her eyes tight shut.

He turned to Ada, who had picked up Rose, and said,' Can you bring her here, Ada please? Rose needs to meet her sister.' He took Rose gently in his arms and placed her beside her twin.

The four of them were still and quiet for a few moments and Ada and Mary withdrew to let them have some time alone.

'We'll get Jim to bring Ronnie and Tilly up in a minute or two then, shall we?' Ada asked.

Kate smiled and replied, 'That would be nice. Ronnie will be surprised to get two sisters.'

'Double trouble.' Mary grinned. 'Poor boy will be outnumbered.'

When Jim arrived with the two children, he was careful to let Ronnie be the first to see his twin sisters. He knew that, given the chance, Tilly would scramble in there first.

Ronnie peeked at the two girls and gently touched each of their tiny fingers.

'Now, we have to think of another name,' Ronnie said.

'How about Annie?' Kate suggested.

They all agreed that Annie suited the little one very well. As Albert took his youngest daughter in his arms, saying, 'Annie it is then,' she opened her eyes and looked at him. To Albert that look said, Where's my cradle, Dad? and Albert immediately left the room calling for Jim and Henry.

'Where are you going in such a hurry?' Kate asked, surprised at his sudden departure.

'I've got work to do and I need some assistance if Annie is to have her own cradle sooner rather than later,' Albert said.

27

When Dot received the news that Kate had given birth to twins, she rushed home as soon as she could. The college granted her a leave of absence and she packed her bags to stay at Mead Cottages until Kate had recovered from the birth. Most of the weight of her bags came from her books so that she could continue her studies. She had no idea of how long she might be needed or indeed if she would have any time to study but she must try to keep up or face the prospect of failing her course. She couldn't bear that thought.

It was a long, cold journey. The brisk walk from the crossroads warmed her but the sun could not chase the ice away from the puddles and her fingers were beginning to go numb despite her warm gloves. When she walked up the slope towards Mead Cottages, she noticed a wisp of smoke rising from the chimney of her home. She hoped there wasn't a problem with the flue. The neighbour's chimney was belching twice as much into the wintery air. The kitchen range could be temperamental and sometimes the chimney didn't draw as well as it should.

When she opened the back door, the family, all crammed in to the tiny kitchen, looked, as one, in her direction.

'Ah, here she is,' Jim Truscott said. 'Here's our Dot.'

'Congratulations, you two,' Dot said, putting down

her basket and looking at Kate and Albert who both seemed subdued. Any further greetings were halted as Dot was overwhelmed by the excited rush of Tilly and Ronnie. The two children, wrapped around with shawls on top of several layers of clothing, threw their arms around Dot's legs and she hugged their padded forms close. When she let them go, they looked up at her, the usual question in their eyes.

'Look in there,' she said, indicating her basket that she had placed by the door. The two children fought to be the first to lift the cover and two pairs of hands fumbled amongst the contents. Tilly pulled out two gingerbread men and Ronnie, a paper bag holding cubes of sticky fudge.

'For sharing,' Dot said. 'Now, where are my new nieces?'

Dot came straight to her sister, who was sitting closest to the range with Rose across her knees, rubbing her back. She raised her face to Dot and Dot kissed her. Dot was shocked at how pale and listless Kate was.

'Clever Kate,' Dot said. 'Not just one babe but two.'

'Double trouble. Twice as many nappies and half as much sleep. We wouldn't have it any other way though. Would we?' Ada said, jiggling one of the babies over her shoulder.

Kate smiled weakly and reached for Dot's hand. 'Mum's got Annie and this is Rose,' she said. 'Would you take her for a bit, Dot? I'm so tired.'

'You go and have a rest, Kate,' Ada said. 'We'll stoke the fire up now Dot's here. Henry, go fetch some more from the coal hole. Jump to it now.'

Henry reluctantly took the coal scuttle out into the cold and Dot took hold of the tightly wrapped shape that was Rose. Albert got to his feet to move towards Kate but she ignored him and started up the stairs.

Dot exchanged a look with her father. Something was not right. The feeling of joy that Dot had expected to pervade the house was absent and the air prickled with tension.

'I think I should check on the kindling stock in the shed,' Jim said. 'I may need to chop some more. How about you come out with me, Albert? Leave these ladies to get on with settling the twins.'

Albert got reluctantly to his feet, his usual smile of greeting for his sister-in-law smothered in a frown.

Once they were out of the door, Dot felt free to speak. Her father had understood the situation and his encouragement to Albert to join him had left Dot time and space to talk to her mother.

'Is Kate all right?' Dot asked. 'She seems very low. And Albert too. Has he started back at the farm yet?'

'She's been in a permanent state of exhaustion since the twins were born,' Ada explained. 'And Albert's job has been filled by a labourer from Nately. Albert has taken so long to recover that they really had to employ someone else. Worst of it is that the whole country seems to be in a bad state. Unemployment is the highest it's ever been and the war has caused it all. Wages are so low it's hardly enough to live on.'

Dot understood now why the fire had been so feeble when she arrived. It was nothing to do with the chimney and everything to do with the family's lack of money for fuel. The money from Mrs Humboldt had kept them going for a while but now things had obviously become harder. It was clear that they had been waiting for her to arrive to set a blaze going and now she was here, she was going to be depleting their

161

resources even more. She had to do something to help.

When both babies had been persuaded to sleep and the children were happily playing, Dot helped prepare the evening meal. She tried to keep the conversation light with her mother, telling her stories of life in Mrs Cooper's lodging house. The evening passed in a more subdued atmosphere than was usual when Dot returned home. When the family retired to bed, Dot sat beside the last embers of the fire and wondered what could be done. In the morning, she would go to see Miss Clarence. She needed to talk. If only Miriam was here. She would know what to do. But Miriam had returned to Eastbourne for the winter. Her friends had offered her a place in their newly acquired artist's residence. At least they called it that. Miriam's letter had revealed that her room was 'a draughty artist's garret' and her descriptions did not encourage Dot to go and join her there before the spring. When she crept up the stairs to join her mother in the double bed, she lay awake for a long time until she drifted into an uneasy and restless sleep.

28

Miss Clarence's sitting room was warm and cosy.

'How lovely to see you, Dorothy. Do come in, please,' Miss Clarence said, taking Dot's coat and inviting her to sit by the fire. 'I'll make us a nice warming pot of tea. It's a dull, grey day out there.'

Dot sat and gazed into the flickering flames, letting them draw her in. She hadn't expected to find such difficulties waiting for her at home. The letter from her mother only told of the joy of the safe delivery of the twins. She stretched her hands to the fire and let her body warm through. So many problems. So much easier to enjoy the moment, escape and let her mind wander into warmer, more comforting thoughts. The glowing coals seemed to burn deep into her brain and the small bursts of steam escaping hissed a musical accompaniment to the ticking clock on the mantelpiece. Miss Clarence was lucky to have such a comfortable home, such a comfortable life. She used to feel sorry for Miss Clarence, that she had no husband and no children, but perhaps it was the better way to be, better at least than the situation her sister was in now.

'Ah! That's good. You've warmed up. You looked frozen when you arrived. Surely you hadn't been walking the fields in this awful weather?' Miss Clarence asked, placing the tea tray on the table.

'Just the short walk from Mead Cottages. The house is so cold and . . . well . . . that's what I've come to talk

163

to you about. Things are not good over there. In fact, they are the worst they've ever been,' Dot explained.

'How so?' Miss Clarence asked. 'I thought the arrival of the twins was cause for celebration.'

'Of course, they are happy that the babies are both fine but feeding two is draining my sister. That's not the worst of it, though,' Dot continued. 'Albert's lost his job. My father is the only breadwinner now. They don't have enough food and what they do have, I know they're giving to the children.'

A shudder passed through Dot as she thought of the continuing winter cold and the prospect of an empty larder and grate. They'd never been a rich family and never would be but they'd always had enough to eat. Her summer in Eastbourne, the opulence of the Queen's Hotel and the obvious wealth of the ladies promenading along the front, made her feel guilty. What right had she to go rubbing shoulders with the gentry, when her family were suffering in this way?

'I have to give up teaching and find a job,' Dot said, her eyes filling with tears.

'We've been here before, Dorothy,' Miss Clarence said, 'and a solution was found, wasn't it?'

Yes, it was, Dot thought, but at a cost. If she hadn't gone to Eastbourne, if she hadn't gone to the dance, if she hadn't drunk so much. The tears fell as she felt once more that man's breath on her neck, his hands holding her firm, his saliva sliding down her chin. Miss Clarence could never understand the full extent of the feelings that were making her tears flow.

'Please don't upset yourself, Dot. There will be a way out of this and we will find it. No more talk of giving up teaching. Leave it with me. Now, let's enjoy our tea before it gets cold,' Miss Clarence said.

Dot wasn't sure what she expected Miss Clarence to be able to do. As she pulled on her coat and said thank you for the tea, she didn't hold out much hope that a simple solution could be found. She prepared herself for the worst. It would be easier for her to give up her ambitions to become a qualified teacher and take on a position as a governess. Kate had always said that her life in service was a time she never regretted. If she hadn't been a nursemaid, she would never have met Philip and fallen so deeply in love. She would never have had Ronnie.

Over the following few days, Dot wrestled with the question of what to do. She'd been granted leave from the college but she couldn't stay in Micklewell forever. She had no time to be bored or think of what she was missing. There was plenty to occupy her: washing and ironing, cooking and cleaning. She became adept at making the most out of minimal ingredients. Suet puddings sprinkled with a few bacon pieces, rolled in white cotton rags and steamed, helped fill hungry mouths.

One evening, as the sun hung low in the trees and the frost began to nip at exposed ears and noses, Jim Truscott came in with his shotgun crooked over his arm and a brace of pheasants over his shoulder. He threw them down on the table and said, 'See what you can do with them. My choice would be a casserole with onions and carrots and plenty of gravy.'

The whole family clapped and cheered. Henry, who had gone out with his father, held the birds up by their feet and said, 'They're still warm. I'll get started on plucking them right away.'

'Pheasant's best hung for a while before eating,' Ada said.

'Well, I'm too hungry for that,' Jim replied.

'So am I,' Albert agreed. 'Where did you get them, Jim?'

'Tell me you haven't been poaching on the estate,' Ada said. 'If the next knock on our door is the game-keeper . . .'

'I haven't been poaching,' Jim replied. 'Is it my fault if the birds don't know which side of the fence they're on? Walked right out in front of me they did. Pheasants have no sense of direction. Isn't that right, Henry?'

Jim winked in Henry's direction and Henry nodded.

'Because it's no good telling your son off and then doing the same thing yourself, is it, Jim Truscott?' Ada snapped.

When the banter was over, the food preparations began and that night they sat down to the best meal they had eaten in a long time.

'Oh, I almost forgot,' Jim said, wiping gravy from his chin. 'I saw Miss Clarence earlier, Dot, and she said for you to call by on Saturday.'

'Can we go too?' asked Tilly.

'No, you can't,' said Ada. 'It's Dot's invitation, not yours.'

'They only want to go because there might be some cake on offer,' Henry said, 'or bread pudding, that's their favourite. I've seen you two hanging around at the end of school asking if there are any jobs she wants doing and the slice of bread pudding in your fists you get by way of a thank you.'

Ronnie looked across at his parents and blushed. Tilly didn't.

'Miss Clarence says we're very helpful and we

deserve it,' she twittered.

'I've never seen them with any bread pudding,' Albert said.

'That's because they eat it all before they get here,' Ada replied. 'They're not daft.'

'They'll go far those two,' Jim commented, grinning.

Dot was relieved that some lightness had entered the room. That was probably due to the heaviness in their bellies. The huge meal had put a smile on all their faces.

29

The rain was cascading down the windows on Saturday morning, dripping off the sills and collecting in puddles in the yard. Dark rainclouds blotted out the sun and the wind whipped the trees at the bottom of the garden into a frenzy.

'I don't think you'll be going anywhere in this. Awful weather,' Ada said blowing her nose and coughing. 'This damp gets right through to me.'

'Try to keep that cold away from the twins, Ma,' Kate said. 'We don't want them coming down with anything.'

'It might ease up in a bit,' said Dot, trying to put a positive face on things.

'The rain or my cold?' Ada replied.

'Both, I hope,' said Dot.

Tilly appeared with her raincoat on, opened the back door and was about to run outside when Ada caught hold of her collar and said, 'Oh no you don't, young lady. You haven't got your boots on and it's raining too hard. You'll get soaked through to the skin.'

'But I like jumping in puddles,' Tilly said, looking up at Ada. 'Please, Ma?'

'Don't try soft soaping me, my girl' Ada said. 'You're not going out until it stops and that's that.'

Ronnie came to join Tilly and the two of them climbed on the back of the chair under the window and pressed their noses against the window pane.

'Rain, rain, go away. Come again another day,'

they chanted.

Dot told them the story of the Sun and the Wind to keep them entertained while Ada helped Kate change and dress the twins.

As if it had been listening, the sun showed its face and the clouds started to disperse as quickly as they had arrived, skimming across the sky in teams. The sunbeams played hide and seek with the raindrops and the sky lit up with an arc of beautiful colours.

'Oh look,' Ronnie shouted, 'a rainbow.'

'No, two rainbows,' Dot said. 'Look, one beneath the other.'

'Can we make a picture?' Tilly asked.

'All right. You get the wax crayons from the dresser and I'll find you some paper. I think I've got some in my college bag.' Dot said. She smiled as she thought of how her nephew and her little sister enjoyed one another's company so much. It was as if her mother and Kate had timed their births to perfectly coincide. The notion that Tilly was Ronnie's aunty still amazed her. How time and circumstance could play tricks.

Once she'd got the children settled, she looked out to see if the rain had stopped.

'Finally,' she said. 'Right, I'm off to see Miss Clarence.'

'Give her my best regards,' said Kate. 'Seems like an age ago that I was her pupil teacher.'

Dot detected a note of regret in Kate's voice. Did she sometimes think that she might have trained to become a teacher if she hadn't taken a different path?

'And wear my galoshes. It's pouring out there,' Ada remarked.

Just as she was getting her coat on, the children

169

suddenly leapt up and began dancing around Dot and singing:

'It's raining, it's pouring, the old man is snoring.
He went to bed and bumped his head and couldn't
get up in the morning.'

As they were careering around, Ronnie and Tilly lost their balance and fell awkwardly against Albert's injured leg. Albert let out a gasp of pain.

'Can't you play somewhere else?' he shouted at the children. 'There's not room in here for you to be flinging yourselves about.'

'They have to play somewhere, Albert. I'm sure they didn't do it on purpose,' Kate said.

Dot was startled by the anger in Albert's voice. For a moment, the sudden burst of aggression took her back to the encounter with the dreadful man at the dance hall. This was so unlike Albert, he was usually such a gentle man.

'Then I'll be the one to move,' he replied.

He grabbed his stick and hobbled towards the door.

'Where are you going in this weather?' asked Kate.

'To the wood shed,' Albert said. 'There must be something useful a man with a useless leg can do.'

'Then at least take your jacket and scarf,' Kate replied.

He grabbed them from behind the cupboard door and took himself outside to the wood shed.

Kate let out another deep sigh and looked at her sister and her parents.

'It's his place of refuge when he's feeling low and he's suffering at the moment. I don't know how to help him,' she said.

'There's none of us can,' her father replied. 'He's not the only one without a job. There's Peter Barclay and Thomas Mitchell both been laid off at Hodder's Farm. I saw Peter just last week and he says to me, 'Last time I'll be bringing the horses down to the forge, Jimmy. Old Hodder's letting me go.' He's always called me Jimmy, since we were kids,' Jim Truscott continued. 'Apparently, the government farm subsidies set up after the war have stopped. The other hands have had to take a drop in wages too, so Peter says.'

'There'll be even more men out there looking for a job now,' Ada said.

'So what chance has Albert got with a bad leg?' Kate added.

There were no words of comfort to be said and Jim, Ada and Dot gave none. Their silence and exchange of looks betrayed their feelings of helplessness.

★　★　★

Dot side-stepped the puddles in the lane and made it to the schoolhouse without getting her feet wet. When Miss Clarence opened the door, she said, 'Ah, Dorothy. I'm pleased you've managed to get here between the cloud bursts. Come in, come in. Let me take your coat.'

Miss Clarence ushered Dot into the sitting room and sat down opposite her. She folded her hands in her lap and leaned forward slightly with a serious look on her face.

'I've given what you told me about your family and their difficulties a great deal of thought,' she said. 'I didn't tell you my own, more cheerful news during

171

your last visit because you seemed so weighed down by your troubles. But now I see that a great opportunity has arisen. I can help your family out, if they will accept my proposition.'

'I'm sorry, Miss Clarence, but I don't follow you,' Dot said.

'I'm not explaining myself very well, am I?' Miss Clarence replied. 'I will say it plainly. I've asked you here this morning to tell you that I have applied for a new position, on the Isle of Wight. It's the headship of a bigger school. I will be earning more money and I've decided that I should use this good fortune to help some of the needier families of this village.'

'Oh, Miss Clarence, congratulations! I'm pleased for you, of course, but the parents and children of Micklewell will miss you greatly. The Isle of Wight is such a long way away.'

'Not so far,' Miss Clarence insisted. 'Only a short ferry ride from Southampton. Now, to get back to the job. If I am successful, I will take up my new post in September. I've been informed that I will need another teacher for the start of the autumn term, as the current holder of the post is to be married in July. She will, of course, then have to resign her position. By then, you will have qualified. I should like you to apply for the post.'

'But Miss Clarence . . .'

'Please let me finish, Dorothy. Believe me, the best thing you could do for your family is to continue your training and become a teacher,' Miss Clarence insisted. 'In the meantime, I can make a small contribution to your family finances but I fear that it may not last many months. Do you have any other relatives or friends who would be in a position to help?'

172

'Unfortunately, there's no one,' Dot replied. 'Your offer is most generous, Miss Clarence, but I feel sure that my parents would never agree to such a thing. They'd be ashamed to accept charity, even from you. We are all so appreciative that you've helped and encouraged me to become a teacher but they could not hold their heads up in the village if word ever got out.'

Miss Clarence remained silent for a while and then said, 'I understand, although sometimes we should heed the advice of the proverbs regarding pride coming before a fall, I think. There is perhaps another way. I have lately been engaged in conducting my own research into methods of teaching, Dorothy. At the end of last year, I had the good fortune to attend a very special meeting in London, where I heard about a new method of educating children. The speaker was an Italian woman named Maria Montessori. She is pioneering an entirely different approach to teaching and I was captivated by her talk. Her methods are controversial but I have obtained one of her books describing her methodology and it is extremely detailed. I don't have a great deal of time to read it at the moment but I would very much like to know the main points and what you think of the approach. I am willing to pay you for your time. Shall we say ten shillings for the first payment?'

'That's very kind of you,' Dot replied. 'I will do my best.'

'Thank you,' Miss Clarence said, looking pleased with herself. 'And we will stay in touch. You can post me sections as you finish them. Now, I insist you take the payment in advance. I'm sure your family can make use of the money right away.'

Dot intended to object but Miss Clarence was ahead of her. She went to her bureau and handed Dot the money with a decisive order. 'No arguments, Dorothy. If you wish me to recommend you to become my assistant teacher, then I must warn you that I expect my teachers to carry out my instructions to the letter and I instruct you to take this money.'

Dot smiled inwardly. There was no doubt about it, Miss Clarence was a force to be reckoned with. No wonder she'd never married, any man would be in her shadow and that was a place no man would concede to be. She was more calculating than devious, though. Dot decided that she could do worse than to learn from Miss Clarence's approach to problem-solving. There was a dogged determination in her personality that would never allow her to give up.

30

Dot walked back down Frog Lane. The leaves had fallen off the trees long ago and their skeletal arms reached up in search of a sun that had disappeared. The rain had stopped but there were runnels of water trickling down the sides of the road and a mournful lowing was coming from one of the barns on Addison's Farm. Most sensible folk were in their houses on such a dark and wet day.

Dot continued walking, lost in thought. As she rounded the bend, she saw Albert walking slowly towards her.

'Thank goodness the rain's stopped,' Dot said, wondering where he might be going. 'Just getting a breath of air, Albert?' she asked.

'Aye,' he replied.

She noticed that his hand was shaking, whether with the cold or with the frustrations of what had happened earlier, she wasn't sure. She knew that men who had served in the war could suffer in their mind and that Albert had survived one of the worst battles of the war. What he had seen must haunt him sometimes. She knew that feeling of not being able to close your mind to events of the past. She had her own struggles sometimes but what had happened to her came nowhere near Albert's sufferings. Kate had told her of his bad dreams and how she sometimes needed to comfort him even now, four years after the end of the war.

Dot could see that Albert was battling with what-ever preoccupations and feelings had brought him out into the wind and weather and now she was here interrupting his need to be alone. If she could have shared his thoughts, she would have seen what he could not stop seeing. There were times when Albert's mind drifted back to France, when he was once again in the trenches, waiting for the order to go over the top. Those times were coming back to him more frequently since his accident. He relived the fear of waiting for the command and the horror of what awaited him. His compatriots falling all around him and the constant dread that the next enemy bullet could be for him.

'Are you all right, Albert?' Dot asked, when she saw the wetness in his eyes. He wasn't really looking at her but seemed to be elsewhere.

Albert gazed blankly at her as she waited for him to reply. Eventually he spoke.

'I should be providing for my family,' he said, looking downcast and lost. 'This damned leg.' He banged his fist against his hip.

'It's not your fault that you've been left with this injury, Albert,' Dot said. 'You were lucky to escape with your life.'

'If I'd have been driving the traction engine, then I wouldn't have gone under the wheels,' Albert replied. 'But I wasn't. I'd just handed over to Tom Garvey.'

'But you could've been killed, Albert. Thank God you weren't. It's going to take time for you to recover. Your leg's improving gradually, isn't it?' Dot said.

'Not quickly enough,' Albert replied. 'I need to work.'

'You're helping Pa out down at the forge, aren't you?'

'His idea,' Albert replied. 'But there's not enough work there for two. I know he's just taking me on out of the goodness of his heart. Sometimes I think it would have been better if . . .'

'Don't say that,' Dot said. 'If you'd seen how distraught Kate was when you were lying broken at the side of the road, you wouldn't even think such things. She loves you, Albert, but she's struggling too.'

They stood for a while longer, until the cold began to creep into them.

'Come on,' Dot said, shivering. 'It's getting colder. Let's get home in the warm.'

As soon as Dot entered the kitchen, she could tell that Kate didn't want to engage in any conversation. She didn't even look up when the door opened. Ada was occupied with adding to the rag rug she had started last winter and still had not completed, Dot's father was sharpening his razor on a leather strop and the children were playing underneath the table, trying to stay out of everyone's way. There was an unsettling quiet about the room and Dot wondered if Kate and Ada had had words. Ada was never very patient but there must have been sleepless nights since the twins were born and Dot had noticed that her mother did not have the strength that she used to have. By the prickly atmosphere, Dot guessed that Kate and Ada had fallen out over something.

'About time,' Ada said. 'I've been waiting for you to get here to cut me some more strips. I'm running out. Kate's feeding Rose, your father's occupied and the children can't manage the big scissors. I'll never get this finished this side of Christmas at the rate I'm going. Always so much to do around here, never get time for my own jobs!'

Ada spat these words out in a continuous stream. She began to cough and fought to get her breath. The cough took hold of her and she got red in the face. She threw down the rag and made her way to the door.

'Some air,' she said. 'I need some air.'

Dot looked at her with concern and followed her outside.

'You shouldn't stay out here too long without a hat and coat, Ma,' Dot said. 'The air's damp and it sounds as if you've got a bad chest already.'

Ada inhaled deeply, which only seemed to make her cough more.

'Don't . . . tell me . . . what to . . . do,' she gasped.

Beads of sweat were forming on Ada's forehead and she pulled at the high neck of her dress. Dot took hold of her arm to steady her and tried to coax her back inside.

'Let me make you some tea,' she said. 'We could all do with a cuppa, I think.'

Ada began to shiver and reluctantly agreed to go back inside.

Dot determined to talk to her father about the coughing fit. Ada had not looked well for some time now. She was always very good at covering such things up but Dot knew that something was seriously wrong.

31

Ada and the children had retired more than an hour ago and Dot could hear Kate and Albert pacing the floor upstairs. The fire was dying in the grate and Dot wrapped a second shawl around her shoulders. Father and daughter were sitting in silence, both looking into the last embers that glowed and darkened in turn.

'You usually bank up the fire for the night, Pa,' Dot said. 'Are you too tired tonight? Shall I do it?'

'Not enough coal,' Jim Truscott replied. 'Got to make it last.'

Dot looked at her father. He had aged. Since she'd arrived home, he'd tried to keep the spirits of the family up but this evening he had let his guard down. He hadn't shaved his grizzled beard and his eyes were dull and lifeless. He sat with his shoulders slumped forwards, giving him a stooped look. She had intended saying that she was going to go back to Chichester but her father looked so downcast and worn out that she didn't have the heart. She couldn't stay much longer, though, or she would lose her place at the college. She had been given leave to come home for only a few days.

'I should get off to bed,' Jim said. 'I'm taking Albert to the forge with me again tomorrow and we need to get an early start.'

'How's Albert doing, Pa? Is he of any help to you?' Dot asked.

'Well, it takes him a long time to do things. That

leg doesn't seem to be healing as quickly as we'd all hoped. Have to face up to the fact that it may never be right. But I can't stand seeing a good man go down like he has. He's still capable with his hands.'

Dot suspected that the money the two received for their work, however, was no greater than for one man's labour. Her father could probably do the jobs as quickly by himself.

'We have to pull together,' Jim said as much as to himself as to his daughter.

The depth of meaning in those words did not escape Dot. She saw the concern etched in her father's face. He had enough worries. Should she mention the decline in her mother's health? The dim light of the gas lamp and the last flickers of the dying fire cast deep shadows across her father's face. He gazed into the darkening space and a future that he could not predict. She stood to go upstairs and was about to say goodnight, when her father said, 'Your mother's not well, Dorothy. I don't know what I can do to help her.'

She sat down again. He had voiced her own thoughts.

'I'm worried about her too, Pa. That cough of hers is getting much worse.'

'She really should see a doctor but how can we afford the fees?' Jim replied, his voice barely audible.

Dot knew he was right. A doctor was out of the question. They barely had enough money to live. It was down to her to do something. It pained Dot to think that she'd come this far and would now be forced to throw it all away but she couldn't sit by and see her family suffer.

As she lay next to her mother that night, she

listened to her hoarse breath and waited for the next coughing fit to rack her weakened body. She feared that it was tuberculosis and if it was, then there would be no getting better. She tried to tell her racing mind to rest but it would not. There was no one she could turn to for help.

Ada was always up first and when Dot awoke, the space next to her was empty. She looked across at the place where her mother's head had been and noticed a small red spot on the pillow case. If her mother had been coughing blood, she'd done a good job of covering it up. The truckle bed was empty too and she could hear Henry shouting at Ronnie and Tilly downstairs to get up to the table and eat their porridge. She poured some water out of the jug into the bowl and splashed her face. She took off her nightclothes, exposing her fair skin to the frigid air. The hairs rose on her lower arms and she pulled on her undergarments as quickly as she could, wincing at the coldness of them next to her skin. After putting on her dress, which smelled a little under the arms, she raked a comb through her hair and twisted it up onto the top of her head, holding it with clips.

It was a school morning and when she got downstairs, Ada was making sure that the children had a good breakfast before going out into the cold. Dot noticed that her mother was still seeing to everyone else first and not eating anything herself. Kate was coaxing and cajoling the children to get ready and they were complaining that they wanted to stay at home with Dot.

'Stop your grizzling, you two,' Henry said. 'You're going to make us all late if you don't hurry up.'

Dot sensed that she needed to calm the tension in

181

the room and said lightly, 'If you have your coats on by the time I count to twenty, then I might even come and meet you at the gate at lunch time. But you'd better get a move on.'

Peace returned to the house when the door shut behind them and the work could begin. The morning soon disappeared with everything there was to be done in a household of five adults and five children. There was a constant pile of washing and ironing and a continuous round of cooking and cleaning. The chickens needed feeding and the twins needed nursing. Then there was the worst job of all, the nappies needed soaking in the stinking bucket in the outhouse.

As Dot poked the slimy heap of towelling nappies under the surface of the greenish water with the wooden tongs, the pungent mix of washing soda and urine made her nostrils wrinkle. This side of bringing up children did not bring her any closer to wanting to be a mother. She loved rocking her two nieces and singing to them and when they looked up at her with their appealing and dependent eyes, she could almost see herself holding her own baby one day, but this particular aspect of mothering did not appeal in the least. No, for the moment she was happy to look after the older ones, from Ronnie and Tilly's age up. Besides, she'd not yet found a man whom she could envisage marrying and maybe she never would. Her experiences of men had made her wary. The memories of the dance hall sickened her and she didn't know if she could ever trust a man again. It would take a very special person to convince her of his true affection. She pushed the idea out of her head. There were more important things to occupy her thoughts and once this unpleasant job was done, she would get on and write a letter to Miriam. She needed to tell her how much everything had changed here in Micklewell and how that could mean changes for her too.

The kitchen was quiet when Dot went back indoors. Kate was rocking one babe asleep with her foot on the cradle and holding the other in her arms. Ada was darning the same pair of socks that had been darned several times before and both men were down at the forge.

Her father's words echoed in her head and she knew he was right. They all had to pull together and she would do her bit too. The offer from Miss Clarence would be a help but she needed more. If she was to continue her training and help the family, then she would have to think of another way.

That night she lay awake for some time, trying to find a solution. She still hadn't written to Miriam and now she wondered what would be the point? Miriam had no money of her own, she relied upon her aunt. She recalled Mrs Humboldt's words when they parted back in the summer, '*Should you wish to accompany me on any sojourns in the future, I would be only too pleased to have you with me.*' But she didn't wish to go anywhere except back to Chichester. Perhaps Mrs Humboldt would consider giving her an advance if she were to suggest spending the summer holidays with her, prior to taking up her first teaching post — if she managed to obtain a teaching post. What Miss Clarence was suggesting was by no means certain. She would have to convince the Board of Education that she was the right person for the job too. It wasn't only up to Miss Clarence.

She didn't see that she had any other option open

to her. Doing nothing would get her nowhere. She would go to see Mrs Humbolt in the morning.

32

Dot rang the doorbell at the main entrance to Frog Hall and waited. Elsie opened the door wide and invited her to come inside.

'Please wait in the library, miss,' she said. 'There's a fire in there. The mistress is still in her room. She's not been feeling too good but I'll tell her you're here. I'm sure she will want to see you.'

Dot stood beside the fire, too nervous to sit down. Knowing how slow Mrs Humboldt was, she expected to wait quite some time. So, when the door swung open a few moments later, Dot was taken by surprise for there was Miriam, a wide grin across her face.

'Dot, my dear Dot. You must have read my mind. I woke up thinking of you. I intended to come to Mead Cottages today and enquire after you but here you are.'

Miriam bounded across the room and flung her arms around Dot, squeezing the life out of her. Just as she was beginning to think her chest would be crushed, Miriam drew back and took Dot by both hands. Dot felt uncomfortable, she was still feeling resentful about what had happened with Douglas. And now, here Miriam was back in her own environment with not a care in the world while hers had turned upside down.

Dot looked down at her hands, now dry, rough and cracked. Her nails were split and she noticed there was dirt under some of them. She pulled back and

185

held her hands behind her back to hide them from Miriam's gaze. What did Miriam know of the kind of problems her family were suffering from? Hers was a sheltered life. She had known no privations, never had to fend for herself. She had the safety net of a wealthy aunt and would never experience the sort of difficulties her family were facing.

'How wonderful to see you,' Miriam said. 'As you see, I made arrangements to come and stay with my aunt. She's been a little under the weather lately and in need of some companionship. So here I am. But I'm wittering on. What brings you here?'

'Actually, I came to see your aunt about the possibility of some more work,' Dot began. 'Is she not well enough to see me?'

'She's fine really, she makes a fuss about nothing. Just wants some attention. But you're a glutton for punishment. I'm here on sufferance but you actually want to spend more time with her?'

'Perhaps need is more accurate. I need to find employment,' Dot said, beginning to get impatient with Miriam's cheeriness.

'Really? But where are my manners? I haven't offered you refreshment. I'll ring for Elsie.'

'No, don't ring just yet,' Dot said. 'I won't stay if your aunt isn't available to see me.'

'Nonsense,' Miriam replied ringing the bell anyway. 'What can be so urgent that you can't manage a cup of tea with a friend? Now please sit down and tell all.'

Elsie arrived promptly.

'I've told Mrs Humboldt that you're here, Miss Dorothy,' Elsie announced. 'And she says that she will be with you as soon as she can. I see Miss Miriam has found you, though. She'll keep you company until

Mrs Humboldt arrives.'

'She most certainly will and a pot of tea to warm my friend and me, with plenty of shortbread, would be marvellous, Elsie. Thank you. Now, how are you and how are things with your family, Dot? Has the baby arrived? Is that why you're back in Micklewell?' Miriam asked.

'My sister had twins,' Dot replied. 'I'm home for a while to help out.'

'Ah, how wonderful.' Miriam sighed. 'So, everything's fine in the Locock household, that's good news.'

'No, it's not good news, Miriam,' Dot said. 'And everything's not fine. If anything, things are worse. My sister's exhausted, my brother-in-law is still out of work and now, my mother is ill. Miss Clarence has offered to help by paying me for a research task but it won't be enough. I have decided to write to the college. I have to find a job. I must give up my training.'

'You're going to give up, with only a few months until you finish?' Miriam asked.

'I have to,' Dot replied, reaching for her handkerchief. It was at that moment that something snapped inside her. Everything that she'd been feeling poured in anger-filled waves out of her mouth.

'I really don't know why I'm telling you all this,' Dot said. 'You have no understanding of how most people live, Miriam. You drift from one social scene to another whenever it pleases you. You dabble in painting and people, never settling in one place or committing yourself to any one thing. You've never had to do a day's work in your life and you will inherit all this when your aunt has gone. Your life is as far removed from mine as it is possible to get at the moment. What on earth am I doing here?'

187

Miriam's eyes widened and her face went pale. She got up and began pacing up and down the room. She went to the bay window and looked out over the lawns. She stood silently in that position for quite some time, until Elsie came in with the tea tray. Dot wondered if she'd said too much. She hadn't intended to sound so angry. Miriam thanked Elsie and returned to the fireside. She poured the tea, lost in thought and passed Dot her cup and saucer.

'You're right, of course,' Miriam finally replied. 'I'm going to do something to help.'

'What?' Dot asked. 'What can you possibly do?'

'I've been thinking for a long time that I should mount an exhibition of my work,' Miriam said. 'I keep producing all these paintings and they're just stacking up, cluttering up my room and doing nothing. They could be earning some money. I'm never going to be a great artist but I've been told my work is very saleable. As you know, I've had a few commissions. I've just been too lazy to get anything else organised. My aunt has always said that I've got talent but no business sense. Perhaps what I've needed all along is a reason to get off my backside and do something. You've given me that reason, Dot. I want to organise an exhibition of art work and give the money raised to you. It's the best way I know that I can help your family and help your situation.'

'But that will all take time,' Dot replied. 'My family need money now.'

'I've thought of that, too.' Miriam smiled. 'I'm going to ask my aunt to loan me some money, which I will repay.'

'And how do you think she will take that?' Dot asked.

'Well, we shall see. I think my plan has the best chance of working if you're here with me when I put my proposal to her. Will you stay? Please? She'll be down from her afternoon rest very soon, I think.'

Half an hour later, Mrs Humboldt sailed into the room looking refreshed from her afternoon nap. She greeted Dot with enthusiasm.

'My dear, so lovely to see you. No, no, do not get up. You stay right there and Miriam will organise some more tea. Ring for Elsie, Miriam,' she commanded with her usual authority.

She evicted Miriam from her warm seat and then launched into a series of exclamations and questions which she threw in Dot's direction. 'But whatever have you been doing to yourself? Those bags under your eyes! Not flattering. Are you not sleeping well? And what are you doing here? I thought you went back to Chichester.'

In the brief pause, Dot explained that she'd come to see her two newly- born nieces.

'Twins!' Mrs H gasped, her voice two octaves higher. 'Children are difficult enough to deal with one at a time but when they come in packages of two then I pity the parents.'

'Yes, it's not easy. I've been helping out,' Dot said.

Miriam instructed Elsie to bring more tea, pulled another chair up to the fire and sat between the two women.

'Talking of helping out,' Miriam said. 'There's something I want to discuss with you, Aunt.'

Mrs Humboldt shifted her attention towards her niece, tilted her head and raised her eyebrows.

'As you have quite rightly pointed out, Dot should be in Chichester finishing her training. The reason she is still here is because she's going to give up her place at college and find a job. Her family have had a deal of problems to contend with over the past few months and now there are two more mouths to feed and Dot's mother is ill.'

Mrs H pursed her lips and stared impassively at Miriam.

The lack of response made Miriam continue, explaining her plan carefully and glancing towards Dot occasionally. Both young women looking for any clue as to what Mrs H's reaction might be.

Elsie brought in the tea tray complete with some slices of Victoria sponge cake. She asked if she should pour the tea but Mrs H replied, 'Miriam will do the honours,' and then remained silent until Elsie had gone.

'Mmm,' Mrs H grunted. She paused to sip her tea and Miriam offered her a slice of the cake. She seemed to be relishing the moment. Finally, she addressed Dot. 'I see you continue to have a positive influence upon my niece, Dorothy, and that, in my opinion, is a good thing,' she said, the corners of her mouth lifting.

Then, turning to Miriam, she said, 'I never thought I would see the day when you were prepared to do more than the occasional commission and actually earn some decent money from your painting. What is even more surprising, is that you are offering to put in all this effort to assist another. Therefore, Miriam, I agree to your proposal and will summon my solicitor, in due course, to draw up an agreement.'

Dot could see from Miriam's expression that she'd not expected such a response.

'An agreement,' Miriam said, her voice tentative.

'Yes, an agreement,' Mrs H replied. 'As you seem to be more open to learning lessons in life, my dear, I have another one for you. Never agree the terms of debt repayment merely by shaking hands. Always have financial transactions written down, preferably by someone au fait with such legalities. Now, let us enjoy our tea and reminisce about our wonderful trip to Eastbourne. We will come to the money matters later.'

33

Dot left the house early. The rainy weather of the previous week was a soggy memory and the air was now fresh and crisp. The spreading Jack Frost fingers on the window pane had prepared her for the cold journey that was to come and she had accepted an additional shawl from her mother to 'keep out the cold'. She was glad of it now as she slipped and slithered up the lane to catch the carter's wagon to the station at Hook. Her father had wanted to come with her, to help carry her bag, but she'd insisted that he get to his forge and start the fire going. He couldn't afford to keep any customers waiting.

The tall stalks of last season's cow parsley were rimmed with frost and the seed heads sparkled in the morning light. They stood erect, their former green and white verdant beauty now gone but now each dead stalk was transformed by a silvery, white gown. A few remaining leaves in the hedgerows hung petrified, stubbornly clinging on despite the freeze. A robin greeted her with his cheery call and she was, for a moment, distracted by his flash of red. She stood for a while, captivated by the scene, but the creeping cold soon penetrated and she moved on. Beneath her feet, solid ruts left by cart tracks and hoof prints refused to yield. A turned ankle would not be welcome, she thought, and she turned her attention from the frozen splendour of the winter world around her, to the icy ground.

On reaching the junction of lanes, she waited for the carter's wagon to take her to the station at Hook, shifting her weight and stamping her feet to keep them from freezing. She waited and waited and was about to give up and go back home when the cart rounded the bend. A few figures sat shivering on the bench seats and she climbed up to join them. No one spoke very much and the thirty-minute journey in the frigid air dampened her spirits. She was glad to see the station come into view and after buying her ticket, she headed straight for the waiting room where she hoped a bright, blazing fire would be burning. She had about fifteen minutes to wait for her train, time enough to warm up.

She looked through the window and could see a stern-faced woman sat in one corner. She was dressed in black with a purple and green hat and had a child by her side who shifted about uncomfortably. The child was wrapped up in so many layers, she looked as round as a plum pudding. The other person in the room, a slim man with a tartan scarf around his neck, was poking the fire, trying to stir it into action. He turned as she came through the door.

'Good day to you,' he said. 'If you're hoping to get warm, then, sadly, you're about to be disappointed. The coal's damp and there's more smoke than there is fire at the moment. I've opened the vent to give it some encouragement but it's still very slow.'

She closed the door behind her, dropped her bag and sat down opposite the woman and child. The woman glanced at her but didn't smile and the child wriggled into the side of her mother complaining of the cold. Dot pulled her shawl up around her neck and removed her gloves which had failed to keep her hands warm. Blowing on her hands and rubbing them together began to bring life back into them but sitting still was proving to be the worst thing she could do, so she decided to go back outside. At least walking up and down the platform would get her circulation going. As she rose to leave, the young man spoke to her again.

'Don't give up on me and the fire just yet,' he said. 'I believe I see a flicker of life here.'

Dot looked towards the fireplace. There was indeed a flame spreading through the coals. She was hesitant but decided to return the smile the young man was sending in her direction, whilst at the same time noting his black, curly hair and deep-set eyes. His skin had a rugged look as if he'd spent a good deal of his time outdoors and yet his clothing was not that of a workman but a gentleman. His voice had a soft lilt and its effect on her was to make her feel comfortable in his presence.

'Come closer,' he said. 'You won't feel any benefit from there.'

Just as he extended his invitation, the child whispered something to her mother and the two of them got up and left. Dot felt a sudden desire to follow them. She would be left alone in the room with this stranger and that made her feel uncomfortable. She wasn't sure whether to stay or go.

The stranger looked at her, opening his eyes wide and gesturing with a theatrical sweep of his arm towards a bench next to the fire. The corners of her mouth turned up in amusement and slowly she began to feel more relaxed. She realised that her fears were unfounded. She was perfectly safe. The waiting room had two large windows and glass in the upper part of the door. Even though they were the only two people in the room, they could be easily observed from the platform. She told herself that she really couldn't go on letting the past rule her life and smiled back.

As Dot moved towards the fire, two strong scents filled her nose, the soot from the station chimney and the sweeter smell of cologne emanating from the young man.

'Have you got long to wait?' the stranger asked.

'My train should be here in a few minutes,' Dot replied.

'Mine too,' he said. 'We must both be travelling in the same direction. I'm William Martin. How do you do?'

He extended his hand and Dot took it. 'Dorothy Truscott. Pleased to meet you.'

'I'm going to Chichester on business and to visit my family,' William said. 'I've been living in Scotland for the past three years and this winter has chilled my bones, so I've come back south to warm up. If you think this is cold, then you should go to Scotland.'

'I don't think there's much likelihood of me travelling to Scotland, Mr Martin, but should I ever get the opportunity I will make sure I go in the summer time.'

'Oh, not the summer time, Miss Truscott. The midges will eat you alive,' William said.

'It seems as if Scotland has little to recommend it,' Dot said.

'Quite the contrary,' he replied. 'Scotland has much to recommend it. The views of the mountains and lochs are stunning. There's nothing remotely like it in the south.'

'Well, I think the South Downs are beautiful,' Dot replied.

'I don't disagree,' William said. 'But I have a particular love of painting landscapes in my spare time and an aspiring artist needs to broaden his scope, wouldn't you agree? There is something dull and unadventurous about staying in the same place all your life and doing the same thing.'

Dot smiled to herself. This young man would get on very well with Miriam, she thought. They both enjoyed painting, both belonged to the same social class and both had the same lack of knowledge about working people's lives.

'Some of us have no choice but to remain at home,' Dot said. 'And if we do travel, it is to earn a living and put food on the table for our families. Now if you'll excuse me, Mr Martin, I believe my train is due any minute. Good day to you.'

William rushed to the door and held it open for her. 'Miss Truscott, I hope I haven't offended you. It was wrong of me to make assumptions. Please forgive me. The train journey would be so much more agreeable if you would allow me to share it with you, but if I have caused offence in any way, then I quite understand if you would prefer not to share a carriage with me.'

Dot paused just to make him reflect upon his forwardness but there was something about the hurt on his face that made her will crumble. Yes, he had been presumptuous but then she did not feel inclined to rebuff him. Apart from anything else, she rather liked the way he looked at her and he was extremely attractive. She found herself transfixed by his dark

196

eyes and amused by his flop of dark curls escaping under the brim of his hat. Somehow, she felt unable to turn him down.

'Apology accepted, Mr Martin,' she replied.

'Thank you,' he said, his relief showing in the disappearance of his frown and the beginnings of a smile. 'Please allow me to carry your bag for you. I believe I hear the train approaching.'

As the steam engulfed the platform, they headed towards one of the front carriages and he opened the door for her. He placed her bag on the overhead rack next to his own and they sat facing each other. She smiled shyly at him, secretly hoping that the train journey would not be over too quickly. She needed to find out certain details from him without seeming too forward.

'There will be a wait at Eastleigh,' he said. 'Would you allow me to buy you some refreshment at the station buffet? There is time, I believe.'

'Thank you,' Dot said. 'That would be most acceptable.'

As the train pulled out of the station, she found herself being pleased that he stopped her from walking away. There was something about him that made her want to know more. She prepared to ask him about himself and just as if they had a simultaneous desire, they both began talking at once. They laughed.

'After you,' William said.

'No, you go first,' Dot replied.

'Do you plan to stay in Chichester long?' William asked.

Exactly what I was trying to find out, thought Dot. 'I'm returning to finish my teacher training,' she said. 'I've a few more months to go and then I will be a qualified teacher. If I pass my exams, of course.'

'So, your family is back there in Hook?' William asked.

'Micklewell, actually. You've probably never heard of it,' Dot said.

'Oh, but I have! My cousin and I have enjoyed many a glass of ale in the Queen's Head. I've had several holidays in the area whilst staying with my uncle and his family at Tylney Hall, Rotherwick.'

'Your uncle lives at the Hall?' Dot said, her voice faltering, for the building was known to her in circumstances that now brought a blush to her cheek. She recalled how she used to go with Kate and a few other children from the village to explore the grounds, play hide and seek amongst the rhododendron bushes and try to sneak a look at anyone coming or going. She remembered how they used to watch, unobserved, while finely dressed ladies paraded in the garden and children played on the lawns. There was one occasion, when they spotted a young couple kissing behind one of the yew hedges and she'd giggled so loudly that Kate had put her hand over her mouth. Too late though! They were discovered by the young man who chased them through the shrubbery calling them 'trespassers' and 'peeping Toms'. He might have caught them, if he hadn't fallen. He tripped on the laces of his shiny shoes and landed flat on his face in a flower bed, while they ran for their lives down the gravel drive and away through the pine trees.

'Yes, my uncle is Major Grazer. He owns a shipping line based in Glasgow,' William explained. 'I've been working for him up in Scotland. He bought the Hall just three years ago. I think he's looking to expand the Clan Line in the south. In the meantime, I'm learning the business alongside his son, my cousin, Nicholas.'

Dot was relieved to hear that the Grazer family would not have been the ones in residence when she'd been roaming the grounds without permission. She felt strangely uncomfortable about talking to someone whom she might have been observing without his knowledge. Now she knew that her nine-year-old self could not have been watching William in a passionate embrace, for he looked about the same age as her and would have been living far from Tylney Hall.

'I'm staying in the Chichester area for quite a while. It could be a month or more,' William said. 'There are two reasons for my extended visit. I'm being allowed extra holiday time as I haven't been home to see my parents for so long. In addition, I've been asked to carry out some work in Southampton for my employer. The shipping business is expanding and there are plans to establish a new base in the docks. I've been entrusted with attending preliminary meetings and reporting back to Major Grazer.'

'Sounds like you've been given a big responsibility. You'll be very busy then, during your stay,' Dot said.

'Not all the time.' William smiled.

A comfortable silence settled over them. Dot allowed a smile to creep across her lips too, as she realised the possibilities that the next few weeks could bring.

'I know it's incredibly forward of me,' William continued, 'but would you consider meeting me again while I am in Chichester? I would be so delighted. I could take you to tea perhaps? Do you know Shepherd's Tea Rooms, just around the corner from the cathedral?'

'Yes, I do,' Dot replied.

'Then may I suggest this coming Saturday at three o'clock?'

Dot accepted William's invitation and a feeling of light headedness immediately swept over her. This was a spur of the moment decision but, as William had said, life would be dull and unadventurous if everything stayed the same.

34

Dot's arrival back at her lodging house was greeted with a great deal of complaining from Mrs Cooper.

'It might be helpful, Miss Truscott, if when you disappear you could give me some idea of when you might return. I have shopping to do and meals to plan. How can I run an efficient lodging house when I don't know who is here and who is not? You'll be lucky if there's enough to go around for dinner. Your room has been shut up for so long it needs an airing. I would have changed the bedlinen and dusted, all ready for your return, if only you'd let me know.'

No, you wouldn't, thought Dot, who was well aware that Mrs Cooper did not excel at the art of house-keeping or any of the finer comforts in life. But she didn't want to agitate her landlady any further, so she simply said, 'My apologies, Mrs Cooper.'

On the staircase she came face to face with Maud Fitch, a fellow student, from the room next door to hers. 'Welcome back to paradise,' Maud said. 'Have you seen Mrs Smiley yet? I would avoid her if you can. She's in a right stew today.'

'Too late, she's already had a go at me for not telling her when I was coming back. No enquiry about my sister and the babies,' Dot replied.

'It wouldn't occur to her,' Maud said. 'She had her compassion removed with her gall bladder.'

The two young women giggled in their shared dislike of Mrs Cooper, whose demeanour was often the

201

reverse of her nickname.

'Looks like I'll have to go without dinner this evening,' Dot said. 'She's not prepared enough apparently.'

'Well you can have mine.' Maud grinned. 'I'm off out. Forgot to mention it to our lovely landlady. Don't worry, I'll tell Mrs Smiley so you don't have to suffer two poisonous encounters in one day. Lillian Spencer has invited me to her house. It's her birthday. Her mother's a wonderful cook. With any luck her brother will be there. Have you seen him? He's so handsome!'

She swept past Dot. 'Enjoy your tripe and onions,' she called.

Dot smiled to herself as she recalled her chance meeting with William. He's handsome too, she thought. Should she tell Maud about their arrangement for Saturday or keep it to herself? Maud was fun to be with but she was a great talker and Dot didn't really want the other guests in the house knowing about William as it might get back to Mrs Cooper and then there would be an interrogation she really didn't want to face.

After unpacking her bags, she sat down at her desk, pulled some paper and a pencil out of the drawer and opened the copy of *The Montessori Method* that Miss Clarence had given her. She had intended to make notes as she went along but the content of the book so fascinated her that she found she had read several chapters and had not picked up her pencil. This certainly was a totally new approach to education. Dot was going to enjoy this research and she was getting paid for it too. Miss Clarence, Miriam and Mrs Humboldt were all so kind and supportive. A weight had been lifted from her mind.

Dot was so happy to resume her studies. Losing herself in her books helped keep her mind off the difficulties at home and the rest of the week went by very quickly. After breakfast on the Saturday morning, Maud suggested they might go for a walk as the sun was shining.

'That would be lovely,' Dot said.

'I've got an essay to write for Monday though,' Maud said, 'and I haven't even started it yet. Shall we go after lunch?'

'I'd prefer this morning, if you could do your writing this afternoon,' Dot replied.

'Ooo! Secret assignation, is it?' Maud teased.

Dot blushed. Maud had caught her off guard. She didn't know what to say.

'Why Dorothy Truscott, I do believe that you are meeting a young man.'

'Sssh,' Dot whispered. 'Keep your voice down. I don't want the whole house to know.'

'Where did you meet him? How long has this been going on? You've kept that under your hat. You're a sly one, you are,' Maud continued, winking at Dot.

'We met on the train when I was returning from Micklewell,' Dot explained. 'And that's all I'm saying.'

Maud was not to be rebuffed. 'Where are you meeting him? What time?'

'As if I'd tell you,' Dot replied, smiling.

The two of them enjoyed their walk and Dot made a very good job of keeping the conversation firmly on safe ground. They talked of her visit home, how their teaching course was going and plans for the future. Maud was taking her teaching qualification too but she made no secret of the fact that it was her mother who had pushed her into it. Her sights were firmly set on getting married as soon as possible. The trouble was, she was trying a bit too hard and most of the time her courtships ended prematurely. Dot thought that the eligible young men were probably frightened off by her constant chatter.

Dot slipped out of the Gables and arrived at the Shepherd's Tea Rooms at five minutes to three. William was already at a table and caught her eye as she came in. A waitress greeted her and then showed her to the table, saying she would give them a few minutes to decide.

'The toasted teacakes are very good,' she said, as Dot sat down. 'And we have a delicious Victoria sponge. I'll be back in a few minutes.'

'I'm so pleased you came,' William said, when the waitress had gone.

Dot smiled and said, 'I always keep my promises.'

There was an embarrassed silence between them for a moment and then they both spoke at once.

'Shall we have . . .'

'Would you like . . .'

They laughed.

'You go first,' William said.

'Shall we have the teacakes?' Dot asked.

'Yes, that's a good idea. With some jam?'

Dot nodded. The waitress returned and they placed their order. While they waited, William asked how her teaching course was going and Dot asked about whether he had been able to see his mother.

'I made a brief visit but my mother was unwell, unfortunately,' William replied. 'I have decided to take rooms in a hotel. Staying at the family home might be too much of an imposition. It will be . . . difficult.'

Dot thought it a strange use of words, to be an imposition upon your family but she didn't comment upon it. The tea tray arrived and while Dot poured the tea, William changed the subject and began to talk enthusiastically about his work and life in Scotland.

'You know they call us English people Sassenachs up there. It's a derogatory term they tell me but the Scots I work with seem very friendly people and I so love the countryside. The scenery is wonderful.'

'I thought you said it was too cold in the winter,' Dot said.

He looked puzzled, the fine lines in his forehead and the tilt in his head giving him a boyish look.

'When we met at Hook station, you said it was cold in the winter and there were midges in the summer.'

'You have a good memory, Miss Truscott,' he replied.

'Call me Dorothy, please.'

'Well, yes. The weather can be harsh but it can be kind sometimes too and it is such a beautiful part of the British Isles. I've taken a few trips to see the famous sights, Loch Lomond and the Trossachs. Are you a person who likes the outdoors, Dorothy?'

'I like walking, if that's what you mean,' Dot replied.

'Then we must take some walks together, if that would be agreeable to you?'

'That would be most agreeable,' Dot said, passing him a teacake and fixing her eyes on his. She felt herself being drawn in. His tongue flicked across his lips, removing a crumb that had settled in the corner of his mouth. For a moment she lost the thread of the conversation as she imagined what it would be like to touch those lips.

'So, what do you think?' he asked.

'I beg your pardon?' Dot said.

'You were miles away,' William said. 'I asked if you would like to meet at the Bishop's Palace Gardens, tomorrow afternoon?'

'Yes, that would be lovely,' Dot replied, her whole body glowing.

35

As February moved into March, the weather became warmer and the spring bulbs began to show pale green spears above the surface of the ground. The puddles in Priory Park became shallower and the pavements around the greens more accessible. A few brave souls ventured out onto the bowling green on sunnier days and the dog walkers were able to bring their animals for daily exercise until after five in the evening.

After that first walk in Bishop's Palace Gardens, Dot and William met two or three times a week. They often walked in the park in the late afternoon, when lectures had finished or on Sundays after church. They also took tea together in various establishments across the town and attended a recital in the cathedral. Dot was enjoying William's company. She found that they had a lot in common. They both enjoyed walking and classical music and were interested in history and historical buildings. William revelled in being her tour guide around the city, introducing her to places she had known little about, for her studies had taken up most of her time.

One afternoon they were strolling around the gardens, when Dot commented how beautiful the camelias were.

'There are even more stunning gardens at West Dean,' William replied. 'I should love to take you there but they are best seen in the summer months and I must return to Scotland before then.'

Dot didn't reply. She knew their time together was limited and there was nothing she could do about it. She was sure that William enjoyed her company as much as she liked being with him but what would happen now? William must have seen her downcast expression even though she'd tried to hide her disappointment.

'So, I will be sure to come back in August and take you there,' he said, lifting her chin and looking into her eyes.

'I don't know where I shall be in August,' Dot said, a tinge of sadness in her voice. She pulled away from him. 'I may have secured a teaching job by then. It could be anywhere in the county. I may even be on the Isle of Wight.'

'Then I will come and seek you out and whisk you away on an adventure. School term doesn't begin until September, does it?'

'No but . . .'

'I will not listen to any buts. We can write to each other until then and you can tell me everything that you are doing. As long as it's not spending time with another young man or I shall be on the first train from Glasgow to come and sort him out.'

Dot smiled but it was a smile of resignation not of joy. Yes, they could write but what would be the point of that? She needed to get on with her life as it was now, not live in a dream that only existed in fairy tales.

If Dot's nervous smile showed her fears, then William seized that moment to try to dissolve them. He took her in his arms and kissed her with such passion that Dot could have no doubt as to his sincerity and depth of feeling for her. When he released her from his hold, her resolve almost melted away. She'd intended to tell him that letters were no answer to their problems and that writing would only prolong a difficult situation that would only cause them heart-ache in the end. Somehow those words would not form. She kissed him back and they held onto each other in the mutual hope for tomorrows that might never come.

She went home to her lodgings that evening with confusion in her head and sadness in her heart. Her good sense was telling her to stop this now and her emotions were pulling her in quite the opposite direction. She would write to Miriam and arrange for them to meet as soon as possible. She needed some advice that she hoped Miriam could give, impartially and with a detachment which she was unable to attain for herself at that moment in time.

36

'So how long have you known this man?' asked Miriam as they walked from Dot's lodgings towards the city centre. 'Two weeks, three?'

'Almost a month,' Dot said.

'Oh, almost a month. Well those few days will make all the difference,' Miriam quipped.

'My mother always told me that sarcasm is the lowest form of wit,' Dot replied.

'Well, motherly advice is not always the best to come by,' Miriam said. 'Some of us didn't even have a mother. Well not one who was present anyway.'

'It's not exactly helpful to turn my problem around and make it yours, Miriam. It's not my fault that your mother sent you away to boarding school,' Dot snapped. 'Now, are you going to help me resolve this or shall we just talk about something else? Your plans for an exhibition for example, remember?'

Miriam picked up the pace and Dot matched her stride for stride.

'I can't talk about anything until I've had some lunch,' Miriam said. 'I missed breakfast this morning. Lead me to an eating place before I expire.'

Dot sighed. Would Miriam ever be any different? She despaired of her friend. Miriam always managed to make herself the centre of attention. Dot was beginning to lose patience and her diminishing tolerance was threatening to turn into an irritation bordering on anger. She was about to say something, when she unexpectedly caught a glimpse of the past and Miriam holding her while she wept. Although Miriam's reaction at the time had annoyed and upset her, she now realised that she mustn't let what had happened with Douglas colour all her impressions of men or spoil a close friendship. William was quite different to Douglas, to Ralph and to Jack. Perhaps Miriam was right about learning from experiences.

Miriam was a good friend then and she was a good friend still, despite her tendency to be selfish. This realisation, and the fact that they were approaching a café that served the best pies in Chichester, decided Dot that she would wait until the right moment to explain herself fully. Also, she was beginning to feel hungry herself. Her appetite had been poor the last few days and so had her concentration on her work. If filling Miriam's stomach was the price to pay for getting her attention, then they needed to sit down and order as soon as possible.

The steak and kidney pie, when it arrived, was delicious. While they ate, Miriam listened as Dot told her about the circumstances of her meeting with William. She described his character and the reasons for him being in Chichester. She played down the importance of his job and the fact that he would be returning to Scotland within the week.

'So, what exactly are you asking me, Dot?' Miriam finally replied, laying down her knife and fork and dabbing her mouth with a napkin.

'What I should do?' Dot replied, trying to keep the exasperation in her voice in check.

Miriam paused and her face took on a reflective look.

'I'm probably not the best person to talk to about

affairs of the heart with the opposite sex, as you are well aware. However, it seems to me,' she said, 'that you have to look upon this as an interesting encounter. A dalliance, no more. An awakening of your passions. We all have those moments, Dot, but they cannot always be acted upon and neither are they intended to be made permanent. In fact, nothing is permanent.'

'I don't need you to start philosophising, Miriam. I just need to know if I should agree to writing to William.'

'What do you hope to achieve by it?' Miriam asked.

'A continuing friendship,' Dot replied. 'What harm is there in that?'

'And what good can come of it?' Miriam said. 'He will be hundreds of miles away. His work is there and your life is here.'

Dot was about to say that things might change but she knew that Miriam was right. Miriam was only voicing her own fears. Yet somehow that tiny glimmer of hope would not be extinguished. This talk with Miriam had not really helped at all. The decision was still ultimately her own and she knew that if William asked her to write, she would.

'Thank you for speaking plainly, Miriam,' Dot said.

'That's what friends are for,' Miriam replied. 'Now, let me tell you about the exhibition. The plans are going along well. I've written to some of my former fellow students at the Eastbourne School of Art and I'm inviting them to exhibit as well. One of them, Eric Ravilious, has just been awarded a scholarship to the Royal College of Art in London. He's definitely someone to watch. He'll be famous one day, you wait and see. His work is different somehow. I can't explain it but a variety of work will bring in more potential purchasers. I will take a cut of the sales and give the money to you thereby your coffers will increase and ultimately your family will benefit. What do you think of that?'

'Well, you have been busy . . .' Dot said. She left a significant pause and then added, 'Thinking.'

'More than just thinking,' Miriam declared. 'One of my friends has replied already. He says he will submit eight canvases for my consideration. My aunt suggested Eastbourne as the best place to mount the exhibition. As she put it, 'An excellent showcase for the idle rich to peruse at their leisure and be persuaded to part with their cash.' I have already approached the Eastbourne Council about the possibility of hiring a suitable space. I've heard rumours that they are intending to open a new gallery with the art collection and money left in a bequest by the former alderman of the town, John Chisholm Towner. I believe they have a building in mind to house the collection. If I can persuade them that a representation of local artists would show they are interested in the artists of the present and the future as well as the past, that would be wonderful, don't you think? The perfect advertisement for their new project.'

Dot smiled. *Typical Miriam*, she thought. Nothing if not ambitious but would her achievements match her aspirations? That remained to be seen. Meanwhile, Dot was left with the practicalities of now, not the dreams of tomorrow.

37

'This feels like the Last Supper,' William said as they ordered tea, scones and fruit cake at Shepherd's Tea Rooms.

'Don't say that,' Dot replied. 'That story doesn't exactly have a happy ending.'

'I'm going to Scotland not Calvary,' William said. 'And I'm going back to a job not seeking to save mankind. That's what it is, Dorothy, just a job. I'm not destined to remain north of the border forever but I do need to return. Despite what it looks like, spoilt little rich boy with wealthy uncle, it's not quite like that.'

'What is it like then? You've told me a lot about your job up there in the Highlands and your holidays at Tylney Hall but I know nothing of your parents and your early childhood.'

'You know I was sent away to school. What more is there to tell?' William said.

'You are an only child. Did your mother not want to keep you close? I'm sure if I only had one son I wouldn't want to send him away.'

The waitress arrived with the tea and William broke off the conversation while she lay down the crockery, teapot and cake stand.

'I've brought strawberry jam. I hope that's all right?' she said. 'You didn't say which sort you wanted and I'm sorry I forgot to ask. I can change it if you like. I'm supposed to ask, you see. We have apricot or

214

blackcurrant as well.'

All this was said in a flurry of agitation with the young girl flicking her eyes constantly in the direction of an elegantly dressed woman standing beside the counter who Dot assumed was the owner. All the waitresses wore neat black-and-white uniforms and were bustling about taking orders or carrying trays. When Dot looked back at their waitress, the young woman was busily straightening her starched white cap and trying without much success to poke her pale, wispy hair inside it.

'Strawberry is fine,' Dot said, attempting to ease the poor young woman's discomfort with a smile. The waitress bobbed and took the tray away.

'Shall I be mother?' Dot said.

'Yes. We were talking of mothers,' William replied. 'So, I will tell you of mine. She had a riding accident when I was about five years old. It left her disabled. She'll never walk again. When I said I went to visit my family, that's not strictly true. Not my whole family anyway. I went to visit my mother. She has never really been able to adjust to her life in a wheelchair since the accident. I was sent away to school because my father could not look after me or would not. I'm never really entirely sure. He could have employed a nursemaid but he said he didn't want any more strangers in the house. My mother had to have a nurse, you see. I remember them arguing a lot. She wanted me to have a tutor so that I could be close to her but he said that I should learn to be independent and that boarding school was the answer. That decision was the cause of my mother's mental breakdown. I'm convinced of it. He sent her away, into an institution.'

'So, you didn't go to the family home at all. You

215

went to visit your mother in an asylum?'

'Yes. My father had her committed. Said she was out of her mind, accusing him of infidelity. I'm sure she was right, though. I can't bear to see him anymore. I go to visit her but I'm not sure she really knows me. That place has made her worse, not better. I can't forgive him for that. I really should have explained rather than giving you half-truths.'

'No wonder you were reluctant to talk about your family when we first met. I'm so sorry,' Dot said. 'I didn't mean to upset you.'

'I don't often talk about it,' William replied, 'but I'm glad I've told you now.'

'Keeping such thoughts and feelings inside is never a good thing,' Dot said. 'Thank you for telling me.'

'There are some people who can make you feel at ease. People who you want to be completely honest with,' William said. 'And you are one of those people, Dorothy. Well, you are to me.'

William reached his hand across the table and took hers. 'I would feel very privileged if you would write to me,' he said, smiling at her. 'I want to know everything that you are doing, however dull it might seem to you. Write to me as if you were writing your own diary. Tell me when you are happy and when you feel sad. Tell me how your studies are going. I want to feel as if I were here, right by your side.'

Dorothy laughed. 'I don't keep a diary and even if I did, some things are personal. I can't let you in to all my secret thoughts, can I?'

And that was how Dot's intentions of ending things melted into the air and settled like sleeping dust in the corner of her eyes. For sometimes the silky veil that is the web of attraction becomes the mask that obscures reality. Dot could see no further than that moment and a switch turned off in her brain. She would return his letters and place her faith in a future she could not foresee.

38

March 1923

It was fortuitous that the opening day of Miriam's exhibition was the last Saturday before William had to return to Scotland. Dot was so excited, both to see the paintings and to have William by her side. The two of them travelled down to Eastbourne by train and Dot talked non-stop about Miriam and her bohemian friends.

'Sounds as if you think I've never met such arty types before. Believe me, in my line of work, I meet some pretty unusual and unconventional people. Nothing they can say or do will shock me,' William said.

'I just want to prepare you, that's all,' Dot explained. 'What exactly does your job entail, anyway?' Dot asked. 'You've told me about the shipping line but not the details of what you do all day.'

'It's all really quite boring,' William replied.

'Let me be the judge of the that,' Dot said.

'I meet with businessmen who want to arrange transport of goods and assess the costs involved in order to quote them a price. I've been asked to arrange shipment for things as diverse as engine parts to bales of jute, coal to antiquities. There are some colourful characters, some honest traders and some swindlers and rogues. I have to make sure the company makes money and doesn't accept any questionable transactions,' William explained. 'Import and export laws are stringent and must be followed.'

'It all sounds very complicated. You have a lot of responsibility,' Dot said.

'No more than teaching a class full of children,' William replied.

Dot liked that about him. He respected her vocation.

As they pulled into Brighton, where they had to change trains, Dot looked out of the window. 'I've never actually visited Brighton,' she said. 'I've heard so much about how beautiful the Pavilion is and I should love to walk along the pier.'

'I will make a note of it,' William replied. 'It will be on my agenda to organise a day out as soon as I return from Scotland.'

They arrived in Eastbourne in time for lunch and William insisted on treating her to a meal at the Cavendish Hotel despite her saying that a simple tea rooms would do. The beef Wellington was delicious and Dot chose the apple Charlotte as dessert. She declined a glass of wine with the meal as she wanted to make sure she had a clear head for looking around the exhibition. She also couldn't help feeling guilty that she was here enjoying herself and her sister was struggling to cope back in Micklewell. Life could be a cruel trickster, showing glimpses of pleasure and joy and then snatching them away. Her only consolation was that at least this was all happening for the benefit of the whole family not just herself.

When they arrived, there were already several people in the room, some studiously examining the works of art and some engaged in lively conversation. The atmosphere was one of refined contemplation and a churchlike reverence. The elegant room had high ceilings. Two large windows at either end filtered light into the ample space. People moved around freely, some examining paintings close up, others standing well back and contemplating from afar.

As Dot and William moved further into the room, she overheard two well-groomed, middle-aged gentlemen talking about one of the art works, a portrait of a young woman.

'Such a command of his subject. It's a wonderful likeness, don't you think? The application of the paint is exquisite. The skin tones perfect,' the taller of the two said.

'And just look at the folds of the dress how they fall across her knees,' the stockier man with a lascivious look in his eye replied. 'One could almost imagine . . .'

He perhaps sensed Dot could hear him and his voice tailed off and he cast a slightly embarrassed nod in her direction.

'Can you see your friend?' William asked.

Dot scanned the faces but it was Miriam who spotted her. She moved towards them, nodding and smiling at people she passed. On reaching them, she greeted Dot with great effusiveness.

'Darling. So lovely to see you,' she said, throwing her arms around Dot. 'And this must be Mr Martin.'

'William, please,' William replied.

She took a long look at William and then extended her hand.

'Pleased to meet you, William' she said. 'Thank you so much for accompanying my dearest friend to the exhibition today.'

'The pleasure is all mine,' William replied, taking her hand.

'I will apologise in advance,' Miriam said, 'for I must circulate. I need to persuade these people to part with their money but I will leave you in safe hands. There are some people here you know, Dot. Remember my friends? The ones you met when we were here with my aunt?'

'Oh, yes,' Dot replied. She felt a wave of awkwardness flow over her. The last time she saw Miriam's friends, she was being helped to leave the dance hall. She hoped no reference would be made to that incident. Miriam must have detected her feelings as she took Dot's arm and whispered, 'Don't worry, I've told them no mention of the dance hall is to be made.'

Florence and Bettine greeted them both enthusiastically and they were soon being swept around the gallery and guided towards the most interesting works of art.

'Are you an art lover?' Bettine asked William.

'Well, I know what I like,' William replied. 'I paint a little myself but I cannot profess to be an expert.'

'Do you like landscapes or portraits, oils or watercolours?' Bettine asked.

'Perhaps Mr Martin has a taste for something a bit different,' Florence said, with a flirtatious gleam in her eye. 'He may be interested in the Eric Gill works perhaps?'

She steered them towards a striking printed image in black and white.

'Girl in a bath, a woodcut,' Florence said. 'Interesting isn't, it? Quite different to most of the works here but then Eric Gill is an unusual sort of man. Or so I've heard.'

William and Dot looked at the print, the fine lines etching the outline of a naked young woman.

221

'It's different, certainly,' Dot said.

'Given that the sitter is his daughter, yes,' Florence replied. 'Not the usual relationship a father has with his daughter, wouldn't you say?'

William looked uncomfortable and Bettine suggested they look at some landscapes. Dot noticed Bettine whisper something in Florence's ear which made Florence glance back at Dot. She looked somewhat embarrassed and said very little for the rest of the time they were together.

Bettine took over their guided tour and introduced them to some of the artists who were present. Eric Gill was not amongst them, much to Dot's relief, for she didn't know how she would be able to look such a man in the eye.

39

'About time too,' said Ada as Kate opened the letter from Dot. 'Well, let's hear what she has to say, then.'

'Shouldn't we wait until Pa and Albert come home?' Kate asked.

'Can't wait 'til then. Open it now,' Ada demanded.

Kate opened the envelope carefully and began scanning the letter hoping to read that her sister would be coming home again very soon. She desperately needed to talk to her. She missed her sister and being able to share thoughts and feelings with her. Kate got on well enough with her parents but living in such close proximity was proving testing at times and now her mother was sick, her usual brisk way of going about daily life had turned into a constant round of complaining and short-temperedness. Kate tried to make allowances for the fact that her mother was in pain but sometimes she just had to get out of the house and try to feel some peace.

'She says that her studies are going well and that . . .'

'No,' Ada said. 'Read her actual words. I want to hear what she has to say directly from her.'

So Kate read aloud:

Dear Mum, Dad, Kate, Albert and children,
You have all been in my thoughts. I hope that you are not feeling too bad, Ma. It was hard leaving you knowing that you are not in the best of health. How is

Albert? I hope his walking is improving. I am working hard for my exams and can report that my tutors are very pleased with my contributions in class and my teaching practice. They have said that I show great promise and that my questions are always challenging. I am quietly confident about passing the course.

'What does she mean, challenging? I hope she's not making a nuisance of herself and being rude to her teachers. Sometimes she doesn't know when to keep quiet and just listen. Always been the same,' Ada interrupted.

'It just means that she wants to know more rather than accepting everything they say,' Kate replied. 'That's a good thing, I think.'

Kate released a long, slow breath and resumed reading.

I'm so pleased that you have been receiving the money from Mrs Humboldt and have been able to make good use of it. It was so kind of her to let Miriam have an advance and I will be forever grateful to Miriam herself for organising the art exhibition. It all went very well. She knows some very talented people and about twenty paintings were sold. She has also taken some commissions and has enough work to keep her busy for months to come.

It's good news that Henry has found some weekend work at Addison's Farm. As long as it's not potato picking, I'm sure he'll enjoy it. I remember you coming home after a day in the fields, Kate, saying you'd rather muck out stables and you didn't care if you never saw another potato in your life.

'Any work is better than none,' Ada said. 'Sounds as if Dot is spending too much time hobnobbing with the gentry. She needs to keep her feet firmly on the ground.'

'You'll like this part, Ma,' Kate said, trying to lift her mother's mood.

I am happy to tell you that I will be able to come for a brief visit during the Easter holidays. I look forward to seeing you all soon. I should be arriving on Palm Sunday, all being well.

All my love,

Dot

Kate could hear one of the babies crying and sighed. She had only just sat down and hoped to be able to just close her eyes for a moment after reading Dot's letter. She was relieved to hear that her sister was coming home, though. The burden of keeping spirits up in 2 Mead Cottages was beginning to drag her down, even with the extra money. She tried not to feel sorry for herself, for life had improved, on the whole. The bills were more manageable now since the regular payments were being received. The family had paid back their rent arrears and were now able to fill the larder and buy more butter and cheese. Ada still stuck to old habits, though. She insisted on scraping the butter wrapping until every scrap was removed and collecting up all the soap remnants to melt down and reuse. Kate found these little things irritating at times. She knew that it was petty to dwell on such small and unimportant details but there were other problems preying on her mind and somehow small things increased her sensitivities. She wished things were different. She wished that Albert had never had his accident, making them so dependent. She wished she could have a home of her own but these wishes were hollow and only served to tighten the knot in her stomach. And now there was an additional worry, one she could well do without.

★ ★ ★

As usual Dot's arrival caused much excitement. There was as much hustle and bustle as Ada could summon the strength to organise. Kate had been kept busy with the preparations for her sister's visit for the past week and Ada, as always, had pushed herself too hard, leaving her weak and exhausted.

'Will you just let me do it?' Kate said, taking the basket of washing from her mother.

'But I need to put clean sheets on the bed. I can't expect Dot to sleep in dirty sheets. You know I suffer from the night sweats, Kate,' Ada replied, coughing and struggling for breath.

'I can do it,' Kate insisted. 'Now go and sit down before you fall down.'

Kate stripped and remade the bed and prepared the vegetables for the evening meal so that all was ready for when Dot arrived. Henry was at the farm and her father and Albert at the forge. She knew that Ada would not be able to cope with the children if she left the house for any more than a few minutes. So, she had asked Mary Suss to come in for an hour or so while she went to meet Dot.

Kate told the children to be good for Mary and that she wouldn't be long. She began to put her coat and hat on and asked Ada if there was anything else she needed before she left. Ada started complaining. 'What's the hurry?' she grumbled. 'You'll only have to stand around waiting. That carter is often late. He stays longer in the Railway Arms than he should. You might be standing there for ages. Mary has got plenty to do herself without acting nursemaid to me.'

'I'm not acting nursemaid,' Mary said, coming in the kitchen door just at the right moment. 'Kate just thought you'd appreciate a bit of company and we haven't had the chance of a gossip for months. Now have I got a tale to tell you about young Polly, old Granny White's granddaughter . . .'

'Well, you'd better come in and put the kettle on,' Ada said.

Ronnie and Tilly made a fuss about wanting to come too but Kate said that they would walk too slowly and make her late.

'It'll be quicker all round if I go by myself,' she said.

As she walked along the lane, she went over the words in her head. How best to explain? Where to begin? Perhaps she should just come straight out with it: 'I can't possibly have another child, Dot. I have to . . .'

Kate hardly noticed the primroses on the banks, forming yellow swathes amongst the green. Their open faces turning towards the sunlight passed her by. The sting of the nettle that brushed against her hand as she stooped to fasten her shoe lace, did not register and the squabbling of the sparrows in the hedgerows, failed to distract her. She formed and reformed the sentences and none of them seemed to be right. Every way she phrased it, the words seemed to emphasise the wrong things, made her sound selfish or without feeling.

By the time she reached the crossroads, her mind was in a whirl and the arrival of the cart was a relief to her, for she could no longer agonise over how to explain, her sister was climbing down from the cart and waving, calling, 'Kate, Kate, how wonderful to see you.'

The two sisters embraced and Kate offered to carry one of her bags.

'It's all right. I'm balanced,' Dot said. 'They're not heavy anyway. You look tired, Kate. You must have a lot to do with Ma not being well. How is she?'

'Much the same. Some days are better than others, I just wish she wouldn't try to carry on as if nothing was wrong with her.'

'You know what she's like,' Dot replied. 'She won't want to give in to it.'

'But that just makes it harder on all of us,' Kate said.

'Tell me everything that's been going on in Micklewell,' Dot said, clearly trying to change the subject.

'There's not a lot to tell,' Kate replied. 'You're the one with the interesting life. You tell me what you've been up to. Your letter was brief.'

'I will only need to go over it again when we get home,' Dot said. 'But there is one thing I want to tell you before we get there.'

Kate sensed that this was of some importance to Dot and something that perhaps she didn't necessarily want to share with their parents.

'I've met someone,' Dot blurted out.

Kate stopped and faced her sister. 'You mean you have an admirer? Are you courting?'

'We have been seeing quite a lot of each other, yes. I think I really like him, Kate. His name is William.

He's related to the family who own Tylney Hall.'

Dot's revelation and obvious happiness thundered down on Kate like a sudden downpour. How could she speak of her worries now? The moment had passed. So, her little sister was courting and someone from a well-to-do family. Her thoughts went immediately to Philip. How strange that the two of them should fall in love with men from a different social class. But she was getting ahead of herself. The two of them had only just met. It was early days yet. She was happy for her sister but she couldn't help but feel a twinge of sadness that her own first love was forever lost to her.

Kate and Dot reached the cress beds in front of Mead Cottages just at the same time as their father and Albert were approaching from the opposite direction. They all greeted one another warmly and walked home together.

'You seem to be walking a little better, Albert,' Dot said.

'Yes, thankfully. The leg feels much better. I only need the stick to walk a distance. I can be of more use to Jim now. I was a dead weight a few months back. Your dad is too kind to admit it but I was a bit of a chain around his neck, I think,' Albert said, glancing at Jim.

'That's enough of that, now,' Jim replied. 'The main thing is you're getting stronger.'

The family group entered the kitchen just as Mary was pouring another cup of tea.

'There we are, Ada,' she said. 'I told you they would smell it brewing. I'd better top it up.'

She fetched some more cups from the dresser, picking her way across a room full of adults talking and children wheeling around calling for their treats from Dot, for she never arrived in the house without them.

40

Several days went by before Kate was alone with Dot.
Kate had been given a pram by Mary Suss's daugh-
ter-in-law. It was more like twenty-second hand than
second hand and it bore all the scars and bruises of
being well used by several babies over the years, but
it served a purpose. The padding inside was yellowing
but a good scrubbing ensured that it was clean if not
pristine and a collapsing wheel on one side had been
repaired and replaced by Albert. It was one of the first
jobs he'd carried out completely unaided by Jim. Kate
had made cotton covers from an old bed sheet and
Ada had provided a crocheted blanket, folded over
several times for warmth.

The two sisters walked along the village street with
the pram, the twins topped and tailed and sleeping
peacefully for once.

'Let's go towards the church,' Kate said. 'We can sit
on the bench around the far side, it catches the sun at
this time of day.'

As they walked they talked of family matters. Of
how tall Henry was growing and how handsome he
was becoming.

'He'll soon be fending off the girls,' Dot said. 'Do
you remember how we used to sigh over Jack White?'

'You wouldn't look twice at him now, Dot, believe
me. He's got a paunch on him and his straggly beard

231

looks like he lost his razor somewhere. He's got more children than he can support and he spends the family's food money on beer. I pity his poor wife.'

'You will never have that problem with Albert. He's such a good man,' Dot said.

'Yes, he is,' Kate replied. She paused and took a deep breath. 'There's something I need to talk to you about, Dot. Something concerning Albert and me.'

'Oh yes?' she said lightly, until she saw her sister's look of concern.

'I'm pregnant again and before you say anything at all, I don't want it. I can't have this baby, Dot. My body is only just recovering and I have so much to do with Ma being ill and the twins constantly needing me and . . .'

Kate's eyes filled with tears and she fought to stop the sobs from escaping from deep within her, but they erupted and stopped her from being able to say any more. She fumbled for a handkerchief in her coat pocket but couldn't find one. Dot produced one from up her sleeve and handed it to her sister.

'Are you sure, Kate? The twins aren't six months old yet. Can a woman conceive so soon after?'

'Yes, they can,' Kate interrupted. 'All the signs are there. At first, I thought I was just tired after the birth of the twins but I've been feeling sick every morning. I just know. I can't go through it all again, Dot.'

'Oh, Kate. I'm so sorry that you feel that way. Bearing a child should be a w —'

'Don't, Dot. Don't say anything. You have no idea what it's like. The broken nights, the sore breasts, the crying, crying, crying.'

Dot took Kate's hand to try to give comfort to her sister. 'What can I do?' she said.

'There's nothing you can do except not breathe a word of this to anyone.'

'What about Albert? Have you told him?'

'No, he mustn't know.'

'But, Kate . . .'

'You mustn't speak of this. Do you hear me? I'm telling you in case anything happens.'

'What's going to happen?' Dot asked, her face grey with worry now. 'Kate, you're not going to . . .'

Kate wiped her eyes and blew down hard. She sat for a while, looking out across the fields. The babies both made mewling noises in their sleep and Kate pulled back the covers to look at them.

'I love them, of course I do, but I just can't go through it all again.'

'Things are getting better, aren't they?' Dot asked.

'Yes, and that's why I can't bear to place another burden on the family, on myself. There's a woman in Nately, who can help. I need to do this soon, Dot, but I can't do it without you. I need you to look after the children while I go. She's told me that she can do it on Sunday.'

'But that's Easter Sunday,' Dot replied.

'I know. The family usually goes to church, so I'm going to say I feel unwell and stay behind.'

'Oh, Kate, it's dangerous. I'm worried for you. Please don't . . .'

'I've made up my mind, Dot. I have to do this. If you want to help me then this is what I need you to do. There will be a gathering after the service. Stop them from coming home as long as possible, keep talking to people and say you just need to have a word with someone else before they drag you away. When you come back there will be a note to say that I've gone to see Granny White for one of her stomach remedies. She stopped going to church long ago, so she won't be there.'

'What if Ma talks to Granny White and she says she hasn't seen you?'

'I can't think about that. Ma always steers clear of her anyway, because she's a gossip and a time waster.'

'Are you sure about this, Kate? I'm worried for you.'

'I'm worried too,' Kate replied, taking Dot's hand. 'But I'm more worried about what will become of me if I don't do this. Will you help me, Dot?'

Dot stared down at their intertwined hands. She squeezed her sister's fingers and looked up. Her head nodded slowly and both the sisters' hearts ached with the pain of what was to come.

41

The sun came up bright and clear on Easter Sunday morning. Tinges of red, purple, pink and yellow bruised the sky and Kate sighed at the beauty of it as she stood at the bedroom window. Albert stirred in his sleep and she heard the bed springs squeak as he turned over. She couldn't bear to look at him.

'Good morning, my love,' he said, his voice still full of sleep.

'Good morning,' she replied, still not turning towards him.

She didn't move as he threw back the covers and each floorboard creaked as he made his way towards her. He wrapped his arms around her and buried his face in her long hair, nuzzling into her neck. She squirmed a little as his breath on her neck always made her shudder, in a pleasant, ticklish sort of way.

'They slept through, then,' he said.

'No, you slept through,' she replied. 'I was up twice, feeding.'

'But the nights are getting better, aren't they?' Albert asked, placing his chin on her shoulder.

She hadn't the heart to get cross with him. It wasn't his fault that he didn't have the flow of milk to feed them. She certainly did and the evidence was beginning to seep through her nightgown. She prepared herself to turn to him. He must believe that she was unwell. She didn't need to pretend, for the deep sadness and fear she felt for what she was about to do showed on her face.

'Are you all right?' he asked. 'You don't look good.'

'I don't feel well,' she replied. 'My stomach hurts and I feel sick.'

'No church for you today, then,' Albert said, holding her at arm's length and looking at her with such tenderness that Kate felt her resolve weaken. 'You can stay here and rest. I'm sure that Dot will help with the children.'

It was all too easy. She hadn't even had to try too hard. Albert was too good. She felt that she was betraying him. The thought of what was about to happen truly was making her feel sick. She couldn't stomach any breakfast and she began to go hot and cold, her heart was racing and she felt light-headed. Albert told her to get back into bed and turned his attention to the twins who were beginning to murmur and wriggle about.

'If you feed them now, will they last until after church? You'll get a better rest if we take them with us,' Albert said, lifting Rose, always the more demanding of the two.

Kate took Rose and fed her, while Albert walked Annie up and down to pacify her.

'Where's Kate?' asked Ada, when Albert entered the kitchen with a contented Rose. 'She's usually first down.'

'She's not feeling well. I told her to stay in bed,' Albert replied. 'She's feeding Annie, then we'll take both of them with us. I hope she'll feel better after some extra sleep. She's not been getting enough since the twins were born.'

'Same for all new mothers,' Ada said.

'Perhaps some extra rest will aid a quick recovery,'

Jim Truscott added.

''Tis only a stomach upset. She'll recover soon enough,' Ada replied. 'Now, the rest of you get a move on or we'll be late for the service.'

Albert was looking for his stick which he was accusing the children of playing with, Jim couldn't find his clean necktie and Tilly and Ronnie were getting in everyone's way. They were climbing all over Henry, begging him to kneel down and give them a ride on his back and the volume of noise in the little kitchen was building to the point when Ada could clearly take no more.

'How many times do I have to tell you two to put your shoes on?' she snapped at the children, her raised voice bringing on a coughing fit.

Dot went upstairs to retrieve Annie and have a quiet word with Kate, away from the chaos in the kitchen.

'Are you sure about this?' Dot whispered, as she sat on the edge of the bed.

'It's for the best,' Kate replied, her eyes downcast. 'I will leave the note on the kitchen table saying I've gone to Granny White's. That will explain my absence.'

Dot lifted Annie gently in her arms, wrapped a shawl around her and prepared to take her downstairs to join her sister. She turned to look at Kate before going out of the door and was about to say something, when Kate interrupted her with, 'Just go, Dot. Don't make it any harder for me.'

Kate lay in bed listening to the hustle and bustle downstairs. She winced when first one of the twins and then the other started to cry. *Please God the family wouldn't decide that someone should stay behind to look after them, rather than take them to yell throughout the service.* Then she heard the calming voice of Dot singing to them, 'Twinkle, twinkle little star' and their crying subsided.

She collapsed back on the pillow in relief as she heard her mother instruct the rest of the family. 'Hush up and let sleeping babies lie.' She listened to every murmur and movement until she heard the back door slam. When they were all gone and the house was quiet, Kate hurriedly dressed herself and scribbled the note explaining her absence. She emphasised the need to settle her stomach so that she could get back on her feet quickly.

Granny White will have a potion that will fix me, she wrote.

She judged that the walk to Nately would take about twenty minutes. The woman had told her to bring some rags for the bleeding. Kate shoved them into a small bag. She looked at herself in the mirror on the wash stand and the colourless reflection that looked back at her didn't seem to be her own.

She left the note in plain view, on the kitchen table propped up against the teapot. She closed the kitchen door quietly and walked around the side of the house, hoping that she would not bump in to anyone. The village street was quiet. Those who were not in church were too elderly or too infirm to be out and about. She could see a figure cycling further down the street but he was moving away from her. She cut quickly across the road to follow the field pathways where she was unlikely to meet anyone. The ploughed fields rolled away in both directions, some slivers of green poking their heads above the ripples of brown earth and stones.

When she topped the rise, she opened a gate through to the next field where some sheep were grazing. One of the ewes had taken herself off, away from the flock. Kate could hear her pitiful bleating and saw that the grass around her was red with blood. As she approached, the ewe tried to get up but could not. She was too weak and the legs of her lamb were protruding from her rear end at an awkward angle. Kate knew very little about birthing lambs but she had seen foals born on the farm where she worked years ago. If she stopped to assist the ewe, it would make her late and then all her plans would be shot to pieces. She tried not to look and walked on.

She could hear the sound of the ewe's distress even after she had topped a rise. She looked back over her shoulder. The sound tore into her and her gut surged. It was too much to bear. She turned and retraced her steps. She knelt down beside the ewe, speaking gently and quietly in a soothing tone. She grabbed hold of the lamb's legs and pulled with all her might. It took some time for Kate to assist the ewe and when she finally saw the lamb lying on the grass and the mother licking away the remains of the birth bag, she sat back on her heels and watched the two of them get to know each other. Her eyes welled.

The little creature struggled to its feet and wobbled about unsteadily. Within minutes the lamb was nuzzling at its mother, seeking out its first taste of milk. Kate thought of her own babies and of the new one growing within her. She looked down at her dress and saw streaks of the sheep's blood darkening the fabric of her skirt. She envisaged the awful process that she was about to put herself through. What if it should go wrong? What if the bleeding would not stop? She had heard of some women dying as a result of trying to abort their babies. She stood and let the tears flow down her face without brushing them away. She looked again at the ewe who gazed back at her with its dull, slit eyes. Such animals had no choices to make in life, they ate, slept, mated, gave birth. Nothing could intervene once their birth cycle had begun, except Mother Nature.

Tears flowed down Kate's cheeks. She had given birth to three children. Her mother had given birth to six, five had survived. She was only ten years old when her baby sister, Ida, had been born and died just moments after she had entered the world. All that remained of that day in her memory were the desperate cries coming from behind a bedroom door, the sound of hearts breaking, her father's footsteps upon the stair and the grey emptiness in his face. In the time that followed, there was a silence that drifted between the rooms and followed her mother wherever she went. The tiny bundle was taken from the house and their family felt the pain of her leaving for years to come.

'Oh, dear God, Kate, Kate! What have you done?'

Dot's voice came to her as if across a void. There was a ringing in Kate's ears and her head throbbed. She looked up at her sister who was staring down at her and her blood-soaked dress.

'I knew I shouldn't have let you go,' Dot cried. 'What was I thinking? We need to get you to the doctor. Can you get up? Let me help you.'

'It's all right,' Kate said, her voice barely audible.

'No, it's not all right. You need help. Lean on me,' Dot said, a note of panic in her voice.

'It's not my blood,' Kate said. 'The ewe, I helped the ewe . . . difficult birth.'

Dot stood apart from her sister and took in what

240

Kate was saying.

'You mean you didn't go?' Dot asked.

'No, I didn't go,' Kate replied.

The two sisters stood looking at each other for a while, breathing in unison. Kate remained still, unable to move or speak. She felt empty inside. When Dot's arms folded around her, Kate's sobs shook her body and Dot could do no more than let her sister weep until there were no more tears left.

When Kate finally stood back and said they really should be getting home, Dot folded her arm into Kate's and they walked back across the fields together.

'Thank you for coming to look for me,' Kate said.

'I was so worried for you, Kate. I don't know if Ma and Pa detected something in my face but they sent me to look for you,' Dot replied.

Kate squeezed her sister's hand. 'Thank you,' she said. 'Thank you for being my sister.'

'But I've done nothing,' Dot replied. 'I can't bear this child for you. I can't take your place.'

'You're here, when I need you most,' Kate said, 'and that's enough.'

Dot wasn't sure that it was. She would soon be leaving again and Kate would be the one left at home. She had to do more.

42

'So, what more do you think you can do?' Miriam asked Dot when they met in Chichester several days after Dot's return to college. Dot had arrived back at the Gables to find a letter from Miriam which her landlady had put in a prominent position on the hall-stand. The substance of the letter was to say that she would be in town for a few days and hoped they could meet. Miriam had spent the first fifteen minutes of their stroll around Litten Gardens recounting how she had met a 'most delicious, young woman called Violet' and how Violet had sat for her on a number of occasions and they had become 'great friends'.

Dot let her ramble on for some time before telling her about Kate expecting another child and how they had only just got back on their feet.

'This is the last thing they needed,' Dot said. 'Kate is beside herself with worry about how she will cope. She even thought about trying to get rid of the baby. Thank God she didn't. I'm worried about her state of mind, though.'

'My God, how awful it is to be a woman some-times,' Miriam said. 'It seems as if our bodies dictate to us how our lives are going to be. I'm just grateful that I will never find myself in such a situation as your sister but you should take great care yourself, dear Dot, that you do not fall foul of the vagaries of the female reproductive system.'

'Really, Miriam, you do have a strange way of

putting things,' Dot replied.

'Let me put it in plain language then,' Miriam declared. 'You must not allow your young man to persuade you to have sexual intercourse with him. The resulting pregnancy will ruin your career.'

Dot hadn't really thought of William in such terms, as a threat to her freedom of choice. She just knew that she cared for him deeply. She was aware of the fact that female teachers were forced to resign if they were married, but she had only just got to know William and she didn't even know if the relationship would stand the test of time and separation. It was too early to consider marriage. William obviously returned her affections but a marriage proposal was quite another thing. As for having a sexual relationship outside marriage . . .

'That's not going to happen,' Dot said. 'What sort of person do you think I am?'

'One with stars in her eyes and a romantic nature that may well get the better of you, Dorothy Truscott. I'm just saying be careful, that's all.'

'I know what I'm doing,' Dot replied. 'I'm not so foolish as to fall into that trap.'

'If you say so,' Miriam said. 'At least when you do get married, whoever the lucky man might be, there will probably be a means of controlling having children accessible to all women. I've heard that there are ways of stopping conception now. There's a clinic in London run by a woman called Marie Stopes. Apparently, there is a device that you insert inside you called the cap which stops the sperm from entering the womb.'

'In London. Well, that's not a lot of use to the women of Micklewell or even Chichester,' Dot said.

'Another case of privilege and geography, if you ask me.'

The two friends debated the issue of how long such changes might take to reach the entire population of women of child-bearing age. Dot became quite heated about the matter and in the end Miriam changed the subject, suggesting that they might go for some tea before the tea shop closed down for the day.

'So, regarding your sister, I repeat my question,' Miriam said, as she finished the last crumbs on her plate. 'What exactly do you think you can do to help? You can't torture yourself like this, Dot. There are some things in life we just cannot change. Being a sister doesn't make you responsible.'

After they parted, Miriam's words kept going around and around in Dot's head. It was true, she wasn't responsible, but neither could she put her concerns about Kate out of her mind. She felt the thin threads of connection between them tighten and she could not pull away.

43

May 1923

With the coming of spring came the lighter evenings. Dot and William had taken to strolling in Bishop's Park after her classes had finished for the day. That particular day the weather had been unseasonably warm and William suggested they sit on a bench and enjoy the last rays of the warm evening sun. He was currently home on leave but was due to return to Scotland the following week and Dot was aware that their time together was limited.

'Close your eyes and hold out your hands,' he said.

She did as he asked her, wondering what surprise she had in store. When she opened them, she was holding two tickets for a concert at the cathedral the following evening.

'You can come, can't you?' he asked, a pleading look in his eyes. 'I hope it wasn't presumptuous of me?'

'I'd love to come,' Dot replied.

'That's wonderful,' he said. 'As it's an evening performance. I'll come and escort you from your lodgings. The concert starts at seven, so shall we say a quarter past six? That will give us time to walk there and get some good seats.'

Dot was standing ready and waiting in the hallway in good time the following evening. In fact, in rather too much time, for Mrs Cooper, her landlady, noticed her outdoor wear and said, 'I see you are going out,

245

Miss Truscott. I trust you will not be late back for I shall be in bed by nine thirty and, as you know, I lock the doors front and back and I don't give out keys.'

'No, I shall not be late back. I'm going to a concert at the cathedral and it will be finished in time for me to be indoors by nine o'clock.'

At that moment there was a knock on the door.

'It's all right, it's for me,' Dot said.

'This is my house and I will answer the door,' Mrs Cooper said, barging past Dot.

Dot knew that it was just because her nosy landlady wanted to see who was accompanying her to the concert. Mrs Cooper had made the rules of the house quite clear when Dot had first accepted the room in the Gables: no gentleman callers. Dot's face coloured but with annoyance rather than embarrassment. She hoped Mrs Cooper wasn't going to make a fuss. William was, after all, only walking her to the concert. She needn't have worried though, for her landlady was sweetness itself. She gushed over William saying that she was pleased to meet such a fine gentleman and would he care to step in for a moment, but Dot caught William's eye and shook her head.

'How kind of you,' he replied, 'but I'm afraid that we should really make our way to the cathedral. We have tickets for this evening's concert but the seats are not reserved so we should really be on our way, or we might end up on the sides where the acoustics are not as good and the sight lines are poor.'

'Of course,' Mrs Cooper simpered. 'Are-cou-sticks are important where music is concerned. Don't let me keep you. Now you be sure to get our Miss Truscott home in good time, won't you? Young women should not be walking the streets late at night, I'm sure you'll agree, Mr . . . ?'

'Mr Martin, William Martin,' William said, taking off his hat. 'Pleased to make your acquaintance.'

'Pleased to meet you, Mr Martin.'

Mrs Cooper stepped back to let Dot through and whispered, 'Nine o'clock, no later,' and then waved flamboyantly as they walked down the street. 'Enjoy the concert,' she called.

They arrived in good time and were able to find seats in an excellent position. Dot was excited and yet the evening was tinged with sadness for her. William was leaving. These meetings would come to an end. There would be hundreds of miles between them and only pen and paper to bridge the empty space. She mustn't dwell on that, though, for it would spoil their evening. She pushed all negative feelings to the back of her mind and, as soon as the orchestra struck up, she let the music take her into another place, happy to escape the reality of what was to come.

The concert ended with the moving notes of Mozart's Lacrimosa and Dot could not stop a tear from escaping the corner of her eye. She brushed it away with her hand and, as she lowered it, William took her hand in his.

'That was wonderful, wasn't it?' he said.

'Yes, wonderful,' she agreed, smiling at him.

It was a moment she wanted to hold in her heart.

They left the towering cathedral and walked past the Cross and the Buttermarket, talking enthusiastically about the concert. They were accompanied some of the way by other members of the audience who were also making their way home. As they progressed down North Street, some people turned off down various side streets until it was just William and

Dot walking side by side.

As they passed a dark alley beside an inn, they halted their conversation and looked at each other with concern. Raised voices could be heard, coming from the shadows. They stopped and stared in the direction of the noise. Just at that moment there was a loud crash and a shout. William took Dot's arm and began to usher her quickly away, when a figure rushed out of the darkness, almost knocking Dot over. The man swore and ran across the road.

Dot was momentarily stunned by what had just happened and William asked if she was all right.

'I'm fine,' Dot replied and was about to walk on, with William firmly holding on to her, when groaning could be heard, coming from the alleyway.

'Someone is hurt,' Dot said, turning back. 'We must go and see if there's anything we can do.'

'It's a street brawl, Dot. These things happen all the time. It's not the sort of thing we should get involved in,' William replied. 'Come along, let's get you home.'

'Help,' the injured man called. 'Someone, please help me.'

'We can't ignore him, William. We should go and assist,' Dot insisted.

William's reluctance was clear but Dot could not just walk away. She began moving towards the cries and William followed her. The man was sitting up, one hand held to his head. Dot was about to approach but William held her arm and said, 'Wait, I will go and look at him.'

From where she was standing, even in the poor light, Dot could see that blood was pouring over the man's hand and dripping onto his trousers.

'Can you stand?' William said, placing his arm

underneath the man's armpit.

Dot wasn't sure if the man's mumbled response was slurred as a result of concussion or drunkenness, but she thought he looked in a bad way. She stepped forward.

'Do you have a kerchief?' she asked the tattered figure leaning against William.

'Beg pardon, ma'am?' the injured man replied.

She was close enough now to smell his breath which stank of whisky and the contents of his stomach which he had thrown up on his jerkin.

'William, remove your necktie and we will try to stem the bleeding,' Dot instructed.

William leaned the man against the wall of the inn. His head lolled onto his chest and he continued groaning but he managed to stay on his feet. William handed Dot the necktie and she proceeded to tie it around his head. The wound on his temple was still bleeding profusely though and the temporary bandage was soon soaked in blood.

'We need to get him to a doctor. I've done my best but I think this wound will need stitching,' Dot said. She then turned to the sorry looking bundle of rags propped up against the wall. 'I'm guessing the man who fled is responsible for doing this to you?' Dot asked.

The string of profanities that came out of the man's mouth told her that this was indeed the case. She reeled from the stench of his breath and the sour odour of his body but she was determined to quash her reaction and do something to assist this sorry heap of misery. The man had been attacked and he was in a bad way. What the two men had been fighting over did not concern her but she couldn't leave him in this alley.

'There's nothing more we can do here, Dorothy. Let us leave now before more trouble ensues,' William said, watching the back entrance in case more drunken men should appear.

'At least let us take him into the inn. He must be known there,' Dot replied.

'I'll take him,' William said.

'Well, I'm not waiting here alone in the dark. I'll come with you,' Dot replied.

Together they managed to get him into a back hallway. An open door through to the public bar allowed waves of raucous laughter and the occasional tinkling note of a piano to escape. A smoke screen obscured their view but William peered around the door trying to catch someone's attention. A young woman, carrying a tray of glasses, finally came towards them and said, 'It's not last orders yet, sir, come along in.'

When she saw past William and noticed the injured man, she turned, placed the tray on a nearby table and said, 'Lordy, Chancer, you're bleeding like a stuck pig! What bother have you got yourself into this time?'

'He's got a nasty cut on his head,' Dot replied.

'I've seen worse,' the young woman said. She took him by the arm and dragged him along with her into the bar without turning back or giving a word of thanks.

'Let's get out of here,' William said.

Once outside, Dot felt relieved that they were in the fresh air. The smoky atmosphere had made her throat sore and she couldn't get the smell of the man out of her nostrils. But she felt they had done the right thing, even though no gratitude had been shown. She could hear the cathedral bells chiming as William turned to her and said, 'It's nine o'clock.'

Dot felt a sudden sense of panic, 'The door will be locked. I'm locked out, William. What shall I do? This has never happened before. Mrs Cooper will be furious.'

'That's what playing Good Samaritans does for you,' William said. 'Next time it might be politic to walk by on the other side.'

'This is not the time for lessons in prudence and quotes from the Bible,' Dot replied. 'This is serious, William. I have no idea what to do. Poking fun at me is not helping.'

They stood in the street for a while, both unsure as to what could be done. Finally, William spoke.

'I will get you a room for the night,' he said, speaking more gently to her. 'We can explain everything to Mrs Cooper in the morning. No point in annoying her more by getting her out of bed to answer the door.'

'I'm not sure what will be worse, a dressing down now or when she finds I'm not in the house at breakfast time,' Dot replied. 'She might even ask me to leave, she's done that to other girls before.'

'I'm sure we can find a way of persuading Mrs Cooper that it was not your fault but we'll think about that later,' William replied. 'We can't stand around here. This is not the best part of the town it seems and we might encounter more of what we've just seen. Let's walk to my hotel and I'll order us a drink. I don't know about you but I'm in need of a whisky.'

'I don't drink whisky but a glass of port would help settle my nerves,' Dot said.

The lobby of the Dolphin and Anchor was quiet.

The attendant at the reception desk greeted William with a smile.

'Good evening, Mr Martin,' he said. Then with a knowing look added, 'Evening, miss.'

William escorted Dot through to the lounge area where Dot took in the surroundings which were even more opulent than the Queen's Hotel in Eastbourne. Stuccoed ceilings hung with pendulous light fittings and the low-level oak panelling was topped with a green leaf patterned wallpaper. Several paintings of countryside views, horses and huntsmen hung from the picture rails and the large room was elegantly set out with small groups of sofas, easy chairs and occasional tables. The predominant colours were cream, green and gold. William indicated two armchairs in the corner beside a large floral display on a pedestal. As soon as they sat down a waiter with a bow tie and slicked back hair appeared at their side.

'Can I get you anything, sir, madam?' he asked.

William ordered their drinks and Dot looked around at the three other groups of people in the room. There were two elderly couples on one side. Then opposite them, a family comprising what she supposed were the parents and grandparents of the one young woman in the group. Tucked away in the far corner was a young couple, who were so fixated upon each other that Dot thought they must be on their honeymoon. She smiled to herself.

'What is it that you find so amusing?' William asked. 'I expected you to be still in a state of high nervousness, given what has just happened.'

'I was looking at the couple over there. Don't turn around just yet but when the waiter brings our drinks, then look. I think they're newlyweds.'

After taking a sip of his whisky, William glanced in their direction and agreed.

'The wedding suite will have cost a pretty penny in a place like this,' Dot said.

'It looks to me that he thinks she is worth it. I know the feeling,' William replied.

Dot could feel herself blushing at his comment but she was secretly pleased at his response. She sipped her port and felt the warmth of it flow through her body.

'I'm going to leave you for a moment to enquire about a room,' William said, getting to his feet.

While he was away, Dot allowed her mind to wander to the possibility of being a bride herself one day. She wouldn't need to have a honeymoon hotel as costly as the Dolphin and Anchor but . . . She stopped herself from daydreaming and whispered a reprimand to herself. This was not her priority right now. There were other more important things to occupy her thoughts, like how to smooth things over with Mrs Cooper.

'It's all arranged,' William said on his return. 'You have the room right next to mine. So, I will be on hand should you wake in the night and feel frightened at being in a strange place.'

'I will not wake,' she said. 'Once I am asleep then only the dawn will wake me. That or an alarm call for breakfast. Did the desk clerk not think it strange that I have no baggage?'

'Politeness and discretion are part of his job,' William replied.

44

The room was small but comfortably furnished. Dot
sat on the bed and it felt firm. She disliked saggy mat-
tresses. She pulled back the curtain and saw that the
window gave out onto the street. She was certain to
be woken by the city preparing for a busy working
day. Saturdays were always busy in Chichester. She
had asked William if an early call could be arranged
just in case, though. She needed to get back to the
Gables before the residents, particularly Mrs Cooper,
were up and about. There was the possibility that
Maud Fitch would come down and let her in before
Mrs Cooper realised that she was missing. Throwing
stones at Maud's window from the back garden was
the only plan she could come up with and William
had agreed that a confrontation with her landlady
should be avoided at all costs.

When she closed the curtains again, she noticed
that there was a connecting door between the two
rooms. She stared at the doorknob but resisted trying
it. William was on the other side of that door. She fan-
cied she could almost hear his breathing, his footfall
across the carpet. There was a bolt on the door. It was
drawn back. She moved to close it but her hand hovered over it and she hesitated. Her first instinct was to
lock the door. Could she trust him? But William was
not like the man who had forced himself upon her.
He was kind and thoughtful and she felt secure in his
presence. She stood for a while, lost in thought and

254

then moved away. The bolt remained unsecured.

Dot prepared for bed. With no toiletries or night-gown, she did the best she could with the soap and towel provided and stripped down to her under-garments, removing her girdle and replacing her petticoat. A brush, comb and mirror set were on the dressing table and she sat down to undo her hair clips and brush her hair. When she'd finished she moved to the far side of the bed to turn out the table lamp.

She pulled back the heavily embroidered, dam-ask bed cover and climbed in between the cool, crisp sheets. The two pillows were too high for her, so she removed one of them to make herself more comfort-able. She lay, looking up at the ceiling for a while, thinking about the course of the day and then turned onto her right side, facing the direction of the con-necting door.

Sleep would not take her. She tossed and turned and sighed as the minutes of the night ticked away. Eventually she gave up and turned on the light once more. She sat on the edge of the bed and the silence of the night flowed around her. Why would sleep not come?

After a while, she was aware of movement next door. William was not asleep either. She listened and could feel him listening too, on the other side of the wall. Her breath came in short, shallow bursts and she shifted on the bed, trying not to make too much noise. She heard the door handle squeak as his hand turned it and the door moved slightly. He didn't open it fully but said in a quiet voice, 'Are you awake, Dot?'

'Yes,' she whispered back.

'I couldn't sleep either. May I come in?' he asked.

'Wait, just a moment,' she replied and pulled her

jacket around her to cover her breasts.

He stepped into the room and moved towards her. Her head pounded and her breath came in shallow gasps. She should be unsettled by the presence of William in her room in the dead of night but instead she felt a ripple of excitement and anticipation that she had never felt before.

He approached her and put his arms around her drawing her close. His kiss was tender and she wanted it to go on and on. She could feel his hardness against her thigh and a sensation of wanting him overwhelmed her. The last time a man had been this close to her it had been quite a different feeling. But all the fear of that memory seemed to melt under his embrace. Before she knew it, she was sitting beside him on the bed and he was caressing her and whispering to her.

'My dearest Dot,' he said. 'I would never hurt you. I will only lie with you if you want me to. Tell me if you don't want this, please.'

'I do,' she replied, without hesitation. Her body had spoken and she could not fight against it.

45

Dot woke up just as dawn was breaking. She lay on her side, her face towards the door almost too fearful to move. She didn't want to disturb William. She felt different. There was now a secret that the two of them shared. She moved slowly and carefully onto her back and turned her head in his direction. In the low light escaping around the edge of the curtains, she could make out the shape of his strong back and broad shoulders. She watched and listened to the rhythm of his breathing, his outward breath emitting a barely audible sigh. She wondered what he was dreaming of.

William stirred in his sleep and turned towards her, his face so close to hers that she could feel his breath on her cheeks. She waited to see if he would wake. A lock of hair had fallen across his eyes and she reached out to move it, her fingers reaching tenderly, her desire to kiss him so strong she could hardly stop herself. As if he sensed her intention, he opened his eyes. She withdrew her hand.

'I'm sorry, did I wake you?' she said.

'Good morning, my dearest Dot,' he replied. 'I'm happy to be awake, whatever the hour, with you beside me.'

He placed his hand on her cheek and stroked it. He moved closer to her and whispered, 'Are you all right?'

She kissed him gently on the lips.

'Please hold me, William,' she said.

He lay on his back and invited her into his arms, her head rested upon his chest and his heartbeat pounded in her ear. She felt as if she was sinking into his body, becoming part of him. The closeness that she felt was more than physical. This man was kind and tender, he was intelligent and hard-working. He made her happy.

Dot would have liked to stay in his arms for the rest of the morning, but with the increasing brightness in the room came the realisation that they could not remain in this position for long. They must get dressed and get to the Gables before the daily routines began.

'We should go,' Dot said.

They dressed quickly and William accompanied Dot through the foyer of the hotel and out into the early morning air. They turned into North Street and as they passed the Buttermarket, it was already bustling with market stall holders who were busy setting up their wares. Carters were arriving with boxes of vegetables from the local farms and barrow boys were loading from the carts as quickly as their skinny arms would allow them. Two women were arranging freshly baked loaves in baskets on their stall and as Dot and William passed by, the warm, yeasty smell lingered in their nostrils.

Hurrying along St Peter's, they barely had the time and breath to talk to one another but when they arrived at the corner of Priory Road, they paused.

'We're almost there,' Dot said. 'I think it best that you leave me here. We don't want any curtain peepers or early morning workers to notice us, do we? Mrs Cooper is well known in this area and so are the faces of her female lodgers. I wouldn't want anything getting back her. I'm in enough trouble as it is. I just hope she doesn't catch me creeping in, that's all.'

William took her hand. 'When will I see you again?' he asked. 'We have so much to talk about and so little time. I leave for Scotland on Friday.'

'Wednesday at four o'clock. The Bishop's Palace Gardens,' Dot replied. 'I'll wait for you at the Canon Lane entrance.'

'I won't be late,' William replied.

Dot kissed her fingertips and placed them upon William's lips.

'Until Wednesday,' he said squeezing her hand.

He turned and walked back down St Peter's. She stood and watched him disappear from sight before continuing along Priory Road towards the Gables where she picked up a handful of tiny stones to throw in the direction of Maud's window.

It was on the third throw that Maud finally opened her window. A bleary-eyed, tousled head hung over the top of the sash which stuck part way down.

'What the hell?' Maud's early morning voice squeaked.

'Shh,' Dot warned, looking across at the other bedroom windows. 'Come down and let me in. Hurry up, Maud.'

Maud disappeared behind the curtain and Dot crept round to the front door. She winced as she heard the key being turned and the bolt drawn back. She entered the dark hallway and Maud closed the door. She was about to relock the bolt when Dot stopped her.

'It made enough noise when you opened it,' Dot whispered. 'She's probably awake already. You get back upstairs. I'll bring the milk in. It's sitting on the doorstep. I'll say I couldn't sleep and wanted to be useful.'

'And you think she'll believe you?' Maud replied.

'More than if it was you that said it.' Dot grinned. 'Go on, before she appears.'

Within seconds of Maud turning at the top of the stairs, Mrs Cooper's door creaked open. She laboured down the stairs, holding onto the bannister with one hand and grasping her dressing gown around her chest with the other. Her head wobbled with its crown of rag rolls, and the flesh of her multiple chins sagged as a counterbalance as she plodded in Dot's direction.

She stood square in front of Dot and fixed her with her black eyes.

'And what is the meaning of this, Miss Truscott?' she snapped.

'I woke early,' Dot replied. 'So, I thought I could . . .'

'Could what?' Mrs Cooper placed her hands on her hips and pursed her lips. 'Wake the whole household to keep you company?'

'Make you a cup of tea and bring it up to you,' Dot replied, smiling and glancing down at the two milk bottles she was hugging to her chest.

Mrs Cooper paused. Dot waited for the look of incredulity to appear on her face but she just grunted.

'Well, that's very kind of you, I'm sure, Miss Truscott,' she said. 'But that's young Lizzy's job. Where is that girl? She should be up by now. Lizzy. Lizzy,' she called. 'If she's overslept again, I swear I'll chuck her out on her ear. Worst day's work I ever did employing her. Most of what she does, she does wrong and I have to do it all over myself.'

Mrs Cooper bustled away towards the kitchen in

260

search of Lizzy. 'Put those on the kitchen table,' she called over her shoulder. 'If you really want to be helpful then you can help Lizzy prepare the breakfasts, otherwise we'll all be late to start the day.'

Dot followed behind smiling to herself, thanking her lucky stars for Mrs Cooper's lack of awareness that she was wearing the same clothes she went out in last evening, and praising Lizzy for being a sleepyhead. Her tardiness and Dot's own quick thinking had diverted Mrs Cooper's attention and redirected her indignation. 'Thank you, Lizzy,' Dot whispered to herself.

46

Dot sat through the last lecture of the day on Wednesday, watching the clock. When the big hand reached ten minutes to four and the figure at the podium was still taking questions from the students who were hanging on her every word, Dot shifted uncomfortably in her seat. The young woman sitting next to her, Vera Thompkins, was always trying to attract attention, always trying to be the one to pose the most interesting question and gain the praise of their tutors. Dot could feel that she was about to ask something and had to restrain herself from grabbing Vera's arm as it shot up into the air.

The actual question that Vera asked reverberated like a hum in Dot's ears, as the surging of her own blood pumped in anger through her body. How dare Vera wallow in her own self-importance when Dot had to go and meet William? How much longer was this going to drag on? Dot was usually keen to concentrate on everything her tutors were imparting to her but today was different. This was her last chance to tell William how much she loved him before he left Chichester. She didn't know how long it would be before they would be able to meet again.

She was in a fog of frustration and couldn't sit still. To stand up and leave when the tutor was speaking would be the ultimate insult. She couldn't do that. She prayed for the lecture to end. When the tutor finally picked up her sheaf of notes and the students began rising out of their seats around her, she realised that it was finally over and she could escape.

'That was so interesting, wasn't it?' Vera turned to her and said. 'Don't you think this new theory from Madame Montessori sounds fascinating? I wonder how we can get hold of her book?'

'Actually, I have a copy. I've read it but it's not mine, so I can't lend it to you. Now I have an important meeting to go to, so if you'll please excuse me,' Dot said, brushing past Vera who, for once, was lost for words.

Dot hurried as quickly as she could to Canon Lane where William would be waiting for her. She was thoroughly out of breath when she approached the entrance to Bishop's Palace Gardens where she expected to see him looking up and down the street, but he wasn't there. She told herself not to worry and stepped through the gateway. Perhaps he was waiting somewhere inside the grounds? She was over twenty minutes late. He might have gone to sit on one of the benches overlooking the lawn. She turned beside a large oak tree and saw two women on the near bench and one man on the far one. She didn't think it was William, surely he would be looking towards the entrance expecting her arrival at any moment. Despite her doubts, she hurried towards him anyway. He was turned away from her and the closer she got, the more she realised that this was a much older man. He looked up at her, his far hand resting on a metal-topped cane. His huge moustache curved upwards as he smiled.

'Good afternoon,' he said.

'Good afternoon,' she replied. 'Excuse me, sir, but have you been sitting here long? Have you seen a young man? He might have been looking at his watch and looking around. I'm late, you see.'

'Well, I've been here a while, my dear,' the man replied. 'But I'm sorry, I've seen no young man. Just those two ladies over there. I do hope you manage to find him.'

'Thank you anyway,' Dot said.

She walked quickly back to the entrance in the hope that he'd returned to the appointed place but he was nowhere to be seen. Dot was annoyed with herself for not getting up and leaving the lecture but she also felt cross with William for not waiting. There were many things that could make a person late. He might have given her a little more time. Then her eyes began to moisten as she tried to reason why he hadn't waited for her. Perhaps he hadn't even arrived at all? There might have been a last-minute instruction from his employer, a farewell to his mother that had not gone well. Perhaps he was ill, or had met with an accident? No, put that idea from her mind. She had to think logically. Do something constructive instead of wondering. She decided to go to the Dolphin and Anchor.

The desk clerk recognised her immediately.

'Good afternoon, miss,' he said. 'May I help you?'

Dot cleared her throat. 'I was wondering if Mr Martin was in his room? I need to speak with him as a matter of urgency.'

The clerk turned and checked the key fobs behind him. He then looked at his guest list.

'It appears that Mr Martin has checked out. He left this morning,' the clerk said. Dot was sure a flicker of a smirk passed across his lips.

Dot's face flushed with embarrassment and anger that she was being treated in such a way. She would not be intimidated by this rude man.

'Please check to see if he left any message,' she snapped.

'And the name?' the clerk sneered.

'Miss Truscott,' Dot replied.

The clerk delighted in slowly checking the shelves beneath the desk and the pigeon holes behind him.

'Nothing, I'm afraid, Miss Truscott,' he announced with a heavy emphasis on the 'miss'.

Dot turned and left. Whatever could have happened? Could she have misjudged William so badly? No, it was unthinkable. She walked slowly back to the Gables and the prying eyes of Mrs Cooper. She had to put on a face that did not betray what she was feeling inside. How she wished that Miriam was with her now, but she was far away on a painting holiday in the south of France. There was no point in sharing her thoughts with Maud for she would simply dismiss her feelings as an overreaction and tell her not to be so hysterical. She wished she could talk to her sister Kate, but she was far away, back in Micklewell, with her own problems to contend with. She had no one to tell of the deep hurt she was suffering and no way of knowing where William was right at this moment. Perhaps he'd had second thoughts about their relationship? She couldn't blame him. After all, she had harboured her own doubts from time to time. There must be a good reason for his failure to meet with her. All she could do was wait.

47

When Dot reached the front door of the Gables, she stood straight and tall and took a deep breath before opening the front door and stepping inside. Thankfully, the hallway was empty of residents and Mrs Cooper was nowhere to be seen. She checked the hall table for any letters or messages and picked up one addressed to her. For one moment, she dared to hope but it was her sister's handwriting. She felt a pang of guilt at being disappointed, placed the letter in her pocket and mounted the stairs.

The dust motes dancing in the air betrayed the fact that Lizzy had been in flicking a duster around. Her cleaning skills were not the best and, when Dot sat down on the bed, she noticed that the dust had been swept into the corner behind the door and not picked up with the dustpan and brush. She unpeeled the envelope and unfolded the single sheet of paper inside.

Dear Dot,

I don't want you to rush home to us, as I know you will feel inclined to do once you receive this letter. But I would never forgive myself if something happened and I didn't inform you beforehand. I must tell you that Ma's condition has worsened. Pa used the recent payment from Mrs Humboldt to call in the doctor who says that she must stop doing so much and rest. You know what she's like though and she carries on

266

until she's fit to drop. Pa was very brave. He took the doctor to one side and asked how long she had got. The doctor says a few months, if she takes proper rest, less if she carries on the way she's going.

She won't listen to anyone. The best thing you could do for all of us, Dot, is to write to her and encourage her to stay as well as she can for your next visit. Give her something to try harder for. She might listen to you. She's so proud of you and your achievements. She needs to stay alive to see you qualify as a teacher. The first in our family to be fully educated and make the best of her talents.

Your loving sister,
Kate.

Dot gripped the letter tightly and held both hands to her breast. She stared into nothingness and felt her chest contract, as if a heavy stone was pressing down on her ribs. Trying to take in the words, she looked at the letter again. The writing undulated in and out of focus. Her mother had been their rock for as long as Dot could remember. She had kept firm control of everything that happened in the Truscott family. She'd suffered the loss of a baby at birth and a son to the bitter toll of war. She'd accepted the illegitimate birth of her grandson and taken Kate and Ronnie back under her roof with pride.

Dot let the tears flow. A few days ago, she could not measure the happiness she felt and now that feeling of lightness and freedom had dissolved into the air. She sat for some time, feeling drained. A surge of hopelessness swept over her. She hated feeling this way. She stood and looked out of the window. Across the road, in the park, she could see groups of people

267

strolling and talking to each other in the early evening sunlight, children playing on the grass and a courting couple walking closely together, whispering to each other. That was her only a few days ago.

She sat down at her desk intending to write to her mother, as Kate had suggested, but the words would not come. Her hands needed something to do, her mind needed to be occupied. She picked up the book by Maria Montessori but could not concentrate on its contents. She replaced the book and walked to her wardrobe. On the top shelf there was a box of small items she had brought with her to Chichester. She carried the box to the bed and opened the lid. She lifted out a neatly folded sampler of cross stitches and embroidered patterns that she had made as a child at school. She recalled how Miss Clarence had singled out her piece as an example of 'carefully executed work'. She remembered that phrase and how it had inspired her to learn as many new words and phrases as she could and practise using them herself. It was the start of her wanting to become a teacher. She mustn't lose sight of that aim. She would write to Miss Clarence and tell her of the worsening situation at home and then she would write to her mother. Kate was right, Ma needed every encouragement to preserve her strength.

Two days dragged by and still no word from William. Dot found it almost impossible to concentrate on her studies but her final exam was looming and she had to find the strength to get on with the task and make sure she passed. She had to finish what she had set out to do. In order that she might be able to work, she began to convince herself that she was never meant to marry William. She and William came from different worlds and if she was to marry then that would be the end of her teaching career before it even started. She couldn't allow her disappointment about William to cloud her vision or stand in the way of her vocation.

Each day she listened for the postman and checked the hall table to see if there was news from Micklewell. Almost a week went by and no letter. Then finally there was an envelope addressed to her! She rushed up to her room and opened it. In her haste she had not recognised the writing. Not from William but Miss Clarence.

My dear Dorothy,

First of all, I'm so sorry to hear that your mother is so ill. Understandably you are worried and want to be there to help your sister with everything there is to do in a household with young children and a sick mother. I note that the doctor has advised that if she takes more rest then she can expect to live to see you successfully complete your training. That gives her every incentive to obey the doctor's orders. Try to hold on to that hope. You are doing the right thing by remaining where you are and finishing your qualifications.

To allay your fears, I have decided to offer help to your family. As you know, I have been considering for some time fostering children and supporting a local family in need. I can think of no better cause than your own. I hope this will not be received as disagreeable interference from your family. I have not spoken to them yet about my thoughts and will be guided by your opinion. Please let me know what you think as soon as you are able.

To return to your own situation, I am pleased to say that I have now been given the authority to employ a second teacher for our school as the numbers of children are increasing. I want you to apply. I am sure that the interview with the Board of Education will be a formality that you will sail through. I will of course help you prepare for the event which is likely to take place in late July or early August.

You spoke in your letter of having worries outside those attached to your family situation that were causing you to reflect upon your future. I do not wish to pry but please know that I am there to support you, should you wish to talk about those concerns. I look forward to seeing you when you return to Micklewell.

Best wishes,
Amelia Clarence

Dot had mixed feelings about the letter. On the one hand, the affirmation that she must continue along her chosen path was just what she needed. On the other, the suggestion from Miss Clarence regarding fostering worried her. Ronnie and Tilly liked Miss Clarence but living with her and moving away from Micklewell was quite another thing. Besides her mother would never agree to such a suggestion. Wondering how all this was going to end, she pulled on her jacket and went for a walk around the park. When her head felt muddled in this way, being in the outdoors and close to nature helped her.

Dot loved to walk beneath the tall trees lining the edge of the park. At the entrance she passed her favourite, the Tulip Tree. Its uniquely shaped leaves fascinated her and the yellow-green flowers with their orange centre made her feel warm inside. She instantly

270

felt calmer and the glimpse of a smile passed over her lips. The park was quiet, it being close to the evening mealtime and she enjoyed the solitude. Passing the elegant Golden Rain Tree with its drifts of yellow, she came to the giants of the park. The towering London Plane trees provided cover in the autumn rain and shade from the hot summer sun. That evening, a gentle breeze sang in the leaves and the dappled light played on the path under her feet. She paused beneath them to look at the beautiful olive-green bark, the large plates on the surface peeling back to reveal the creamy underside. She veered off the path to go and touch the trunk of one of the trees, her fingers searching the textures, her mind calming. She wrapped her arms around the tree and pressed her face against it. There was a strength there that seemed to seep into her, the branches above her reaching for the azure sky, the roots beneath her holding firm.

Restored and ready to return to the Gables, she made herself a promise. No more predictions. She would take each day at a time.

48

At the same moment that Dot walked out of the examination room feeling confident that the first of her three exams had gone well, her sister, Kate, was preparing to go and see Miss Clarence.

'What do you think she wants?' Albert asked her, as she took off her apron and pulled her shawl around her shoulders.

'If I knew that I would have told you,' Kate replied. 'Now I won't be long. Remember, if one of them wakes then be sure to lift her out of the pram before she sets the other one off. One crying babe is easier to cope with than two.'

Miss Clarence had asked Kate to come and see her when she had walked past the school the previous evening, pushing the pram over every bump and ridge to try and joggle the twins to sleep.

'Nothing to worry about, Ronnie is doing very well and Tilly too,' Miss Clarence had said when Kate frowned. 'I'm so sorry to hear that your mother is seriously ill, Kate, and I want to do something to help. I have a proposition to put to you and it might be better if we could talk quietly together,' she explained, nodding towards the cries coming from the pram.

'Do you think Albert could look after the little ones after school finishes tomorrow?'

Kate wondered what on earth Miss Clarence

272

thought she could do to help. If it was an offer of money, her father would not accept it, his pride would not allow him to. It had pained him enough to accept charity from Miriam and Mrs Humboldt. Any offer to pay for treatment was useless as the doctor had said that, at her mother's stage, there was nothing more that could be done. The bitter truth was that TB was a disease that, once advanced, could not be halted. Money could not buy a life.

'Ah! Good afternoon, Kate,' Miss Clarence said as she opened the door of the schoolhouse. 'Please come in. Would you like some tea?'

'That would be lovely but I'm afraid that I can't stay too long,' Kate replied.

'I quite understand. Then we will get straight down to talking about why I have asked you here today,' Miss Clarence said. 'Please come through to the sitting room.'

As Kate entered the room, she was taken back many years to the time when she sat here as a young woman who needed comfort after her brother, Fred, had been killed in the war. She recalled how she'd had to return to her job as a nursemaid and leave her grieving family. Now here she was again. She waited to hear what Miss Clarence had to say.

'I am a single woman and know nothing of the demands of bringing up a family, Kate, but I do know something about children. Your Ronnie is a bright boy and he and Tilly have a strong bond. They do everything and go everywhere together. Ronnie helps Tilly with her number work and she helps him with his spelling. When sides are picked for a game of football in the playground, Ronnie always makes sure they are on the same side.'

'I know they are inseparable,' Kate interrupted. She couldn't see what Miss Clarence was trying to say.

'Now I've given this a great deal of thought. I've been watching families in this village struggle for some time with the problems of rural unemployment and low wages for those who do have a job,' Miss Clarence continued. 'I've been wondering how I could help and have decided to foster a child or children.'

'I'm not sure how this affects . . .' Kate began and then she realised.

'Are you saying you want to foster Tilly?' Kate asked.

'I wouldn't think of separating her from Ronnie,' Miss Clarence explained. 'As I said, I know how attached they are to each other.'

Kate was silent. What was Miss Clarence thinking? How could she possibly consider letting Ronnie be looked after by anyone else, even by someone as kindly as Miss Clarence? She was stunned. However much they were struggling, it was unthinkable.

'But you're leaving the village. You're taking a new job. On the Isle of Wight, isn't it? How is it going to help us by you taking our children away?'

'I know it sounds like a drastic measure but so much is falling upon your shoulders at the moment, Kate. Let me help carry some of that burden, please.'

'Ronnie is not a burden, Miss Clarence. Besides, Dot will soon qualify to become a teacher and she will be able to help,' Kate said, her voice betraying her agitation and confusion.

'Dot will no doubt pass her examinations, Kate,' Miss Clarence replied, 'but when she finds a job, it may not be in the local area. She will most likely be asked to move to some other area of the county. You and the family should prepare yourselves for that.'

Did Dot know about this? Was she planning to go with Miss Clarence and had not told her? Kate was shocked by the idea that Dot might not be coming back home. She had the feeling that Miss Clarence was not telling her the whole story. She didn't know what to say. She was stuck between the offer of a way out and her devotion to her son. A maelstrom of emotions overwhelmed her. She was angry with Dot for escaping, for not being here to help. Yet at the same time she was proud of her sister for all she had achieved. She could not stand in her way. What should she do? An image of Ronnie waving goodbye to her clouded her vision and pierced her inside. Before she had really considered her response carefully, the words escaped her lips.

'It's kind of you to offer to help us but we couldn't possibly let them go with you. I couldn't sleep at night wondering how my Ronnie was and, as for Ma, she would flatly refuse to let Tilly go.'

'I understand how you feel,' Miss Clarence began.

'No, you don't,' Kate snapped. 'You don't understand at all. You're not a mother.'

Kate saw the hurt on Miss Clarence's face and regretted those last words.

'Please, let me explain,' Miss Clarence said. 'I understand more than you know. I was sent to live with my aunt when I was only five years old. My father was a drunkard and a bully and my mother decided to leave him and was forced to take a job in service. It was impossible for me to join her, so her sister took me in and I was raised as part of their family. I saw my mother only very occasionally, perhaps three or four times a year. Your Ronnie and Tilly would not be with

275

me forever, Kate, just to help you all out over this very difficult period.'

Kate didn't know what to say. This revelation about her teacher's previous life was totally unexpected. She remained silent.

Miss Clarence looked at Kate, clearly embarrassed by her lack of response. 'I realise this offer of mine will have come as a shock to you, Kate, but it may be the best solution for the family, at least in the short term. Talk it over with Albert and your father but perhaps not your mother for the moment, she doesn't need to be further burdened by such concerns. I don't need an answer right away.'

Kate was still taking in the full impact of what Miss Clarence had to say when she realised that she was clenching her hands together so that her nails dug into her skin. She relaxed them and stood up.

'I should be going now,' she said.

'Will you consider what I have suggested?' Miss Clarence asked.

'I don't know what to say,' Kate replied.

'Perhaps when Dorothy returns, you might discuss it with her,' her former teacher added, trying to ease the tension between them.

Kate didn't reply but moved towards the door.

'I do hope I haven't spoken out of turn,' Miss Clarence said, as she held the door open for Kate. 'The last thing I would want to do is upset you.'

As Kate closed the schoolhouse gate behind her, she tried to imagine what life would be like without the sound of Ronnie and Tilly playing in the house. An empty space that only they could fill. She decided not to tell Albert and Ma and Pa about Miss Clarence's suggestion. If Albert asked, she would tell him that Miss Clarence had wanted to talk to her about arrangements for the school fete. There was enough on their minds without adding to their problems.

49

There was little Dot could do in Chichester now that her final examinations were over. But although she wanted to get back to her family as soon as possible, she was torn between waiting just one more day in case she heard from William and getting on a train. She had already given in her notice to Mrs Cooper and said her goodbyes to Maud. The letter she had written to Miriam to tell her that she was returning to Micklewell was in the post. Miriam would receive it when she returned from France. Dot was tidying away her writing materials and books and packing her bags when she heard the front doorbell ring. She opened her bedroom door and stood at the top of the stairs. She heard Lizzy say, 'Just a minute. I'll call her.'

Just as Lizzy shouted Dot's name, Dot careered down the stairs in such a hurry she nearly tripped over the worn section of stair carpet that she usually carefully avoided.

'It's for you,' Lizzy said, stepping back so that Dot could see the figure on the doorstep.

Dot looked straight into the mischievous face of a young boy, his cap falling over one eye and his trousers hitched up by his bicycle clips.

'Telegram for Miss Dorothy Truscott. Is that you, miss?' he said.

'Yes,' she replied.

He extended an envelope towards her.

The boy hovered in the doorway and Dot realised

he was expecting a tip. She asked him to wait and rushed upstairs to fetch a few coins. She thanked him and returned to her room to read the message in private.

Sincere apologies. Mother gravely ill. Please write and send home address. Thinking of you. William Martin. Grazer Irvine Co Ltd Glasgow

Dot sat down with a sigh of relief. It had taken him a long time to get in touch but at least he had eventually sent word. She felt some comfort in knowing that he had been thinking of her. The situation with his mother must have been serious. She would write to him but for now she must devote her whole time and attention to her family.

* * *

The familiarity of the lane from the crossroads to 2 Mead Cottages settled her. There had been so much that had changed in her life since she had initially taken this journey in reverse and first set out for Chichester and her training to become a teacher. She could have walked this route blindfolded for she knew each sound and smell along the way. The muck heap at Wellhouse Farm, the lavender lining the path towards the Taylor sisters' front door, the rasping of a saw and the smell of fresh wood shavings from the carpenter's shop. It felt like she was home. As she crossed the footbridge at the ford and approached the pond, she heard the splash and discordant fretting of ducks disturbed by a dog. The owner was encouraging it to come out of the water with little success. As

279

she got closer, she recognised Mary Suss.

'Do you need a hand there, Mary?' Dot asked, putting down her bags.

'Dot, what a joy to see you. Just a minute while I get this animal under control,' Mary replied. 'Gus, come here, come. Blasted dog!'

Mary finally managed to get the dog to come to her and scolded him.

'He's always been disobedient,' she said, placing a rope lead around his neck. 'I told Walter that he should have got rid of him when he was a pup but, well, you know what men are like.'

She brushed her hair out of her eyes and stood up straight.

'I'm glad I've run into you,' she continued. 'I guess from the bags that you haven't been home yet.'

'No, I've just arrived,' Dot replied. 'They're not expecting me. Last time I wrote I just said I would come as soon after my exams had finished as I could.'

'In that case, I think I should warn you that your ma has gone downhill a lot since the last time you were home and your dad is taking it badly,' Mary said.

Dot paused while she took in the full impact of what Mary was telling her. Kate's letter had raised her concerns but now Mary was confirming all that she'd feared.

'Thank you, Mary. You're a good friend to us all,' she replied, her eyes beginning to well up.

'Just remember I'm there if you need me,' Mary said, placing a hand on Dot's arm.

Dot picked up her bags and walked slowly on towards the watercress beds and Mead Cottages. She didn't know what she would find there but she knew she had to be strong for all of them.

The children were still at school when she arrived at number two. She opened the back gate and saw the pram under the shade of the apple tree. Kate was down the garden pegging out the washing and when she heard the back gate click, turned to face Dot. She immediately dried her hands on her apron and came down the path to greet her. The two sisters held each other for some time before looking into each other's eyes. The hurt in Kate's eyes mirrored the hurt in her own.

'How is she?' Dot asked.

Kate just shook her head and then said, 'She'll make a supreme effort when she knows you're here but don't be fooled. We've made a bed up for her in the front room. All that going up and down stairs was exhausting her. Come on in and I'll just go and see if she's stirring. She's sleeping a lot.'

'Before we go in,' Dot said. 'How are you, Kate? You look tired.'

'I am tired but there's nothing to be done about that,' Kate replied.

'Have you told them about . . . ?' she asked, placing a hand gently on her sister's belly.

'Yes,' Kate replied.

'And how did Albert take it?'

'Well, he's pleased, of course, but he's also concerned about how we'll cope, how I'll cope with another one to care for.'

'I'm sorry I couldn't come sooner,' Dot said.

'You did what you needed to do. How did the exams go?' Kate asked.

'I think I did well but we must wait and see. I get the results next month.'

The two sisters entered the kitchen and Kate

opened the door to the front room as quietly as she could. A stew was cooking slowly on the range and the smell was delicious. There was a bowl of broad beans on the table still in their furry coats and a colander waiting for the shucking to begin. Dot smiled as she recalled how her mother's fingers were often brown at this time of the year with the shucking of beans.

She heard Kate say, 'There's someone here to see you, Ma.' She peered around the door and beckoned Dot in.

The room was dimly lit with the curtains closed to keep out the bright sunlight. Dot moved towards the bedside and was immediately shocked by the change that had come over her mother. Her hair was lank and stuck to the sides of her head. She was bathed in sweat and tried to sit herself more upright but sank down again onto her pillows. Her eyes were glazed as if she couldn't focus on Dot's face. Dot bent over and kissed her.

'Dot, my Dorothy,' Ada whispered, her voice cracked and rasping. 'You're here. I'm so glad you've come.'

Even those few words made Ada start coughing. Dot could hear the rattling in her mother's chest and watched helplessly as her sister wrung out a cloth from the bowl of water beside the bed, mopped her mother's brow and wiped the blood spatters from her lips.

'Let's try sitting you up, shall we? That helps when she starts coughing,' Kate explained. 'Give me a hand Dot, would you?'

Kate showed Dot how to lift their mother to cause her the least discomfort and, after a while, the coughing lessened. The two sisters stayed with their mother for a while until Kate heard the twins crying and went to see to them. Dot tried to stay cheerful, for her mother's sake, and told her about her final exams and her farewells to people in Chichester. She left out the part about applying for a job. She tried to put that thought from her mind. She had a while yet to try to justify that decision to herself and explain it to her family. Probably best not to mention William yet either, too many complications. One thing at a time.

At that moment she looked at her mother's pale and sunken cheeks and tried to imagine what life would be like without her. She was overwhelmed with feelings of guilt for having been so happy in Chichester, while her mother lay dying and yet she knew if she didn't keep going with her plans to teach, then all of her training would have been in vain.

Ada's eyes began to close and Dot moved to leave her to sleep, when Ada's arm reached out and held Dot's sleeve.

'Always remember I am proud of you, Dot,' Ada whispered. 'You have achieved more than anyone in the Truscott family could dream of.'

'Please, don't try to talk, Ma,' Dot said. 'You know it makes you cough.'

But Ada ignored Dot's caution and struggled to say what she wanted to say.

'I know you love me,' Ada whispered. She paused to get her breath. 'And I love you but my time is coming to an end and yours is just beginning. Don't waste it, waiting.'

Those whispered words that came from Ada's lips while Dot was struggling with her conscience, gave her the encouragement she needed. Her mother had given her daughter the freedom to make her own choices and build her own life. Dot hoped the rest of the family would be as understanding.

There wasn't a moment to spare when the children came home and Jim and Albert returned from the smithy. The usual banter was missing, however, for everyone was aware that Ada could not join them and that cast a sadness over them all. Dot responded to the family's enquiries about how her exams had gone but the conversation soon fell flat and they turned to practical matters.

'I'm afraid the sleeping arrangements are going to be cramped,' Kate said, 'but we'll make do. I can sleep downstairs with Ma. I often need to get up to her in the night anyway. You can go in the big bed with Tilly and Ronnie, Dot. Pa and Albert will have to make do in the small room.'

'It's too much disruption, Kate. I can ask Miss Clarence about the possibility of my sleeping at the schoolhouse,' Dot replied. 'And I won't hear any arguments.'

Kate cast a look at her sister. Neither knew what the other was thinking. For the first time in their lives, there was a guardedness between them, each wondering what the other was withholding.

The following morning Dot set off to see her mentor and friend hoping that her suggestion would not be too much of an imposition. It was a fine morning and, as she walked down Frog Lane, she delighted in hearing the early morning sounds of birds singing and the occasional rasping call of a magpie from the top of the maple tree. She was only a few minutes into her walk when she stopped, mesmerised by the scene in front of her. The surface of the road seemed to be moving. The lane was covered in hundreds of froglets, hopping over each other. A flapping sound to her left, drew her attention to a huge, white heron rising into the air from the trout farm. In his beak he held his prize, a small brown trout. The froglets were safe for the moment.

She picked her way carefully through the frolicking frogs and smiled as she did so. Her mother's words had helped lift the burden of her worries a little, although there was still much to talk over with her father, Kate and Albert. She entered the garden and knocked on the door of the schoolhouse. Miss Clarence opened the door to her and invited her in.

'So, it's all over. Just have to wait for the results,' Miss Clarence said. 'I'm sure you've done well.'

They went through to the kitchen where Miss Clarence had cut flowers on the table and was half-way through arranging them in a vase. Aquilegia and alliums interspersed with greenery were forming a lovely pink and purple display.

'Don't let me stop you from your arranging,' Dot said. 'I can talk while you finish. I'm here to see you because it's been a while since we met but also because I need to ask a favour,' she began.

She had decided to get straight to the point and asked if she could stay.

'With my mother downstairs and only two bedrooms . . .'

'No need to explain any further,' Miss Clarence said. 'If you hadn't asked, I was going to offer. So that's settled then, bring your things over this afternoon. Now it's my turn to ask a favour,' she continued. 'I need you to talk to Kate and Albert. As you know, I wish to help your family. Well, I decided to put my idea to Kate. I've offered to take Ronnie and Tilly with me to the Isle of Wight. Kate said she would think about it but I've heard nothing from her. Has she mentioned anything to you?'

'No. I didn't realise you'd already spoken to her. You said in your letter that you were thinking of fostering but I had no idea that you'd already broached the subject. It's a difficult time for them . . .'

'It's precisely because it's a difficult time that I'm offering. Have you told them about the job yet?'

Dot shook her head. 'I didn't think the time was right.'

'We are running out of time,' Miss Clarence replied. 'The summer holidays will be here and gone before we know it. I have to make moving arrangements. You need to tell them, Dorothy.'

'But how can I when the exam results are not out? I might not . . .'

'Of course, you'll pass,' Miss Clarence said. 'I have no doubt. The education authority will put the offer in writing to you and you need to prepare your family for the outcome. You do still want to do this, don't you?'

'Yes, I do,' Dot replied. 'But there are other problems.'

'Then we'd better talk about them,' Miss Clarence said.

It was half an hour or more before Dot finished relaying all the events of her final weeks in Chichester and her feelings for William. Miss Clarence listened without interruption and when Dot had finished, she took some time to respond.

'So, you see, Miss Clarence, I am torn in so many different ways. My family, my career and the man I love. I'm in an impossible position. What can I do?'

Dot prompted.

Miss Clarence folded her hands together in a precise manner and looked directly into Dot's eyes.

'Firstly, you need to give him a chance to explain, Dorothy, and secondly, what is it we say to the children? Anything is possible? Remember the words of St Francis of Assisi. 'Start by doing what's necessary; then do what's possible; and suddenly you're doing the impossible.' So, start by doing what's necessary. I will get the spare room ready for you and later I have something to tell you about the choices I had to make at your age. They might help you see things in a different light. We are more similar than you might know.'

50

'I've asked Mary and Walter Suss to have the children this afternoon so that I can talk to you all,' Dot explained to her father. 'Henry has offered to walk them there before he goes back to the farm.'

Ronnie and Tilly were jumping around with excitement shouting, 'Do you think they'll let us play with Gus? Have they still got their rabbits?'

'Can we stay for tea?' Tilly asked. 'Mrs Suss makes the best shortbread biscuits.'

'Just hurry up and finish your lunch,' Henry complained. 'Or you'll make me late.'

When the children had gone and Kate had managed to get the twins off to sleep, the family sat around the kitchen table. All faces turned to Dot.

'Well?' Jim Truscott asked. 'What's this all about? If this is so important that Albert and I need to be here instead of back at the forge, shouldn't we be including your ma in this conversation?'

Dot glanced towards the slightly open door. 'She's resting. I wanted to discuss this with all of you first,' she replied.

'Well get on with it then,' Jim said, his tone a mixture of concern and impatience.

'There's no easy way of putting this,' Dot said, her mouth dry and her heart rate rising.

'I've been talking to Miss Clarence. She's offered me a room at the schoolhouse to make things more manageable here.'

'We're managing, aren't we?' Jim snapped. 'What business is it of hers?'

'Let's hear Dot out,' Albert said.

'She's also offered me a job, subject to the interview with county of course,' Dot continued.

'But she's going to a new school, on the Isle of Wight,' Kate said.

'Yes, the job would be there, with her,' Dot replied.

Jim Truscott's face turned pale. His jaw tightened and he gazed into a distance that he could neither see nor wanted to see.

'It would be good money, Pa, and I would send some of my salary to all of you.'

'So, that's why she offered to help with Ronnie and Tilly because she knew, you knew, Dot, and you didn't breathe a word to us,' Kate snapped, staring straight at her sister. 'When were you going to tell us? Why have you left it until now? You must have known for a long time that it was your intention to leave.'

'What's all this about Ronnie and Tilly?' Jim asked.

'Miss Clarence wants to take them away, foster them. Thinks they will be better off with her,' Kate said.

'What?' Albert asked. 'What do you mean, take Tilly and Ronnie?'

'I was going to tell you but I thought you wouldn't even consider it. Besides, I couldn't let Ronnie go. Dot has sprung all this on us. She can do the explaining now,' Kate replied, glaring at her sister.

'But she's not offering for her own benefit, can't you see?' Dot said. 'And I will be there with them.'

'Times are hard,' Jim said. 'But not so hard that we can't look after our own. It would kill your mother.'

Dot had expected them not to take the suggestion

easily but she felt their opposition so strongly that she didn't know what to say next to persuade them that this was the right thing to do.

The opening of the front-room door turned everyone's attention. Ada stood, leaning against the door frame in her nightgown and shawl, her frail body barely allowing her to stand upright.

'I heard it all,' she said. 'I'm not so sick that I don't still have my hearing and my faculties. Don't treat me as if my opinion doesn't count.'

The last few words provoked a coughing fit and Kate and Dot rushed to support their mother.

'Now see what you've done,' Jim shouted.

'She's doing what is best for the family, Jim,' Ada winced as she was helped into the most comfortable chair.

'Don't think for one minute that I want to see our little 'uns sent away. I'm sure none of us do but sometimes the hardest decisions have to be made,' Ada said.

She coughed into her handkerchief and took a while before she could speak again. 'Tilly and Ronnie . . . will be together. They will be . . . getting . . . a good education and they will be with our Dot. Besides, with another babe on the way, there will be a lot of extra work for you, Kate,' Ada said, pausing frequently for breath.

Jim got up from his chair and helped Ada sit down. The family sat looking at her and at each other, all trying to take in what had just been thrown down in front of them. All surprised at Ada's reaction. Ada's breath came in short bursts but the determination to continue showed on her face. She had more to say.

'Now Kate, I want you to listen to me. I know the

pressures that a woman is under and I see how they are telling on you. You will soon have four children of your own and Tilly to look after. I know all about that but at least I had a time to recover between each birth. You need to think of your own health, Kate. My advice to you and Albert is to consider carefully what would be best for you all in the long run.'

Dot looked across at her sister. Would she agree to let Ronnie go? Dot could see the anguish on Kate's face. She was struggling with the decision.

'But how often will we see them? The Isle of Wight is so far. It might as well be the moon. We can't afford to pay ferry crossings,' Kate said, her chin and lower lip quavering.

'I will make sure they write and I will bring them home for the summer and Christmas holidays, at the very least,' Dot promised.

If Dot could have shared her sister's thoughts, she would have seen how Philip's face and Ronnie's, at that moment, merged into one, the two impossible to separate. She could read the mixed emotions on Kate's face, the thought of separation from Ronnie, the knowledge that another life was growing inside her, another mouth to feed, the failing health of their mother. All this Dot could see and she felt for her sister. What she could never share was the return of a memory that would always be there for Kate, the moment she had learned of the loss of her dear Philip.

'Perhaps it's for the best,' Kate said, reaching for Albert's hand. 'It's just that . . .'

'We don't have to make any decisions now,' Albert replied. 'We need some time to think about this.'

'And how are Ronnie and Tilly going to take the idea of moving away?' Jim asked. 'Has no one thought about that?'

'Oh, they will see it as a bit of an adventure if we explain it the right way,' Ada replied.

Dot admired her mother's strength. She had accepted what could not be changed and was prepared to do what was necessary. That strength had passed through her to her daughters. Dot was both grateful and relieved for her mother's support. In time she hoped that Kate would forgive her for not being completely honest with her. Whatever happened they would look after each other as a family, Dot was confident of that.

51

A day later Dot moved her sparse belongings into Miss Clarence's spare room. It was agreed that the family would give Miss Clarence their decision regarding Tilly and Ronnie by the end of the week. Dot was pleased that they were taking the offer of help seriously and hoped they would eventually agree to Miss Clarence's suggestion.

Dot's room at the schoolhouse was quiet compared to the busyness of 2 Mead Cottages. She sat on the edge of the single bed and smoothed her hand over the silky eiderdown. She looked around her at the neat and prettily decorated room. Her few possessions fitted easily into the chest of drawers and the three practical dresses she owned dangled from their hangers in a wardrobe that was empty enough for her to fit inside.

Miss Clarence had placed a small vase filled with delicate flowers from the garden on the small writing desk under the window and Dot recalled her words on showing Dot the room.

'All teachers need a writing desk,' she had said as she pulled the curtains back. 'But they also need colour and light and a reminder that there is a world outside the classroom.' Dot sat down at the desk to write to William. She wrote of how pleased she was to hear from him and how sorry she was to learn of his mother's illness. She explained her situation regarding the family and her impending interview for the

293

job on the Isle of Wight. Then she put down her pen and rested her chin on one hand. The complications of continuing to stay in touch with William were only going to get worse. She couldn't deny her feelings for him but neither could she see any future for them together.

It causes me much distress to say this, my dear William, but the distance between us is too great.

She paused with her pen lifted from the paper at that point and did not sign her name. Something was holding her back. When Amelia Clarence called up the stairs to ask her to come down for tea, she placed her pen in her writing box and left the note on her desk.

They ate together talking of the news in Micklewell, who was marrying, who was courting, the preparations for the coming village fete and whether Tom Pavey would win the champion vegetable grower prize again this year. When they had exhausted all the local topics and eaten their fill, Amelia Clarence poured the tea. She handed Dot her cup and said, 'I thought I should elaborate on what I said to you regarding us having more in common than you realise.

'I wanted to tell you something of my own situation when I started teaching. My first job was in a small village near Winchester. I met a young man, Sidney Hyams. His family were friendly with my aunt. I was lodging with her for the first few years of my teaching career. Sidney was training to become a solicitor and we met as often as we could. My aunt insisted we were chaperoned, of course, but a few times we managed to shake our companion off when we were walking.'

At this, Amelia raised her eyebrows and Dot smiled.

'I'd only just started my job and he would not be earning good money until he qualified. We knew that we couldn't marry or I would have to resign my position. Luckily for us, I had a friend who was prepared to let us meet at her house and so our relationship continued on that basis for several years. When I obtained the post at Micklewell in 1911, that caused us some difficulties but we were able to spend some weekends and school holidays together. In 1916, Sidney, like so many other young men, was called up. We saw one another when he was on leave but Sidney died in the Battle of Cambrai, just a few months before the end of the war,' Amelia said.

'I'm so sorry. I didn't know,' Dot said.

'Your family had their own troubles, every family did at that awful time and no one here knew about Sidney. We had to keep our relationship quiet. What I'm trying to tell you, Dorothy, is that it is possible to love someone and keep your liaison out of the public eye, especially if you are outside of Micklewell where no one knows you personally. It sounds as if you really love this young man and, if he loves you, then I'm sure he will find a way to be with you. There are always possibilities, Dorothy.'

Was Amelia right? Should she continue to hope? Dot would never know whether she and William had a future together unless she tried, unless she redrafted her letter and waited for his response.

★ ★ ★

After several rewrites, Dot finally put the letter in the post. While she waited for a reply, she spent as much time as possible at 2 Mead Cottages. The neighbours made enquiries after Ada's health whenever Dot passed them in the street and several sent over vegetables from their own gardens or the occasional pie. Even though money was short for many families within the village and many men were working reduced hours, they still found some way of showing their sympathy for the family and giving help and support where they could. Dot finally received two letters in the post and immediately recognised one as Miriam's handwriting. The second was an unknown but elegant and carefully formed hand. Could it be?

She opened that one first and her eyes swept to the signature. It was William's reply.

My dear Dorothy,

How can you ever forgive me for abandoning you in the way I did on what should have been our farewell evening together? Please believe me that my intention was that it only ever should be a farewell and not a goodbye. The reason I could not meet you was that my mother had a stroke and the sanatorium contacted me at the hotel. I left immediately. As you can imagine, I was in a state of shock and stayed with her at her bedside until the doctors could reassure me that she was out of danger.

By the time I left her, I had missed my train to London and connection to Glasgow. I knew I was expected back for an important meeting. I should have left a note for you but I just didn't have time. I'm so sorry. I want to make it up to you somehow and I've been giving it some thought. Then I knew I had to do more than just think. So, I've been making enquiries about joining the Union Castle Line in Southampton.

Your letter explains very clearly the situation with your family and I am so sorry to hear of your mother's diagnosis. You have commitments to them which I fully understand. I respect your dedication to your teaching career and would never try to persuade you do anything but continue with that vocation. What I can say for myself is that my love for you is sincere and I am prepared to wait. Neither of us know how long that might be but I'm asking you not to give up on me, Dorothy. We are young and time is on our side.

With fondest love,
William.

Dot wasn't sure he was right about time. She was twenty-three now and was determined to continue teaching until she was at least thirty. By then, if they were still with her, Ronnie and Tilly would be thirteen. But by then, Albert might be back in full employment, the twins would be in school and her mother, her mother . . . She didn't want to think about that. She was doing it again, mapping the future. She must stop and concentrate on what she knew to be true. William loved her. He could foresee them being together. He was prepared to move closer to her. She should take comfort in that.

She turned her attention to Miriam's letter which was full of tales from France, the people she had met and the places she had seen. She was returning to England with some regrets. France was so much freer. She had joined life drawing classes and 'explored

297

the female form'. Dot smiled at that phrase. Miriam would have found many ways of doing just that, she was sure. She missed the light-heartedness of their friendship. Perhaps they would find the opportunity to meet before the summer ended.

52

As the summer heat seethed and writhed around the Hampshire hills, the people of Micklewell sought shade in every darkened corner and under every broad-leaved tree. The wheat in the fields turned from green to a golden brown and corncrakes hid amongst the stalks. Nests slowly emptied and fledglings took to the air. Sparrows squabbled in the hedgerows and the stream slowed its progress through the tangled roots of the watercress beds.

On the fourth of August 1923, the evening sun dipped below the horizon and Ada Truscott's life ebbed away. A stillness crept through the lanes of Micklewell and a mantle of sadness settled upon 2 Mead Cottages. Jim Truscott held his wife's hand, until the rasping breath that kept rhythm with his own beating heart, stopped. The sounds of the ending of the day receded as if he was no longer a part of that world. He could only sit and be with her, nothing else mattered.

When the living-room door creaked slowly open, more than an hour later, he had no sense of time. He turned his head. Through a mist of tears, the faces of his two daughters came closer.

'She's gone,' he whispered, before the rack of pain stopped his broken voice.

Kate and Dot placed their arms gently around

their father's shoulders, his once strong and broad chest heaving with the deep sorrow that was engulfing him. The sisters' tears mingled with his own and they held on to each other, their only comfort being a sharing of each other's grief.

Albert made sure the children didn't come downstairs if they woke, while Kate and Dot washed their mother's body and brushed her hair for the last time. They lifted her frail form and dressed her in her favourite pale blue dress with its darker floral pattern and lace collar. They kissed her tenderly and told her how much they loved her. The two held each other while the tears of one wetted the cheeks of the other. When they drew apart, Dot placed a hand on her sister's belly.

'She would have so loved to meet her next grandchild,' Kate sobbed.

They stood for a while looking at each other, then both placed a kiss on their mother's forehead and turned to leave their mother's body. They had done the last thing they could do for her, with love.

The family sat together in the kitchen, unable to find words to express their grief. Albert finally was the one to ask if he should fetch the doctor to confirm Ada's death and Jim agreed that he should. Little sleep was had that night. As the dawn broke and the chorus of life began, the Truscott family moved into their routines and began the sad task of arranging for Ada's funeral. The responsibility fell to Kate and Dot, as their father could not face having to deal with seeing people. Henry, Ronnie and Tilly were told of Ada's death and, although Henry was old enough to take in the meaning of the loss of his mother, Tilly and Ronnie were too young to grasp its full impact.

Henry, realising this was a time when things could not go on as normal, said that he would go to the farm and tell them he couldn't work for a few days. He knew he would be needed at home.

And so, the necessary arrangements were made. Neighbours learned of Ada's death and sent messages of condolence. Mary Suss had the children as much as possible and the family held in their grief and got through their days. The funeral was to be on the 9th of August and there was much to do. Somehow Dot found the time to write to Miriam, care of Mrs Humboldt at Frog Hall. She didn't expect Miriam to receive it before Ada's burial.

On the day of the funeral, the church was packed with villagers. Ada was well respected and the attendance at the service reflected that. When the vicar gave the eulogy, speaking of her love for her family and how her devotion showed in her hard-working nature, a ripple of quiet acknowledgement passed around the church. Kate and Dot looked at each other, their eyes full of tears and Kate reached for Ronnie's hand, remembering how her mother had embraced him on their return to Micklewell when he was only three months old.

Ada's body was laid to rest beside the baby she had lost and Jim Truscott vowed to raise a proper headstone for his wife and Ida as soon as he was able. How would he ever manage without his strong and courageous companion?

As people drifted back to their homes, Dot remained for a while kneeling at the graveside. Albert and Kate had taken the children home and her father was talking to an old friend at the lych gate.

Dot was aware of someone placing a posy upon the

301

grave and looked up to see Miriam standing there.

'I'm so sorry, Dot,' Miriam said.

Those words broke Dot's silence and her spirit. She'd been holding all her emotions deep inside her, in order to get through the past few days and now they were all released in a torrent. Miriam took Dot in her arms and she sobbed until there was nothing left, she was exhausted.

'Shall we walk a little?' Miriam asked.

'I should go home with Pa. I don't want to leave him to walk home alone,' Dot replied.

'Then I will see you tomorrow,' Miriam said. 'Do you think you could meet me here about three?'

Dot nodded. Miriam handed her a lace-edged handkerchief. 'Keep it,' she said. She bent down and removed one of the daisies from the small posy, which she tucked into Dot's hair and kissed her.

'I've always felt we are sisters, Dot. You are the sister I never had. The daisy is a flower of sisterly love and I will always love you.'

The following day, Dot met with Miriam as arranged. She hoped that Miriam wouldn't start talking about France, she wasn't in the frame of mind to hear about Miriam's frivolities. But Miriam was quite restrained and showed Dot a gentle consideration for her feelings. They walked and talked of Micklewell and Miriam's plans now she'd returned. She would stay with her aunt for a while, she explained.

'But I must think seriously about my future,' she said. 'I can't be a student for the rest of my life. I'm considering applying for a position as an art teacher. What do you think?'

Dot couldn't imagine Miriam in front of a class of children but she didn't want to dissuade her from finding something less self-indulgent to do with her life.

'I'm sure there are some private schools for girls who would welcome your expertise,' Dot replied.

'That reminds me,' Miriam said. 'Have you had your results yet?'

'Yes,' Dot smiled. 'I passed. At least I was able to tell Mum before . . .'

Miriam placed an arm around Dot's shoulder and then took her hand.

They walked on together up past the chalk pits. They sat upon that same bank, where they had rested a year ago, amongst purple vetch and dancing butterflies.

'Do you remember when we first came here?' Dot asked.

'How could I ever forget?' Miriam replied.

The two friends sat side by side, each holding on to their own thoughts.

'Will you still move to the Isle of Wight,' Miriam asked, 'with Amelia Clarence?' She paused. 'And what about William?'

'As I told you in my letter, I think the move will be for the best,' Dot said. 'It will be hard for Ronnie and Tilly to begin with, I'm sure, and Pa will miss the sound of their laughter in the house. But it will also help lighten some of the burden of his money worries.'

'Are Kate and Albert agreeable then? To let Ronnie go with you?' Miriam asked.

'They've accepted that it will help them cope, given there's another child on the way,' Dot replied. 'Things are improving for Albert too. He's walking without his stick now and learning the blacksmith's trade alongside Pa. Henry has one more year at school and then he'll be old enough to join them. I'm not sure how many more years Pa can continue working, before his strength fails him.'

'My dear Dot, you are such an organiser,' Miriam interrupted, smiling at her friend. 'And what lies ahead for you? I suppose you haven't had much time to think about that.'

Dot didn't reply immediately. She was imagining herself sailing across the Solent and William watching the boat disembark from the quay, the two of them waiting for the time when they could be together again. She saw herself standing before a class of children during the daylight hours and whiling away her evenings beside the fire, reading to Ronnie and Tilly and writing letters to her beloved William.

'Who knows?' she replied. 'There are numerous possibilities but there's much for me to do here in Micklewell before I can put my mind to anything else. I need to concentrate on the here and now.'

The two friends returned the way they had come. They walked on in silent companionship and at the village pond they parted company. The promise that they would keep in touch with each other was sealed with an embrace.

'And remember,' Miriam said, as she walked away, blowing a kiss, 'as soon as anything exciting happens, I want to be the first to know.'

53

Two weeks after Ada's funeral, William arrived at Hook station on the midday train, after travelling on the overnight sleeper to London and then on to Hampshire. When he stepped off the train and onto the platform, carrying his suitcase, Dot had already been waiting for nearly an hour. She ran towards him, weaving in and out of the other passengers into his open arms. They held each other, oblivious to everything that was going on around them, until the train moved off and the clouds of steam enveloped them.

'I'm so sorry to hear about your mother,' William said, once they were alone on the platform.

'Thank you,' Dot replied, holding back the tears. She pulled back from him and felt her heart surge in her chest. Might it have been better not to have seen him at all? Now she was here, beside him, she didn't want to leave him but she must. Her family and Miss Clarence were depending on her.

'I can't stay long, I'm afraid,' she said. 'Kate is the only one who knows that I've come to meet you. I haven't told my father and Albert yet. It's all been too much to deal with . . .'

'No need for explanations,' William replied, taking her arm. 'You have had so much to cope with and now you must prepare to leave and start your first teaching job. Not only that but you have two young-sters to take with you. I'm so grateful that you could find the time to come and meet me, my dearest Dorothy.'

She clasped his hand.

'I've reserved a room at the Raven Hotel,' he continued. 'I leave for Southampton tomorrow and I start my new job in two days' time. Our meeting is going to be all too brief. Can you come and eat some lunch with me? Just for an hour or so?'

Dot agreed. 'The carter who brought me here says he can wait until half past one but no longer.'

As they sat together in the dining room of the Raven, William talked of his success in obtaining his new job in Southampton and Dot told him of her preparations to travel with the children and join Amelia Clarence on the Isle of Wight.

'So, your family have come to terms with your leaving?' William asked.

Dot nodded, her eyes downcast. She let out a sigh.

'And they have accepted that Tilly and Ronnie should go with you,' he continued.

'Yes. It took a while for them to see that it was for the best. I think it was hardest for Kate but with the twins and another child on the way, Albert finally managed to persuade her that she needed to accept some help. I can't imagine how hard that decision must have been.'

'But he and Tilly will be together and they will be with you. I know that you will look after them both and you will be a wonderful teacher too. Is there anything you're not prepared to take on, Dorothy Truscott?' William smiled.

'Well, that remains to be seen,' Dot replied, smiling back at him.

'So, exactly where are you going to be on the Isle of

Wight?' William asked.

'Whippingham School. It's not that far from Cowes. When we get to the port we will need to get the chain ferry across the River Medina, apparently,' she explained.

'You've become quite the adventurer, Dorothy Truscott.' William grinned.

'I am amazing myself, even,' she said. Her eyes glazed over for a moment. 'If only Ma could have been here to wish me well.'

She couldn't say anymore, as her eyes filled with tears.

'She would be proud of you,' William said.

'She was proud of me. She told me that before she died,' Dot replied.

William reached for her hand across the table. 'It will be all right,' he said. 'As soon as I'm settled in lodgings, I will write to you.'

'Do you have a pen and paper?' Dot asked.

'Not on me. Just a minute,' he said, beckoning the waitress over.

The neatly dressed young woman bobbed her acknowledgement and disappeared into the reception area. She returned a few moments later with the pen and paper. Dot wrote down the address that Amelia had given her and William slipped it into his pocket. They finished their lunch, talking non-stop about how the next weeks and months might unfold for both of them.

At the appointed time, Dot stood beside the carter's wagon bound for Micklewell. She smiled a broad smile at William and, when the carter's attention was on his horses, she kissed William full on the mouth. William kissed her back. When he pulled back from her, he took her hand in his and kissed it gently.

'Will you marry me, Dot?' he whispered.

Dot threw her arms around him.

'Yes, oh yes!' she said.

He lifted her off her feet and twirled her around.

'Those leaving with me best get on board now,' the carter shouted.

'Until the autumn then,' William said, helping her aboard the wagon. 'I'll write to you as soon as I have an address.'

This time, Dot knew that he would keep his word. She trusted him. Now she could prepare for her departure from Micklewell with a lighter heart. The evening ahead would not be easy, she knew, but she could face it now with greater confidence. She had agreed with Kate, Albert and Pa that they should tell the children together that evening. Dot anticipated that Ronnie and Tilly would be confused about what was to happen and why they needed to go with her. Perhaps there would be tears when they finally packed their bags and left, but she was sure that they could all get used to the new way of living, in time.

As the carter clicked his tongue and slapped the reins, Dot turned to see William standing and waving until the wagon was out of sight. The next time she would see him would be beside the Solent. The horse plodded on down the backstreets and out into the Hampshire countryside. As they crossed the River Lyde, the Michaelmas daisies nodded in the afternoon breeze and Dot breathed in the sweet smell of newly mown hay. The rest of the day might be a challenge but the weeks and months ahead had possibilities and she was ready to explore them.

Acknowledgements

My thanks to:

My first reader Margaret Colyer.

The author of the following book of non-fiction: *The Montessori Method* by Maria Montessori translated from the Italian by Anne E. George

My agent, Saskia Leach and the team at the Kate Nash Literary Agency.

Kate Lyall Grant and the editorial and publishing team at Joffe Books.